ADVANCE PRAISE

"Only an experienced social worker with a heart for social justice could have written a thriller of this caliber. In a novel that challenges a radioactive core of secrecy, Dorothy Van Soest has deftly shaped a protagonist who balances integrity and idealism as she attempts to save lives and herself."

> — Carol Masters, *You Can't Do That! Marv Davidov, Non-Violent Revolutionary* (2009), *The Peace Terrorist* (1994), *Dear Descendent* (2019).

"Some books entertain, some inform, some inspire. *Nuclear Option* does all three. This story weaves the lives of troubled, courageous, ordinary people who struggle to avenge and heal harms by challenging powerful corporate and government powers. Even more than most historical fiction, this is an exceptionally meaningful book for students, clubs, and study groups to discuss the timeless, universal question: why, what, and how are you willing to fight or die for?"

> — Beth Brunton, Earth Care not Warfare

"Nuclear Option captures so well, especially in sleuth Sylvia Jensen, the brilliant and passionate peace and justice activists I have known over the years who are driven by heart and conscience to create the world we want to see. Kudos to Van Soest for conveying, in a bite-size and very personalized form that we can take in, the difficult and scary information about the nuclear threat we need in order to save the world."

> — Marybeth Gardam, Women's International League for Peace & Freedom U.S. Section Committee Chair, Iowa Women for Peace co-founder, Iowa PSR

"Few writers are more deft at intertwining mystery with social issues of urgent concern than Dorothy Van Soest. *Nuclear Option,* her latest novel, reunites that unlikely duo, Sylvia Jensen and J.B. Harrell, as they investigate how a lethal past, both personal and national, detonates into the present. With results that are explosive!"

> — Carol Mossman, Author, *The Narrative Matrix, Politics and Narratives of Birth, Writing with a Vengeance*

"This thrill-packed *Sylvia Jensen* mystery reminds us of the costs the world has paid and continues to pay for maintaining nuclear arsenals that threaten unimaginable horror. Dorothy Van Soest immerses us in the world of ordinary people who won't go quietly into oblivion."

— Charlie Cooper, Democracy and Justice Advocate, Baltimore, MD

"*Nuclear Option* shines a light on a little known history of when the U.S. government conducted nuclear tests in the Marshall Islands and exposed military troops to radiation for research on its effects on humans. Van Soest's novel follows the inter-generational family of an Atomic Veteran whose outrage at the results of his direct exposure leads to their persistence to hold the government accountable. Helping to guide the activism of father and son is the anti-nuclear activist Sylvia Jensen, who has her own struggles related to her involvement in the antinuclear movement. *Nuclear Option* is a love story and a thriller in its own right. Anti-war activists will be intrigued with the struggles within the antinuclear movement to find right strategies and the challenging ethical decision the heroine is compelled to make. The novel made me sad and angry and it also gave me hope in the courage and creativity of people confronting a historic injustice and the lessons they learned. Enjoyable and thought provoking; highly recommended."

— Dan Gilman, Past President, Seattle Veterans For Peace

"How do you reconcile memories of the distant past with the realities of the present? This intriguing question structures this story of Sylvia Jensen's journey from active anti-nuclear protestor in the 1980s to reluctant participant in the politics of the 21st century. Like the afterlife of nuclear fallout, passions from long ago linger in Sylvia's life and lead her to relive unresolved decisions and pathways. In this fascinating mixture of memoir, fiction, and history, author Dorothy Van Soest guides us through Sylvia's haunting encounters with people and events that force both her and the reader to wonder if we can ever stop challenging the selves we constructed so long ago."

— Dr. Louise Krasniewicz, University of Pennsylvania. Author, *Nuclear Summer: The Clash of Communities at the Seneca Women's Peace Encampment*

"Don't start Nuclear Option unless you have sufficient time to read this absorbing and twisting mystery from the first page to the last! You will be pulled into an intricate plot that links the atomic tests of the 1950s and 60s, thousands of victims of those tests, and the inner workings of both antinuclear activists and the FBI. Dorothy Van Soest once again keeps you on the edge of your chair as you ride the curves and dangers of this stirring book".

— Frederick L. Ahearn, Professor Emeritus and Former Dean, National Catholic School of Social Service, The Catholic University of America, Washington, DC

"During the 1950s and '60s, thousands of US military personnel were deliberately exposed to ionizing radiation from nuclear bomb tests. For years the physical and emotional suffering of these Atomic Veterans remained hidden, due to government denial and veterans' initial reluctance to speak about their experience. Dorothy Van Soest's engaging novel *Nuclear Option* makes that experience real through the interwoven lives of an Atomic Veteran, his son, and a social worker activist. Their painful struggles mirror the stories of actual radiation survivors and their supporters. The heartbreak of radiation's genetic impact and the survivors' powerlessness to protect their children fuel the outrage that drives the novel's action. Mobilizing against the massive force of the nuclear industry, some intriguing characters enter the story. Ominous developments threaten a tsunami. But as the novel surges to a dramatic finish, we are left with a glimmer of hope."

— Priscilla Ellis, Ph.D. co-author, "Atomic Veterans and Their Families: Responses to Radiation Exposure". American Journal of Orthopsychiatry. 60 (3), July 1990

"I was brought up short by how much I identified with the main character in *Nuclear Option*. Sleuth Sylvia Jensen's tortuous inner tension is captured in a vivid action-packed story with atmospheric detail that plunges you right into the middle of her friendships, romance and protests. A must read!"

— Betsy Bell, Author, *Open Borders: A Personal Story of Love, Loss, and Anti-war Activism*

"If you take love and compassion seriously in the face of the world's injustice, you may be disarmed by the wounded-ness of some of the characters in *Nuclear Option* and tempted to despair about whether what they can do will make any real difference. But the twists and turns of plot keep revealing deeper realities that will force you to re-think your reactions as the story draws together multiple layers of suffering caused by our military policies and practices, especially some nuclear ones that may surprise you. Expect to stay up late reading this captivating and thought-provoking mystery."

one of America's favorite genres, making it a pleasure to read and decode. Her characters are complex and surprising—how many female sleuths dare admit being a recovered alcoholic over seventy with a friend at *The New York Times*? Her plot is rooted in real sources and possibilities, its facts astonishing enough that an embellished climax seems believable. Best of all the writer delivers hope to temptations of despair and adds a wealth of added resources and allies any book group will value. Savor it and share it."

— Rickey Gard Diamond, author of *Screwnomics*

"*Nuclear Option* is more than just an investigative work, but a story replete with social and political inspections of nuclear issues. Readers interested in a strong woman-centered suspense thriller centered on individual responsibility will find it an unusual, astute read that brings to life the revitalized purpose of a single woman who reassesses her choices and impact upon the modern world. Its story of sacrifices and saving lives will linger in the mind long after sleuth Sylvia Jensen's final revelations."

— D. Donovan, Senior Reviewer, *Midwest Book Review*

"A perceptive thriller set in an offbeat milieu . . . a well-researched, compassionate, and exciting blend of social commentary and political thriller."

— *Kirkus Review*

"*Nuclear Option* sheds light on an unconscionable secret atomic veterans were forced to keep, the outcome of this catastrophic time still bleeding into society today . . . Wow. When I finished reading it I literally sat motionless, stunned by what I had just consumed, thinking how is this the first novel I've read by Dorothy Van Soest? This is a novel of excellence, written by an author gifted with extraordinary talent."

— *Reader Views*

ALSO BY DOROTHY VAN SOEST

FICTION
Just Mercy
At the Center
Death, Unchartered

NON-FICTION
Diversity Education for Social Justice: Mastering Teaching Skills
Social Work Practice for Social Justice: Cultural Competence in Action
The Global Crisis of Violence: Common Problems, Universal Causes,
Shared Solutions
Challenges of Violence Worldwide: An Educational Resource
Challenges of Violence Worldwide: Curriculum Module
Incorporating Peace and Social Justice into the Social Work Curriculum
Empowerment of People for Peace

Nuclear Option

Nuclear Option

A Novel

Dorothy Van Soest

Apprentice
House Press
Loyola University Maryland

This book is a work of fiction. Names, characters, places, and incidents are either products of the author's imagination or are used fictitiously.

First Edition

Casebound ISBN: 978-1-62720-291-6
Paperback ISBN: 978-1-62720-292-3
Ebook ISBN: 978-1-62720-293.0

Printed in the United States of America

Design by Natalie Labib
Promotion by Kyra McDonnell

Apprentice House Press
Loyola University Maryland
4501 N. Charles Street
Baltimore, MD 21210
410.617.5265
www.ApprenticeHouse.com
info@ApprenticeHouse.com

Preposterous

After Hiroshima and Nagasaki
it is preposterous to call
a change in Senate rules
however important, "the nuclear option."
There are no nuclear options
figuratively or literally speaking.

We need to pull the plug
on nuclear power. Unsafe and costly,
it only serves as a fig leave for further
advancement of nuclear weapons
by those wielding power
in nuclear powers.

—Laureen Nussbaum
    Author, *Shedding our Stars*

PROLOGUE

Journal of Norton Cramer
May 4, 1956

I woke up this morning thinking today was the day I would die.

It's not that I'm afraid of death. We all have to go sometime. But I'd like to die someplace other than this godforsaken gray place with no trees, plants, or beaches. My buddies and me call it the Rock, like the inmates call Alcatraz, San Francisco's island prison. It's as bleak as that and more.

We're stationed at a place called Enewetak Atoll, about halfway between Australia and Hawaii in the North Pacific. It's about as far away from anything as you can get, which I guess is why the brass decided it's an ideal place for nuclear experiments. The island is only two miles long, and pear-shaped, and it's still the largest one in the Marshall Islands, a horseshoe-shaped coral reef of thirty small islands that surround a sheltered lagoon forty miles across.

Anyway, this morning, I lay in my bunk for a long time looking at a picture of Shirley and me. She's so beautiful, and I'm just a skinny, pimple-faced kid. I wondered what she'd say if she could see me now, since boot camp pumped me up. I kissed her dimpled cheek and pressed her smiling face to my chest, my heart breaking all over again. Breaking up was the right decision for both of us, though. We were only eighteen years old then, twenty years old now. Too young to get married. Too young for me to die. Too young for her to be a widow.

I tucked the black-and-white photo back under my pillow and told myself I was overreacting. It was just my hangover talking. No one had ever said, or even suggested, that Operation Redwing would be my last day on earth. I told myself it was all in my head.

1

But it's hard not to think that way, when we don't even know why we're stationed on this deserted island. After two weeks with no job to do but maintain the barracks, we couldn't help but start to wonder why we were really sent here. I mean, who wouldn't? And since we were all issued radiation badges to measure our level of exposure during today's test, rumors ran rampant, despite all assurances that the exposure would be no more than getting an X-ray.

Master Sergeant Trayne's voice—"This is it, men! Move! Outside and in formation now!"—got me jumping down from my bunk so fast my insides felt like they had rotted out. From all the gin I drank last night. We all drank too much, I wasn't the only one trying not to think about what would happen today.

I stood outside in formation and checked my radiation badge one last time to make sure it was secured to my belt loop. My fingers were shaking.

"Eyes straight ahead. Arms at your side. Stand tall. Single file. Forward march."

Our barracks are at the thin end of the island, which is only a few hundred yards across, so we had to march to the airstrip at the fat end, which is still only half a mile at its widest, though it counts for 90 percent of the island. My head pounded with each step.

"Backs to the center of the island."

I turned and stood at attention facing the lagoon.

We'd been told the explosion would be one to two miles behind us, and if we faced the blast, our eyes could be permanently damaged, even if we closed them. We were also told there was nothing to worry about. I don't know what kind of fools they think we are. I saw that the officers were wearing high-density goggles. How come we weren't?

"H minus fifteen minutes." A disembodied voice blasted through loudspeakers that had been set up along the water.

I crossed myself. I'm not even Catholic.

Master Sergeant Trayne walked along our rows, looking for any sign of an unshined shoe or a tarnished belt buckle. He stopped and glared at my friend Tom next to me. He flicked his fingers under Tom's chin like he was chastising him for some great offense, but I think he just wanted to look good to the reporters on the nearby *USS Mount McKinley*, here to write about today's test. But even though I thought it was all for show, the master sergeant's cold, unfeeling eyes still sent a shiver up my spine.

"H minus ten minutes."

I closed my fingers around the radiation badge at my waist.

"At ease. Relax."

All around me were the sounds of shuffling feet, throats clearing, quiet conversations, strained laughter. I wasn't the only one who was terrified. I scanned the landscape—nothing but perforated aluminum buildings and concrete slabs. All the island's inhabitants were removed after World War II. The lush tropical foliage was leveled then, too. Now the only color on the island is the bluish-green water of the lagoon and our drab olive-green uniforms. And why were we brought here again?

"H minus seven minutes."

I saw that the water tower had been tied down with steel cables. We'd been told that all structures deemed to be at risk would be secured. I mumbled under my breath to Tom, "Guess they don't think we need to be tied down."

"H minus five minutes."

I felt Tom shaking next to me even though our bodies weren't touching. I started humming a hymn from my childhood. It's not that I was ever religious or anything. It just came to me. *Why should I feel discouraged? Why should the shadows come? For His eye is on the sparrow, and I know He watches over me.*

"Attention!" Master Sergeant Trayne paused. "You all know what attention means!"

"H minus three minutes."

No one talked. No one coughed. No one moved.

"You are not to turn around until an announcement is made over the PA system at zero hour plus thirty seconds."

The words to the hymn in my head got louder. *His eye is on the sparrow, and I know He watches over me.*

"No one, repeat no one, will look directly at the fireball at zero hour."

I held my breath. *Yea though I walk through the valley of the shadow of death, I will fear no evil.*

"H minus thirty seconds."

For thou art with me . . . His eye is on the sparrow.

"Twenty seconds."

I wanted to turn to Tom, grab his arm, but I didn't dare. I shall dwell in the house of the Lord forever.

"H minus ten seconds."

"All right, men." *Master Sergeant Trayne's voice was strained.* "Arms raised and placed over your closed eyes."

All I could hear was my own breathing, the words of the hymn in my head. Thy rod and thy staff they comfort me.

"Five, four, three, two, one."

ONE

2019

"Sylvia! Sylvia Jensen! Long time no see!"

Martin Lind still looks like a stereotype, albeit an aging one. No matter the season, even, like now, in early summer, he wears the same brown sport coat with patches on the elbows, now frayed around the edges, the same threadbare British ivy hat that he's worn like a uniform for fifty-some years of his life. I wave once, tuck a stray strand of gray hair into the bun at the back of my head and scrunch down in the pew.

It's not that I'm unhappy to see Martin. I like him, a lot, and have the utmost respect for him and what he's doing. I just want to make sure that seeing him, as well as other activists here, doesn't arouse in me a feeling that I should be doing more. Not that any of them can or want to make me feel that way. It's my issue, not theirs, one grounded in an old childhood sense of not being enough that, in the past, pushed me to do too much and then left me feeling, always, that it still wasn't enough. I don't want to get sucked back into that pattern tonight. It's an old and deeply rooted character defect I've worked hard to overcome. And now that my life is better than ever, more serene and accepting, I intend to keep it that way.

BERTHA PICKERING 1920–2018 is projected in bold black letters on a giant screen at the front of the sanctuary, and there's a photo of Bertha smiling under the weight of her signature hat, its floppy brim covered with dozens of what she called her kick-ass buttons. She was in her nineties when the picture was taken but looks ten years younger than I do now at seventy-seven.

My iPhone pings, a text from my friend J. B. Harrell. *I'm in town. On a story. Save me a seat.* I put my purse on the bench next to me and respond to his text. *Last row on the main floor, left side.* My history with J. B. goes all the way back to 1972, when I was a thirty-year-old social worker on the reservation and he was a seven-year-old child in the white foster care system. I encountered him again when I was a sixty-three-year-old foster care supervisor in Monrow City and he was a forty-year-old investigative reporter. Our relationship was rocky at first, but we became close after working together to discover the truth about the death of an American Indian boy in one of my foster homes. Later we solved another murder, of a former student of mine in the Bronx who'd gone missing in 1968. So now we're fast friends. I'm eager to see him tonight, as I always am.

People pour into the sanctuary—many I recognize, and some I knew very well in the past but haven't seen in ages. The crowd already numbers several hundred, and more are still coming, filling the balconies, jockeying for places to sit, exchanging greetings and hugs. Their friendly, increasingly boisterous voices echo off the cavernous ceiling and spar with the chants filtering in through the double doors that have been propped open to let in the warm June breeze. *Keep America safe! Keep America safe!*

People outside, many dressed in American flag attire, have come to protest Dr. Darla Kelsey, tonight's speaker. J. B. is probably in town to do a story about her for the *New York Times.* Or maybe he's doing a story about Bertha. That would be nice.

I'll never forget the day I met Bertha, thirty-nine years ago. She held something in her hand that looked like a hollowed-out metal ball. "You know what this is?" I shook my head. "It's a cluster bomb. The Nectaral Corporation designs them." She shoved it in my hand. I almost dropped it. "About six hundred and sixty of these bomblets . . . cute name, huh?. . . are shot out of large bomb containers. Imagine, almost seven hundred of these bomblets spinning out at warp speed all around us, little steel balls exploding from each one, indiscriminately killing, injuring." She paused. I handed, almost threw, the cluster bomb back to her and she caught it with one hand. With her other hand, she held up a photo of a dead Vietnamese baby. "*This* is who they kill." She looked down at the metal shell in her hand. "You see, not all the bomblets explode right away. No, they lie in wait. In the ground. And when little children pick them up . . . Boom!" She whispered the word. "One more dead kid." She lifted the photo higher.

Her big brown eyes drilled into my heart. "You're going to have to do something about it, you know."

She was right. I was never the same after that.

A squealing microphone on the pulpit interrupts my reflections, and a bald white man hunched over with arthritis jumps back like it bit him. He leans forward again. "My name is Henry Williams, and I'm a deacon in this church. We'll be starting in five minutes, so if you would please get yourselves settled?"

The man hobbles off, and conversations come to an end. The young plop down on the floor in the aisles, others squeeze together in the pews, barely able to move, their elbows and thighs pressed together. People push in closer to me in the middle of the pew. I pick up my purse, give up J. B.'s seat.

A man in a nondescript tan button-down shirt and brown chinos passes by, leaving behind a trace of Aqua Velva aftershave cologne that invades my nostrils and moves directly to my heart. The man heads down the middle aisle, turning his head from side to side in search of a place to sit. A full beard, dark brown, almost black. A ponytail halfway down his back. Green eyes. *His* green eyes. But, of course, it can't be him. Norton died more than thirty years ago. So who is this man who looks like him, who has the same distinctive gait, the same slight backward sweep of his left leg, who wears the same cologne? He squeezes into a pew several rows in front of me just as a ghostlike hush falls over the cavernous room.

A tall Black woman steps up to the pulpit. She has a smile that could melt the coldest heart and her ministerial attire—sleeveless lavender vest layered over a long white robe, clerical collar at her neck—could stir devotion in the staunchest nonbeliever and the conservatively religious alike.

"Welcome. My name is Reverend Jeannette Capen. Pastor Jean to most of you. We have gathered tonight to honor Bertha Pickering, a longtime fixture in our city who needs no introduction." She pauses. "But I'm going to give you one anyway." Warmhearted laughter. "Bertha was an unsung heroine, a lead organizer whose tireless work often went unrecognized, a woman who sought to live an authentic human and spiritual life and never stopped trying to do the right thing, even in the face of near certainty that it would make no difference. Bertha Pickering's life was grounded in radical Christian values and pacifism. And yet, she was often denounced from pulpits in this town. Well, not now, not here, not in *this* church."

Excitement mounts as the deacon reappears carrying, with some difficulty, a long rectangular object covered in white silk. He places it on the pulpit, and with a grand sweep of her hand, Pastor Jean pulls off the cloth to reveal a replacement nameplate for the church sign outside. Gasps pass from person to person and turn into clapping hands.

"By unanimous vote of the congregation, the name of our church has been officially changed to the Bertha Pickering United Church of Christ."

The sign's gold letters on black background are projected onto the screen behind the pulpit. People jump to their feet, clapping and laughing and chanting. *Ber-tha, Ber-tha, Ber-tha.*

Pastor Jean waits for everyone to settle down. "And now I invite you to talk about the Bertha *you* knew. Please limit your comments to a sentence or two so everyone has a chance."

People rush to the front in waves, and soon there's a long line stretching all the way down the left aisle. I squirm in my seat, fidget with my fingers, want to join them and don't want to join them. There's no way I could say everything Bertha meant to me in a sentence or two. And the line is already too long anyway. At this rate we'll be here all night.

The first person to step up to the microphone looks familiar, but I can't place her. She's about twenty years younger and a few inches shorter than me, with coal-black hair.

"Bertha was the first woman to chain herself to the door of the Pentagon."

At the sound of her voice I remember who she is. In 1984, I was

8

attached to her at the gate to the Seneca Army Depot in New York. Bertha had been there, too, only that time she was fastened to the gate with yarn, not chains.

An elderly hippie with a headband streaking across his forehead is next. I recognize his face but never did know his name. "My dear friend Bertha Pickering served five years in prison, two in federal maximum security. My friend Bertha was beaten and jailed during the antiwar protest at the Democratic National Convention in Chicago in August 1968. She was under FBI surveillance for decades."

One after another, they speak, and each one stirs a new memory for me. The last in line is Marianne. She's my age, but unlike me, she's still out there protesting. She's shorter than I remember; maybe she's shrunk like I have. All I can see over the pulpit is a shock of pure white hair and steely blue eyes encased in wrinkles.

"Bertha only got irritated with me once. It was on her ninety-sixth birthday." Marianne's deep voice reverberates through the sanctuary. "I told her she should slow down." We all laugh. We know what's coming. "Bertha looked me straight in the eye and said, 'Marianne, I will give up my activism on the day I die and not a day sooner.'"

I'm on my feet, cheering along with everyone else and, at the same time, wondering what Bertha would think if she knew what my life was like today. If she saw me loading and unloading boxes of food from my car during my weekly Meals on Wheels deliveries and doodling away the interminable minutes at the monthly Monrow City Retirement Association board meetings instead of going to all the protests and rallies. Would she think I've given up on the world? I wish she were here so I could assure her that I care as much as ever about what I see and hear—children being locked in cages on our borders, people murdered every day just for daring to be who they are, thousands of people sleeping on our streets and in our parks—and that, like her, I will never quit until the day I die. I would also tell her what I've learned over the years, and that now I'm doing what I *choose* to do, not what I think I *should* do or what I think I have to do in order to be an okay person. I wonder if, like me, she ever got tired, asked if she'd been arrested enough times, spent enough days in jail waiting to be arraigned, been on trial enough times, written enough letters, gone to enough protests and marches. I wonder if she had to learn, like I did, that she was just one person and the only thing required of her was to do her part.

Martin Lind, someone else who will never quit until the day he dies, steps up to the pulpit. The crowd applauds and whistles, then stops when he raises his hands. "On behalf of the Monrow City Peace and Justice Coalition, it's my distinct honor now to introduce tonight's speaker." More cheers. "Dr. Darla Kelsey is a senior fellow with the Arms Control Association. With a master's degree in peace studies and a BA in international studies and political science, she is an expert on nuclear nonproliferation, missile defense, Iran's nuclear capabilities, and North Korea's missile program." He stretches his arms out and opens his hands. "But the most exciting thing about Dr. Kelsey, as you know, is that she is the granddaughter of our own beloved Bertha Pickering."

The chanting outside—*Keep America safe!*—increases in volume but can't compete with the raucous standing ovation inside. Dr. Kelsey, a frequent commentator on CNN, NPR, and MSNBC, would be the equivalent of a movie star to this audience under any circumstances, but for her to be the granddaughter of our heroine sends us over the moon.

She appears older in person than she does on the screen, her long blond hair stringier, with strands of brown that match her brown suit and add a commanding maturity to her bright smile and youthful brown eyes. Bertha's eyes.

"We have nuclear weapons, so why don't we use them? That's the unbelievably dangerous question some politicians are actually asking today." She pauses for effect. "Some of them are even asking why they should have to go to Congress to get approval to use them."

The audience boos. Competing shouts from outside. Someone rushes to close the door. My gut lurches like it does when the news on TV is rife with conflict. But I know what to do now when my serenity is threatened like this: take in a deep breath, start counting, and let the air out through my mouth. After several attempts, my jaw starts to relax.

"North Korea has nuclear weapons capable of annihilating major cities in our country," Dr. Kelsey says. I count to ten. "And now, they are threatening to test a hydrogen bomb over the ocean." A hush falls over the sanctuary as her gaze moves from the upturned faces in the front row all the way to the people in the back. When it reaches the last pew, Bertha joins in and whispers in my ear. *You're going to have to do something about this, you know, Sylvia.* I push back. That old familiar guilt that tells me I'm not doing enough may no longer rule my life, but that doesn't mean it's not crouching around the corner, ready to spring with claws bared given the chance.

The man who looks just like Norton breaks into the silence. "Not gonna happen," he shouts.

Dr. Kelsey nods and smiles at him. "Not if we can stop it."

He jumps to his feet and raises his fist in the air. "And we *are* gonna stop it! Don't worry, we're gonna."

I lean so far forward I almost slip off the pew. The agitated pitch in his voice is as familiar as his appearance, his pattern of speech one I remember only too well.

"With that kind of enthusiasm, I believe we will." Dr. Kelsey smiles at him again and he sits back down. "But not everyone is like you, sir. Some people say there's no need for concern. Why worry, they say, when we have the capability to shoot down any incoming missile before it can reach us."

"Bullshit," the man who is the reincarnation of Norton shouts.

After that, only snippets of Dr. Kelsey's speech—a smattering of acronyms like GMD, THAADS, and ICBMs; a missile defense system that won't protect us; a petition supporting a United Nations treaty to ban nuclear weapons—slip through the images and memories now playing like a movie in my head. About the night Norton and I met. His irrefutable commitment to peace and his knowledge about the issues. His long ponytail and bushy beard. The twinkle in his green eyes. His biceps bulging under a long-sleeved black T-shirt with PEACE in huge white letters on the front. The two of us talking in the bar late into the night, too many glasses of white zinfandel for me, too many cans of Pabst beer for him. Then my mind jumps to the months after, the arguments, misunderstandings, secrets.

11

The man who looks just like him jumps to his feet again, and I'm jolted back to the present. "No! We will not allow it!"

Dr. Kelsey nods. "I know you folks won't. You folks know that to allow nuclear waste to be stored here would be to risk radioactive contamination worse than any plague you can imagine, poisonous pollutants in the air you breathe, the water you drink, and the food you eat."

She steps aside and hands the microphone to Martin Lind. He thumps his hand on the pulpit. "Dr. Kelsey is right, folks. The danger is real. The Nectaral Corporation is planning to store plutonium right here in our back yard." People boo. "They don't want us to know what that means. They don't want us to know the risks." People nod and call out in anger. "They don't want us to know what happened at the Hanford nuclear reservation. Or at Three Mile Island."

People chant: *No they don't. No they don't.* Martin raises his hands. He's on a roll. "They don't want us to know what happened at the Nevada test site." *They don't care.* "Or what happened at Fernald, Ohio." *They don't care.*

Martin lets the chanting continue for a while and then steps in. "So, do you think they care if mutated children are born here?" *No they don't. No they don't.*

Finally, he raises his hands, waits for the crowd to grow silent. "But we do know, don't we?" *Yes we do!* "And we do care, don't we?" *Yes we do!* "But we also know that knowing and caring are not enough. We have to stop them. We have to act."

Stop the madness! Stop the madness! People are on their feet now, shouting, fists in the air. The protesters outside get louder, too. *Keep America safe! Keep America safe!*

Martin shouts over the din. "Our message is clear. No plutonium storage here. No war profiteering here. No nuclear weapons anywhere." People repeat his words. Then he raises his hands and hands the microphone to Peter Minter, the Indian Child Welfare compliance officer I used to work with when I was a foster care supervisor. Peter and I have been friends and allies for years, serving together even now on a state-wide reform task force.

"I want to remind you," Peter says, "that the nuclear fuel cycle in this country began when the mining companies dug uranium from our Indian homelands. Our women had spontaneous abortions. Over half of our babies had birth defects, respiratory, liver, and kidney ailments." He pauses with a swing of his gray braid. "And now that they can't find any other place to store the damned stuff forever, they're going to try to end the nuclear cycle on our homelands, too."

The man who looks like Norton shouts. "Just say no!" Everyone chimes in. *Just say no! Just say no!*

My heart throbs with old passions stirred, screams at me to get in there, get involved, *do* something for God's sake. But my head tells me to slow down, breathe in, breathe out, stay calm. *I am enough. I do enough.*

Martin steps back to the pulpit, and the chanting stops. "It's not a done deal yet. When there's a congressional hearing about the plutonium storage contract, we will be there! Our voices will be heard! We will stop this! Our first action is next Thursday at Nectaral Plaza. Be there! And on your way out, be sure to sign our petition supporting the UN treaty to ban nuclear weapons."

I squeeze through the people crowding into the middle aisle and stand on my tiptoes by the door. My eyes light up when they settle on the man who looks like Norton. "There you are," I whisper. Then everything stops, and with each step the man takes in my direction, I take a step back into another time. One step, and it's 1984 and I'm being introduced to Norton at a coalition meeting. Another step, and I'm sitting across from him in a police van. One more step, and I'm seeing him for the last time as he walks away with two FBI agents.

And then the man who looks just like him is walking past me. I touch his arm and he stops, turns around. "Excuse me, sir," I say. "Is your name Cramer, by any chance?"

He makes a half turn like he's about to bolt, then hesitates and turns to face me. His eyes are narrow, suspicious.

"My name's Corey. Corey Cramer."

"I'm Sylvia Jensen. I knew your father."

13

TWO

1984

It was an unusually chilly spring for the Midwest, cold enough to sleep with my winter comforter on the bed. The sounds of traffic on the street below woke me, and one at a time my eyes let in the bright light, the morning sun. I rolled onto my side. My panties were lying on the floor next to the bed, my jeans over by the door, my bra and blouse out in the hall. I turned onto my other side.

"Norman?" No answer. "Norman?" Had I gotten his name wrong? "Good morning." I reached out to touch his head, thinking I could wake him by running my fingers through his long dark hair or tickling his beard. But the space next to me was empty.

"Damn," I muttered out loud. When a man goes to bed with you and then sneaks out sometime during the night, it's a pretty good bet he went home to his wife.

I rolled onto my back. A spider crawled across the ceiling. What day was it? It must be Wednesday. Last night was the Monrow City Peace and Justice Coalition meeting, always on Tuesdays.

Then what happened at work yesterday slowly came back to me.

"Mommy, Mommy," two-year-old Lucy had wailed. Her face was flushed nearly as red as her tiny T-shirt and her eyes were filled with a panic so palpable it burned every bone in my body. But her mother, slumped over in a drug-induced comatose state, didn't respond, didn't even hear her.

"Come, my love," I said as I gathered the toddler in my arms. "Mommy needs to sleep for a while. We'll take care of you until she

15

wakes up."

In the car, Lucy howled, hysterical. She kept looking back, searching for her mother. At the temporary foster home, she went numb and silent. She had a fever. A child so young shouldn't have to suffer like that. She wasn't equipped. Neither was the foster mother. I stayed to help when Lucy's little body went stiff and she wouldn't eat. We had trouble taking her filthy clothing off so we could give her a bath. I wanted to stay longer, but I had to leave. There were other clients waiting for me. Other children, other foster parents who weren't equipped to deal with the traumas they were forced to face.

Last night, even though my heart was broken and my body exhausted, I went to the coalition meeting after work. And that's where I met him, the man no longer in my bed this morning. A jackhammer pounded at the concrete fog in my head and loosened chunks of the night before in little bits and pieces—a kind and thoughtful man, in his forties like me; green eyes, white teeth, crooked smile; our whispered comments during the meeting, our nonstop conversation over drinks afterward; tripping on the edge of the elevator and staggering down the hall to my apartment, and after that . . . after that . . . I couldn't remember anything after that.

Not that that was unusual. That was my pattern. I poured all my compassion into the foster children I worked with during the day and then turned to alcohol, and sometimes men, for love at night. Well, at least the one last night hadn't just been a stranger I found in a bar. At least I had something in common with this one. At least there was that.

I sat up and glanced at my bedside clock. Shit! Either my alarm hadn't gone off or I'd slept through it. I jumped out of bed and raced to the bathroom, splashed cold water on my face, gulped down a couple aspirin, and ran a comb through my shoulder-length blond hair. I pulled my brightly flowered peasant blouse and long faded denim skirt from the closet, then tossed them on the bed and opted instead for the beige linen suit and navy blue cotton blouse I usually wore to court. If I was going to be late, I should at least look professional.

It was after nine o'clock when I rushed upstairs to the foster care unit carrying a cup of coffee from the café on the first floor of the downtown Health Services Building. I had just slipped into my cubicle when Betsy Chambers, our department administrator, headed my way. I smoothed down my knee-length skirt and tugged at the hem of the suit jacket, ready to tell her I'd make up for my tardiness by working late tonight.

"Good morning, Sylvia." She flashed me a warm smile. "I'll see you at the meeting this afternoon." A little wave and then she was gone.

Whew! Except for my raging hangover, no harm done. She didn't seem to have noticed I was late, and from her friendliness, I was pretty sure I was still her number one choice for the supervisor position after Rita retired. I lifted a stack of files from my bottom right-hand drawer and got to work. Today was my day to do paperwork and update case records.

A few hours later, the phone rang. If it was a foster parent calling to say a child had run away or been injured, or there was some other crisis requiring my immediate attention, I wouldn't be able to finish my paperwork before the staff meeting and I really would have to work late tonight.

"Sylvia Jensen speaking."

"Hi, this is Norton. I didn't have a chance to say good-bye last night."

"Oh." So that was his name. Norton. "Okay."

"That's it? Just, 'Oh, okay'?"

"How about, 'Oh, you didn't tell me you were married.'"

There was silence on the other end of the line for a few seconds. "I am," he finally admitted.

"Was that so hard?"

I listened to him inhale and exhale. "I'm sorry. I should have told you."

"What's her name?"

"Chloe."

"And your children?"

"One. Corey. He's four years old."

A few awkward seconds passed. "Well, no matter," I said. "It was just a one-night stand. Thanks for calling."

"Wait, Sylvia. Don't hang up. Please. I really liked talking to you. I was hoping we could do it again."

"Do what again?"

"Talk."

"Sure."

"Sure . . . what?"

"Sure, we can talk."

He laughed. "Well, okay then. I'll call you."

"Sure." Sure, meaning a married man who just wanted to talk would be a first. And sure, meaning I knew he wasn't going to call anyway.

But he did call, the next day and the next. The following Thursday we met after work to talk. We met again the Thursday after that and the Thursday after that, then before and after the coalition meetings on Tuesdays. It was just talk, I told myself. Nothing more. Just talk. That first night had been a fluke, a drunken mistake, and I really didn't know what had happened anyway. Several weeks went by before I finally asked him.

"I'm embarrassed that I don't know," I said, "but did we have sex the night we met?"

He laughed. "You passed out," he said. "I was drunk, too, but I had enough sense not to take advantage. I tucked you into bed and hurried home."

My initial instincts had been right: he was a good man, a decent man. I told myself there was no reason to feel guilty about our relationship. Norton might be married, but he and I were just friends, that was all. He probably went home and told his wife all about our conversations each week.

For six weeks we met every Tuesday and Thursday, still talking, just talking—mirroring each other's terror about the world being on the brink of the final abyss and raging at Nectaral Corporation's continued manufacture of weapons of mass destruction—always in the same back booth in the same bar with the same drinks, white zinfandel for me, Pabst beer for him. One night he brought his journal and read what he'd written about a dream he'd had.

I'm standing on top of a hill that's almost tall enough to be considered a mountain, high enough to see a mushroom cloud in the distance. There's a fire in the cloud, red, yellow, orange. First there's only one cloud, but then I see another, and then another. It's familiar. I've seen it before, in real life.

A flash of terror crossed his face and he stopped reading, then started again.

At first, the mushroom clouds are far away, but they're getting closer and multiplying. There are people lower on the hillside. They're not high enough to see what I see. I call out to warn them. "The end of the world is here! Hug your children. Hold your loved ones. Tell them you love them. Say good-bye to them." But they all laugh at me. They think I've gone mad. They turn away as if they don't hear and go about their business as if I don't exist.

A woman in a long white robe appears before me with arms outstretched, palms up in a meditative pose. "Do not give power to fear, my dear," she says. "Bring love to your fear." I scream at her that it's not just fear, it's real, and we're all going to die. But she just looks at me with a condescending smile and says "Bring love to your fear" again and then disappears.

Norton tightened his grip on his journal.

A young man in his twenties comes toward me and tells me I worry too much. He talks to me as if I'm a young child or a senile grandfather. "Our military has been on the cutting edge of missile defense systems for the past sixty years," he says. "Nobody's going to get nuked. They won't let it happen." I scream at him, tell him to wake up. Don't you see? Don't you see? He rolls his eyes and walks away, laughing. I fall to my knees and cover the back of my head with my hands just as I was taught to do during atomic bomb drills in public school. I howl. But no one hears me. No one will listen.

He stopped reading and sighed. Then he gathered me in his arms and his dream became mine. We clung tight to each other for a long time, bound together by a shared terror in the depths of our souls, a terror not felt by others.

After that, things were different. Something had changed between us.

"My wife is like the woman in my dream who told me not to give power to my fear," he said after we finally broke apart. "Chloe's a good person, but her only goal in life is to be happy."

"I envy her that," I said.

"It's so different with you, Sylvia. You understand me. We understand each other."

I knew he'd just crossed the invisible line that up until then we'd both honored. And I liked it, despite the tsunami of guilt sweeping over me. I waited for him to continue, wanted him to cross that line again, and he did.

"Chloe and I see most things differently. She's not keen about my involvement with the coalition, to put it mildly. She says she doesn't know why I want to be such a killjoy." I should have stopped him. Instead, I downed another glass of wine.

From that point on our conversations deepened, became more and more personal. Norton told me stories about his son, Corey, whom he adored and lived for, whose future he'd be willing to die for if necessary. I told him about being married to Frank and living and teaching in the Bronx, how we'd moved back to the Midwest to live off the land in a one-room cabin and then divorced after I left for university to get a master's degree and never returned. I told him stories about what it was like to be a foster care worker in a broken child welfare system. He told me stories about people he'd worked with at the post office for twenty years. As time went by, we dug further and further into our histories as if searching for special places where our lives converged, times when similar experiences meant we had somehow known each other before we even met.

It seemed like we could talk about anything, that nothing was off-limits. Until one night, when he said he'd enlisted right after graduating from high school.

"What was it like to be in the military?" I asked.

That was when I learned that a distant look could take someone away from you in an instant. He guzzled his beer, then raised the empty can to signal for another one. When he finally spoke again, he didn't answer my question.

"You know, Sylvia," he said. "It's the accidents and near misses that scare me the most. Like last year, when the Soviets thought a nuclear attack from us was imminent and the officer in charge had only twenty-three minutes to respond. He told his superiors it was a false alarm even though he had no evidence that it actually was." He stared off into space for several more seconds. "That man saved the world, Sylvia. That one man."

Then, without warning, he jumped to attention and looked at his watch. "Time to call it a night."

I longed for him to come home with me, longed to hold him, love him, have him hold me, love me, longed for him to let me in. "One more drink?" I said.

He shook his head. "Tomorrow's Good Friday." He stood up and slapped a twenty-dollar bill on the table. "The vigil starts early in the morning."

I gulped down the rest of my wine, so drunk I could hardly walk, much less do anything else, and went home. Alone. Norton didn't answer my question about his military service that night, and I never asked it again.

##

At six o'clock the next morning we met in front of the sign that said "Headquarters of Nectaral: Worldwide Heating and Cooling Systems." No mention of cluster bombs or guidance systems for first-strike nukes and cruise missiles. No mention of Nectaral being the biggest military contractor in our state. Over a hundred protesters were already huddled together on the sidewalk, bundled up in wool and shivering against a biting early morning wind. Some wore religious attire, their somber Good Friday mood blending with the muted colors of the two- and three-story homes in the historic neighborhood that circled the corporate compound.

The gate to Nectaral Plaza opened onto an immaculately groomed park shaded by large trees. Benches were strategically placed around a profusion of flower gardens for visitors who, unless informed, would never suspect, from such beautiful surroundings, that they were sitting in the belly of an agent of death.

Martin Lind, director of the Peace and Justice Coalition, shook all our hands and thanked us for coming. Martin had told us once that when he was in the army, some guys shouted "Jew boy" at him and then beat him with a duffel bag filled with rocks. I couldn't help but wonder if Norton had witnessed something like that when he was in the military, if that explained his strange non-answer to my question last night.

Martin's deep, booming voice cut through the morning chill. "Even after years of protesting, the monster inside these walls keeps growing and growing. Which is why we have moved from protest to resistance. So . . . how many of you are willing to risk arrest this morning?"

Many of those gathered were in affinity groups, support systems for people planning to commit civil disobedience in orchestrated situations such as this. They had been trained in nonviolent behaviors, strategies, and tactics. Half of the group raised their hands in response to Martin's question, but this time I wasn't one of them. After the police moved in, Norton and I planned to leave and spend the rest of the day together.

Martin smiled at all the raised hands. "My dear friend Meridel Le Sueur says you can't live in this century and be for anything that is true and just without going to jail occasionally."

"So do you think they're going to arrest us today, Martin," someone asked.

"I met with Bigger yesterday, and he didn't tell me how they planned to respond to our action today. Maybe they don't know yet themselves."

Another voice rose up from the back of the crowd. "Who's Bigger?"

"Thomas Bigger is the CEO of the Nectaral Corporation."

Norton let out a snort and commented out of the side of his mouth, "Yeah, the charitable guy who adopted two orphans during the Vietnam War." He snorted again. "Their parents were probably killed by his cluster bombs."

Jim, who was in an affinity group with Norton and me, stepped to the front of the crowd. He had a wooden crucifix strapped on his back to which a replica of a nuclear missile had been nailed. In silence, we formed a single line behind him and with slow, laborious steps walked toward the main administrative building in the middle of the plaza. A soft and mournful soprano voice rose from the line. *Were you there when they crucified my Lord?* I knew the Easter hymn well from the church I was raised in. I tried to sing along, but a lump in my throat blocked the words.

At the entrance to the building, people who were willing to risk arrest formed a circle and fell to their knees. The rest of us stood behind them like a choir surrounding a sacred altar. Father Keagan, pastor of the Monrow City Episcopal Church, taped a five-foot photograph of little children on the double glass doors and then knelt in prayer before it. As I stared at it, the faces of the children in the picture became the faces of the many children I had been unable to save. Markus, a student of mine in the Bronx who had disappeared in 1968 and had never been found. Jamie, a child stolen from the reservation and lost in the foster care system. The words from an old Sunday school song rang in my ears. *Jesus loves the little children, all the children of the world.*

Rhona, Char, and Anita, three biological sisters who were also Catholic Worker House nuns, stepped forward, each of them holding a vial of red liquid, their own blood, which they lifted up and presented like Communion wine.

Oh, o-o-oh, oh, sometimes it causes me to tremble, tremble, tremble.

The three sisters splashed their blood onto the images of the children. At that point I broke away from Norton, joined the inner circle, and fell to my knees.

Were you there when they nailed him to the cross? Yes, I was there. I had been hypnotized once for past-life regression and remembered a former life as a Roman soldier, on the wrong side. I didn't know if that was true or not, of course, only that it felt like it was.

A dozen policemen in black jackets appeared, one of them with a megaphone. "You are on private property. If you do not leave immediately, you will be arrested." Soon three officers stepped into the circle, and they started to confront each resister one by one.

"Ma'am," one of them said when it was my turn, "do you know that

23

you are on private property?"

I looked at him. Unable to answer.

"Ma'am, you have one more chance to leave or you will be arrested."

When I didn't move, one officer grabbed my arms, another one my legs. My body went limp. I closed my eyes and saw the blood-splattered photo of the children as the officers bound my hands behind my back with plastic cuffs and then lifted me from the ground, carried me away, and tossed me onto a bench in a police van. Just before the door closed, Norton was thrown onto the bench across from me.

"I'm sorry," I said. "I know I promised we'd spend the day together."

He winked. "We are together."

At the station, we were separated though, men and women held in different cells. At dusk a judge released us on our own recognizance pending trial, and Norton and I went to our bar. This time we sat side by side in our booth, hip against hip, shoulder touching shoulder, hands brushing hands. When the waitress appeared with my usual glass of wine and his usual can of beer, we both shook our heads.

"Gin and tonic," we said in unison. We hadn't even consulted each other first.

Norton laughed. "I do believe we have become one person."

He reached for my hand and squeezed it. I knew I should pull away but I didn't. He took both of my hands in his and looked at me for a long time, his eyes reflecting the same longing that was in mine. Then he kissed the tips of my fingers and tenderly caressed them one by one. I knew it was wrong. He was married. He had a son. I pulled my hands away and reached for my drink.

After several minutes of silence and another gin and tonic, Norton ran his fingers down my cheek. "It's too late, Sylvia. I already love you. You already love me."

I did love him. I loved everything about him. I loved his serious pontificating. The way he injected his monologues with doses of ironic self-mockery. I even loved his stubbornness. Once he decided what was right, there was no getting him to change his mind. He was like me that way. Maybe loving Norton was my way of loving myself. Maybe it was a way of caring for myself, a way to ward off my fears or at least manage them. Could that be so wrong? And in the face of nuclear annihilation, how important was right and wrong anyway? How could it be wrong to follow my heart?

My hand touched Norton's cheek. "Do you think we have time?"

He nodded, his eyes full.

"Okay, then," I said, my words slurring. "Let's go to my place."

THREE

2019

Crowds of people squeeze past us on their way to the exit while I gaze into Corey Cramer's green eyes, the eyes of Norton, the man I adored, the love of my life, whose leaving, I now realize, I've never fully mourned. The face of his son is like a kaleidoscopic lens of shards from the past. Norton and me climbing a fence at a military base. Forming a human blockade, sitting arm in arm, singing *Give Peace a Chance.* Holding hands. Lying side by side in bed, sharing secrets. Laughing. Together. Always together. Until we weren't.

Corey's jaw is set tight. "You knew my father?"

I brush an imaginary piece of lint from my skirt. "We were good friends."

His eyes see into me. My first impulse is to hide my nakedness; my second is to embrace it, scars and all. He shuffles from one foot to the other. He's going to walk away.

"Your father and I were in the nuclear disarmament movement together in the eighties."

He looks down at the floor. "I was only four years old when . . . I don't remember much, about my dad."

"He talked about you a lot," I say.

His mouth shapes into a pout. He looks just like the child in the picture Norton always carried in his wallet.

"Coffee?" I say.

He doesn't say yes or no, but when I turn and walk out the door, he follows. My left hand grips my long skirt so I won't trip going down the steps. We skirt the edges of the angry protesters, and he cups my right elbow. Just like Norton used to.

"There's an all-night diner around the corner," he says when we reach the bottom step.

I nod. "Nick's. Your father and I . . ." A deep ache in my throat swallows up my words, a longing to go to the diner with Norton just one more time, to feel the warmth of his hand in mine, his arm around my shoulders. For years after he was gone, I drowned my grief in alcohol. Later, after I got into recovery, I tucked our relationship into a compartment of drinking transgressions, labeled it an illicit affair with a married man who shared my passion for justice, sex, and alcohol.

When we reach the diner, I pour my ache for Norton back into its secret container in my heart. Jingling bells on the door announce our arrival; blinding lights reflecting off the steel panels behind the well-worn counter welcome us. We pass the floor-mounted counter stools, walk to the far end of the railroad-like dining car, and sit in the last booth—Norton's and my booth. Corey, unaware of the unfinished grief his presence has unleashed, flips through the list of songs on the tabletop jukebox. He reaches in his pocket for a quarter (it used to be a nickel) and selects *King of the Road*, one of Norton's favorites, then bobs his head up and down in time with the music just like Norton did. Unlike his father, who loved the diner's tacky décor, Corey's face registers distaste for the mismatched red stripes down the middle of the white Formica table, the white stripes on the red wall.

"You look just like your father," I say.

"Hmm." He picks up his menu, pretends to read it.

"He was a fighter," I say.

He looks at me for a long time, then down, his palms pressed into the table. He's not the talker Norton was. Finally, he leans back in the booth with a sigh.

"Mom said the FBI is what got him," he says at last. "But she always changed the subject when I asked what happened. That's what Mom was best at. Changing the subject."

"Your dad did what he did for your sake," I say. "Your future."

"And yet Kim Jong-un still has a nuclear missile launch button on his desk, doesn't he?" He spits out the words like bitter fruit on his tongue.

"I know," I say.

Just then a waitress appears. She plunks two mugs on the table and fills them with coffee without asking if we want any. Some things never change.

"Okay, folks." She pulls out a pencil and order pad from her apron pocket, then taps her foot on the worn linoleum and rolls her eyes. When I order a chocolate malt and Corey orders two eggs over easy with bacon and hash browns, she gives us a *Well, it's about time* sigh and stalks off.

"Your father loved it that Nick's serves breakfast twenty-four hours a day." Corey furrows his brow. I don't tell him he's just ordered Norton's favorite dinner.

My iPhone beeps, a text from J. B. *Sorry I missed the memorial. Got caught up with the protesters outside. Where are you?* I text back, tell him I'm at the diner and invite him to join us. "That was my friend J. B.," I tell Corey. "He's an investigative reporter with the *New York Times*. He was supposed to meet me at the church but didn't make it."

Corey doesn't seem interested. "I s'pose you're going to the protest at Nectaral." His set jaw is a dare.

"I haven't decided." I don't tell him about the tug-of-war in my heart during the memorial service, the struggle between two parts of me—the one that works to remain composed and serene, and the one that surges with passion to act, to be more impulsive, more unstinting. More like I used to be, more like I imagine Bertha Pickering was.

"How about you," I ask. "Are you planning to go?"

He jerks his head from side to side. "Protests don't change anything. No one pays attention."

"I do plan to get signatures on the petition in support of the UN treaty to ban nuclear weapons. One hundred and twenty-two other countries have already adopted it."

He shakes his head. "Nothing but pie in the sky. Another hollow effort. We have to do something to make things change *fast*."

"That's not how change happens, I'm afraid. I wish it did."

29

His face freezes, hard, like a stone. "Then we're doomed."

"Not necessarily." I could cite examples of how things have changed over time after long periods of struggle, but I don't want to get into an argument. "I don't know," I say instead. "Maybe we're doomed no matter what we do. Sometimes it's hard to have hope."

The muscles in his jaw tighten even more. He hisses, "We have to make 'em listen." He looks from left to right as if checking to make sure no one else can hear, then lowers his voice to a whisper. "And believe me, Sylvia, that's exactly what we're gonna do."

The steely determination and deep passion in his voice sound like Norton, only there's an edge of violence to it, like a volcano threatening to erupt. I wonder what he means about *making* them listen? Make *who* listen? *How?* My questions now are similar to the ones I asked Norton when I returned from the women's peace camp in New York in the summer of 1984. Similar also to the ones I asked him when we were on trial for trespassing at Nectaral Plaza on Good Friday, the questions that threatened our relationship.

I flash Corey a conciliatory smile. "Your dad was a skeptic, too."

His response is quick, automatic. "Yeah, well, a lot of good that did him . . . or us."

I hold back, careful not to injure him like Norton and I injured each other with words.

He curls his hands into fists. "Mom kept Dad's secrets, but after she passed, I found his journal. It's all there. All documented. I know everything."

My heart stops beating. He knows everything? Does that mean Chloe, Norton's wife, knew about our relationship? Is that what Corey's rage is about? Do I really want to know?

"That was a long time ago," I mumble.

He reaches across the table and his hand bumps against my mug. Coffee splatters onto my blouse. He leans forward, points his finger at me.

"It's not over," he says through gritted teeth. "Mark my words, Sylvia, it's not anywhere near over."

FOUR

1984

By summer, my love for Norton was more intense than the hot sun; it bloomed brighter than the wildest and most colorful profusion of flowers ever seen in the Midwest. I loved the way his skin stretched down over his high cheekbones and settled into either frown or smile lines on the outsides of his lips, the way his green eyes twinkled with kindness and burned with anger, the tingle of his fingertips on my skin. But as my love for him deepened, so too did my guilt. He was married. His wife, Chloe, thought we were just friends. He had a son, Corey, who was only four years old and needed his father. Many times I told myself I had to let him go, but I never could. Instead, I drank.

A widespread sense that summer, among our activist friends, was that the world was a more dangerous place than ever. Norton and I, to counter our fear that we were on the brink of nuclear annihilation, went to more rallies, protests, sit-ins. We drank more. We made love with more intensity. Our passion for each other and our passion for saving the planet were indistinguishable. We saw ourselves as the warp and woof of a global tapestry without understanding that its design was too complex for us to grasp.

I decided that summer to go to the Seneca Women's Peace Camp in New York, which had been established near a military base where nuclear weapons were being stored. How could I not do my part when women at a similar camp at Greenham Common in England had been protesting the planned deployment of those weapons since 1981? I didn't know that my decision to go would mark the beginning of the end for Norton and me.

He came to see me off. "Do what you have to do." That was his fare-well to me as I boarded one of two buses that would take ninety-nine of us Monrow City women to New York. His voice was firm and he smiled, but the lines around his lips drooped, and he looked unwell. I didn't think of it as an omen at the time. I just thought it meant he would miss me. The bus drove slowly away from the parking lot, and I stuck my arm out the window and waved and waved until he was an indistinguishable dot on the landscape. Then I settled back in my seat.

"Welcome, ladies!" Jennifer, the twenty-something, blue-jean-clad intern from the Peace and Justice Coalition, stood at the front of the bus with a microphone. "Thousands of women will be going to the camp between now and Labor Day, but our contingent is the largest."

Expressions of pride rippled through the bus.

"Will there be enough room for us?" It was Maddie, our resident worrywart.

Jennifer flicked her hand in what could be interpreted as being either dismissive or reassuring, depending on how you felt about the question or the questioner. "The camp is on a fifty-two-acre farm," she said. "Plen-ty of space to accommodate us. But, of course, the size of the camp is nothing compared to the eleven-thousand-acre Seneca Army Depot."

"How many nuclear weapons are stored at the depot?" This time Maddie shouted louder and with a lot more anxiety in her voice.

Jennifer smiled, but she also let out a barely disguised sigh, like she thought everyone on the trip should already know the answer to that question. "The military neither denies nor confirms the presence of nu-clear weapons," she said. "So we don't know."

We passed some middle school boys playing soccer on a grassy field and that got me thinking about the children who lived near the Seneca depot. What would happen to them if there were a nuclear attack or, God forbid, a nuclear accident? I'd read that there were emergency evac-uation plans only for on-base personnel.

Mary Lou, in the seat next to me, poked me with her elbow. "If I lived in the town of Romulus, I sure wouldn't want to be so close to the depot." I attributed Mary Lou's propensity for giving voice to my thoughts to years of experience, given that she was eighty-nine years old and a great-grandmother of six, but maybe she'd always been a reader of people's minds.

"Our briefing materials said that the town is totally dependent on the depot," I said. "The military even controls its water supply."

Mary Lou huffed her disgust. "Yeah. The depot land is valued at two hundred and fifty million, and you want to know how much it pays in property tax?" She didn't wait for me to answer. "Not a cent. Not a single penny."

"So I guess people must depend on the depot for jobs then," I said.

Mary Lou shrugged and raised her hand. "Jennifer? Do you know how many townspeople work at the depot?"

"Only a few," the intern said. "Most of the fourteen hundred jobs at the depot aren't open to local residents."

"You'd think they could at least hire people from the town to do the cooking and cleaning if nothing else," Mary Lou mumbled.

"Two hundred to two hundred fifty of the depot jobs are for military police," Jennifer said. "They're trained in anti-terrorism and authorized to use deadly force." She paused to let that sink in.

Gasps rippled up and down the length of the bus. Moisture seeped into my T-shirt from under my armpits. Would we be considered terrorists? Surely not. We were just a bunch of middle-aged white women, respectable-looking mothers and grandmothers from the Midwest. Surely the military police wouldn't use deadly force against us. Or would they? I scrunched down in my seat with Norton's words—*Do what you have to do*—ringing ominously in my ears.

"Ladies!" The microphone squealed. "Sorry." Bertha Pickering looked a lot younger than her sixty-four years in a blazing orange T-shirt and long denim skirt that brushed against her ankles. "I have something to say. I know that's unusual." She chuckled. "Seriously. We must *not* be pessimistic. Our job this week is to stop the shipment of nuclear weapons to Europe. Our mission is *not* impossible! Remember, we'll be less than fourteen miles from where Elizabeth Cady Stanton lived. Where

Susan B. Anthony traveled, to the first women's rights convention, held right there in Seneca Falls in 1848. So if anyone tries to tell you we're crazy, just ask them what would have happened if those women had given up when they were told that the right to vote was too radical and impossible."

"Right on!" Mary Lou and I shouted to the sound of scattered applause.

"Did you know that Seneca Falls was a station on the Underground Railroad?" Bertha was emboldened, her voice louder.

"Yes!"

"And did Harriet Tubman give up the fight to end slavery when that seemed impossible?"

"No!" we shouted.

"Is eliminating nuclear weapons from the face of the earth impossible?"

"No!"

"Are we going to give up?"

"No!"

"That's all I have to say then."

The bus erupted in laughter and applause. We clapped and clapped. We stomped our feet. We chanted. *Won't give up. Won't give up.* The bus driver honked the horn. Bertha laughed and returned to her seat. I knew she was a force, but I'd never seen her in action like that before.

After several minutes, the bus fell silent, with Mary Lou snoring on my shoulder while I slipped into an optimistic sleep.

We were on the bus for two days, getting off at truck stops for food and, for a lucky few, showers. It was dusk when we finally arrived at the camp. I stumbled down the bus steps with Mary Lou behind, a tight grip on my shoulders to keep from losing her balance. Acres and acres of parched land were visible at the darkest edges of twilight, not yet night, clumps of soil hardened into rock by months of drought, a dizzying new world from which I would return changed in ways I did not yet fathom.

"I thought the mosquitoes were bad at home." Mary Lou swatted her forearm, then waved her hand back and forth in front of her face.

A black Lab sniffed my toes. I leaned down to pat her head, and she licked my hand and wagged her tail like I was her new best friend. To our left, a two-story farmhouse beamed light through open windows, women's voices inside, floodlights outside exposing peeling white paint. Next to the farmhouse, a large open tent with long tables and benches, cooking utensils hanging from a board at one end, wooden shelves, stacks of bowls and plates. Behind the kitchen area, a barn on which were drawn nude female figures with their stomachs painted white, their beautiful bodies connected with black spider web lines.

The screen door to the farmhouse slammed shut. A Black woman in her twenties strode toward us, a long thick braid thumping her waist in time with her footsteps. "Welcome!" She skidded to a halt. "So glad you made it. We've been waiting for you. I'm Janice. From Toronto. I've been here since the beginning."

Several more female figures, semitransparent halos in the dusky mist, appeared in different shapes and colors and smiles of youthful exuberance at the sight of our open mouths and wide eyes. One young woman was topless.

"Hi, my name's Brenda." I stared at her ample pale pink breasts and wondered what I'd gotten myself into.

"And I'm Felicia." She was a heavyset brown-skinned woman in a much too tight T-shirt and much too short jean shorts.

"Welcome, you can call me A." She looked like an ordinary white boy with a butch haircut. "You know, like 'hey there' without the *h*? It's short for Annabelle but I hate that name, so call me A. Just A."

A slightly older and taller woman stepped forward, much more confident than the others, but maybe it was just the way her bright red hair set off her chalk white face that made it seem that way. "Jackie here. Hi."

One by one, the rest of the women introduced themselves, each voice solicitous in its own unique and, in my view, delightful way. They grabbed our tents, sleeping bags, and knapsacks and walked off with our stuff while we trudged along behind.

"Now that we're here," I whispered to Mary Lou, "the average age of the camp just jumped twenty years."

"More like forty." Mary Lou chuckled under her breath.

Someone behind us muttered, "I feel so conservative," and that set off a barrage of responses.

"So middle class."

"So white."

"So boring."

"So clothed."

"Well, I don't care what anyone else does, *I* plan to wear clothes."

That one made Mary Lou chuckle again. "I always wanted to go braless," she said from the corner of her mouth. I laughed out loud. I was secretly envious of these young women, so free and in love with themselves. When I'd been their age, and even now sometimes, I was uncomfortable in my own skin, my too skinny, too pimply, too unattractive, too not-perfect body.

We passed the kitchen area, a row of sinks to which hoses were attached to draw in water. Underneath the sinks were pipes to drain the water into plastic buckets. Beyond the sinks, a row of small tents with a portable toilet inside each one. A respectable distance from the bathroom area, hundreds of tents arranged in small circles. Neighborhoods within a village. In the center of everything, an open pavilion-type building, its roof supported by wooden posts, bales of hay inside arranged in concentric circles. A women's meeting space. On the other side of the pavilion, the young women stopped and dropped our things on the ground.

"Ta-da! The Midwest section!" Janice pointed at the open field with a flick of her long braid. She started to say more, but the sound of a helicopter drowned out her voice. It dropped low enough for me to see the spinning blades and the bared teeth of two men inside, then made a sharp turn and flew off.

"They do that when it gets dark." Janice laughed. "We don't know if it's some surveillance routine or if they're trying to intimidate us."

Butch-haircut-called-A shrugged her shoulders. "You'll get used to it."

"No worries," Janice added. "We patrol the camp every night from midnight to six in the morning. If you like walkie-talkies, you can sign up to cover a shift." Mary Lou grunted. I shook my head. Janice laughed again. "No worries. There are other chores you can do. The sign-up list is next to the fridge on the kitchen wall in the farmhouse. Breakfast is ready at six, put away at nine. If you're hungry now, there are snacks in the house. But first, we'll help you set up your tents and get you settled in. Every morning at ten we meet to plan the day's action at the depot."

I set up my little two-person camping tent next to the palatial tent belonging to the sister nuns Rhona, Char, and Anita, the funniest women I'd ever known. I'd shared a jail cell with them after the Good Friday protest, and they'd had me laughing for hours with their stories. My favorite was the one about the first time Char was arrested at Nectaral headquarters.

"So there's Char," Rhona laughed, "the one who's always preaching about nonviolence, and what's the first thing she does when the officer approaches her?"

"She knees him!" Rhona and Anita said in unison, to peals of laughter.

"I'll be doing penance the rest of my life for that one," Char said. Then she laughed louder and longer than anyone.

My tent was just wide enough for me to walk along one side of my sleeping bag, long enough for my knapsack to fit at its end, and tall enough for me to stand up bent over. I changed into the extra-large T-shirt that I'd brought along as pajamas, but instead of going to bed, I was lured outside by angry voices. A dozen or so women were sitting around a fire pit in the middle of our circle of tents.

"This isn't what I signed up for." Maddie's slightly plump body was hunched over with a flashlight pointed at her lap. "I sure wish I'd seen this handbook before. I thought the camp was supposed to be about creating a nuclear-free world, not a woman-focused one. Have you noticed how everything around here is in a circle? It says here the circle symbolizes our wombs." Her angry finger tapped on the page. "Like it's gospel or something."

"You knew it was a women-only camp when you signed up," someone said.

Maddie's huff emphasized what most of us already knew, that she did not like to be challenged. "I didn't know it was an exclusionary, feminist-only one," she said. "It says here that no male over the age of twelve is allowed onto the main grounds."

"Really?" Mary Lou's voice was strained from exhaustion. "What about my grandson? He's just as firm a believer in the anti-nuclear cause as I am."

"Well, if women are going to be running around naked, you wouldn't want him here, would you?" Maddie's negativity usually wasn't contagious, but tonight, with everyone drained by the long trip, it snowballed into a string of complaints.

"I don't have any problem with lesbians, but I draw the line at public displays of affection."

"To each her own, I say, but I don't want to see it."

"What's with the macrobiotic food anyway?"

My stomach grew queasy with worry. I hadn't come here to sit around and talk about feelings or deal with lesbian/straight differences or work through my own personal issues. Or, for that matter, to build and maintain a community of women.

Pam, our Quaker, stood and made her hands into two stop signs. The silver strands in her gray hair glowed in the light of the fire. "We're having a bit of trouble adjusting, that's all. It's late and we're tired." Her voice was calm and conciliatory. "I suggest we go to bed and get some rest so we're fresh for the action at the depot tomorrow."

"I was just trying to express my feelings," Maddie grumbled. "Does that make me a bad person?"

"Of course not," Pam said.

One by one, we headed for our tents. I tucked myself into my sleeping bag, but a string of worries kept me awake. Would Maddie's attitude stir up conflict? Would we forget why we came? If we couldn't live together in peace here, then what chance was there for peace in the world? And if we couldn't work together, how the hell were we going to stop the deployment of cruise missiles and Pershing missiles to Europe? I longed for Norton, wished I could talk to him. Then I started worrying about him. The last time he told me he loved me, it was with such intensity that I'd wondered if he was thinking about leaving his wife. My heart fluttered at the thought, but I knew it was wrong to want that, wrong to even think that. I sat up and reached into the bottom of my duffel bag for the bottle of bourbon. I needed a nightcap.

Nobody would know. It made no sense for the camp to have an alcohol-free policy anyway. I opened the bottle and took a swig. Then another. One more, and I shoved the bottle back in the bottom of the bag and fell into a deep sleep.

At seven o'clock the next morning, I was startled awake by a helicopter hovering so low it shook my tent. Soon it sounded like several helicopters were circling the camp. I lay there, frozen, barely breathing. This couldn't be normal. Something must have happened. I threw on the same T-shirt and shorts I'd worn for the past two days on the bus and stepped out of my tent. The camp was alive, buzzing with excitement. I grabbed the arm of the first person I ran into, a dark-skinned woman dressed in a purple Indian sari.

"What's going on?"

Her eyes were as wide as golf balls. "Some women got into the Q zone at four o'clock this morning."

"Q zone?"

"The highest security area inside the depot." She stopped to catch her breath.

"What's in the Q zone?"

"Sixty or seventy reinforced earth-covered bunkers *and* a twenty-eight-thousand-square-foot underground, temperature-controlled building for storing plutonium."

"Are they dead? Did the armed guards shoot them?"

Her eyes opened wider. "They didn't even notice. And the women were in there for at least *twenty minutes!* Can you believe it?" Her eyes widened even more.

"How in the world did they even get in there?"

"They climbed over *three* fences!"

"Why? What did they do in there?"

"They hung a banner with a clothesline of purple hearts on the *inner-most* fence and sat there for a while. Praying, I guess. Then they climbed back out, over all three fences. They left a child's stuffed lamb in front of the outside fence with a note attached that said *And the lamb will lie down with the lion*. And no one even noticed!"

Just then a helicopter swooped down and sent everything flying in its wake. I fell to the ground with my hands covering the back of my neck, a perfect duck and cover. The woman helped me to my feet. "They're probably looking for them," she said. "I heard they came back to camp and went to bed."

Over breakfast there was talk of nothing but the women who got into the Q zone. How brave they were. How daring. What a coup it had been. No names were mentioned. The less we knew about who they were, the better. It was for their protection. They were young, someone said, which made me wonder if their action was a sign of courage or simply youthful foolhardiness.

Butch-haircut-called-A puffed up her chest and chuckled. "A depot spokesman has publicly denied all rumors that security was breached. They sure don't want anyone to know a bunch of women—girls, to them—got inside. Undetected." She snorted, then laughed so hard she started to choke.

Bertha Pickering sat down next to me on a kitchen bench. "Quite an exciting coup, hey?"

"But if there's no news coverage," I said, "what do you think their action accomplished?"

She shrugged her shoulders. "Maybe it was just something they had to do," she said.

There it was again. *Do what you have to do.* But what did that mean for me? Did I have to risk getting shot, maybe even killed, like those young women had?

"I don't know if I can do what they did. Maybe I'm too old," I said.

Bertha laughed. "Never too old to do what has to be done. And the older you get, the less you worry about the consequences."

At ten o'clock, during the meeting to plan the day's action, I thought about what Bertha had said. Whenever suggestions were made that felt risky or scary to me, I imagined what I would be like in my fifties, sixties, and seventies if I already allowed myself to be overly cautious now at only forty-two.

At noon, one hundred twenty of us walked to the depot in a single file along the side of the highway. An army truck drove past and a hand popped out from under the tarp, its fingers flashing a peace sign. We all cheered. We walked through the town of Romulus, and some people waved to us, others gave us the finger. I smiled and nodded to all of them, feeling secure in the truth that what I was doing was what I had to do in that moment.

Three rows of soldiers stood at the gate to the depot. Straight and tall, billy clubs in front of rigid bodies. Stone faces with no expression. On the other side of the road, forty or fifty white townspeople, young and middle-aged men, angry-faced women, teenagers.

"Go home, bitches," a woman with big blond hair screamed.

Aiming an American flag at us like a weapon, a young, clean-cut man shouted, "You're nothing but a bunch of Communists, feminists, lesbians, and . . . and vegetarians!"

I laughed and poked Mary Lou with my elbow. "I'm not any of those things," I said. But then two teenage boys threw rocks at us and one fell just short of my foot. I stopped laughing.

"Disperse!" an MP in full riot gear shouted into a bullhorn. "Disperse or you will be arrested."

A soft, mournful song, in Pam the Quaker's voice, arose from the middle of our group.

Child, child, child, child,
Will I ever see you grow?
I am fighting for your future
I love you so.

A few of us sang the first line again, then others repeated it after us, and soon our voices rose in a round, the words and melody alternating a message of love. Tears streamed down my face. I wiped them away and more kept coming.

41

The crowd across the road started singing, *Oh beautiful for spacious skies*. We fell to our knees and joined them. *America, America, God shed His grace on thee.*

"Hey, that's *our* song," someone yelled.

"Yeah, shut up, you don't give a rat's ass about America!"

"Why are you kneeling?"

"Yeah, you don't even believe in God!"

The song ended and we stood up. We walked over to the depot fence and started hanging items that symbolized what would be lost in a nuclear holocaust. Norton had sent his army uniform with me, to do with it whatever was needed, he'd said. I fastened it to the fence with clothespins and then cut it into tiny strips with a pair of scissors from my backpack. Soon the fence was covered with precious items that broke my heart— baby shoes, a hand-crocheted baby blanket, a pendant worn by one of the nuns for forty years, a banner from a casket that said Mother on it, photographs, children's toys, a diary, medals.

Someone took my hand and pulled me into a circle. In the middle, three lithe young women danced, their legs slowed by grief, disbelief, and shock, their arms outstretched, begging, mouths shouting out, raging at death.

NO! NO! NO!

We shouted back with hope for life.

YES! YES! YES!

One of the dancers stopped mid motion. "The bomb has just dropped," she said, "and you have five minutes to say good-bye to everyone and everything you love."

A moment of stunned silence. The eyes of the three dancers closed. Then their mouths opened to an intense mournful wailing, a keening expression of grief traditional for women in many cultures. Others joined in, their howling sharp and shrill. The sound swelled, died down, swelled again. Hands were thrown up, striking our breasts as we grieved together with a high-pitched divine madness that sounded like howling alley cats as large as lions.

The terrible, unpleasant din was more than the townspeople could bear. They surged across the road, started yanking our things off the fence. We dropped to our knees.

One of the dancers raised her palms to the sky. "Living day to day and knowing that you have no future makes your heart a rock," she said. "Crying cracks the rock so something can grow again."

We held on to each other and swayed from side to side. The sound of our keening lurched over the depot gate. It drove the townspeople back to the other side of the road. Then a horrifying scream pierced my ears. A howl so terrifying and from a place so deep it consumed me with unspeakable pain. A grief beyond words. A sound that silenced all other sounds. It was only when I felt gentle fingers touching my face and arms encircling me that I realized the scream had come from deep inside me.

Everything happened fast after that. I was bound to a woman on each side with nylon wristlets that cut into my skin. Hands reached around me and over me, winding brightly colored yarn around my body, weaving me to other bodies, to the gate. An MP's helmet got caught in the yarn's web and he cursed, shouted "Disperse! Disperse!" as he struggled to untangle himself.

Other MPs in riot gear repeated the warning. "You are trespassing on federal property. If you do not leave, you will be arrested."

Women stood outside the yellow line chanting their support. *The whole world is watching! The whole world is watching!* A news reporter took notes, a photojournalist took pictures. The MPs charged: "Disperse!" The supporters responded: *The whole world is watching!*

To the sound of a banjo playing *America the Beautiful* across the road, my hands were cuffed behind my back. Hard fingers dug into my armpits and the backs of my knees. My body was carried away. Supporters cheered. Townspeople jeered. I was thrown onto an army bus. Driven away with military police jeeps on each side of the bus. Taken to a makeshift detainment center, fifteen women in a plywood and chicken wire cell. Ushered out one at a time. Fingerprinted. Photographed.

"Identification, please."

I shrugged. *It's over. It doesn't matter anymore.* Rough hands on my shoulders. Pockets of my shorts pulled inside out, emptied of nothing.

43

"Your name?"

I shook my head.

"So you want to do this the hard way, huh?"

I was pushed onto a chair off to the side while others were processed. For crossing the yellow strip on the road that separated federal and Seneca County property, they were given a "ban and bar" letter. If they came back to the depot, six months in a federal prison and a $500 fine. Two women who were repeat offenders were carried away. The others were released. Then I was the only one left.

"So, are you ready to tell us who you are now?"

I opened my mouth, tried to say *Jane Doe*, but my lips were stuck together. What was I doing? I hadn't planned to resist, hadn't even planned to risk arrest. I had no driver's license or ID with me. I had no control over what I was doing. I raised my shoulders and they froze up like I'd gone catatonic.

"Okay, sit there until you're ready to cooperate. All night if you want."

The MPs talked among themselves. What should we do with her? Should we call someone to come get her? No, we can't let them think they can get away with this. Do you think something's wrong with her?

A tear trickled down my cheek. My hands are cuffed. Can't wipe it away. No matter. It's over. I'm dead. We're all dead. Nothing matters any more. The bomb has already dropped. It's too late.

I was pulled up from the chair. I opened my mouth. Air rushed in. I'm dragged into a tiny room. There are no windows. Plastic cuffs cut off my wrists. The door slams shut. Is it night or day? I close my eyes. I lie on the floor. Hard. Concrete. My back hurts. My legs cramp up. My feet.

Hours pass. Maybe days. I rolled onto my back and opened my eyes. Pitch-black. A brief flickering of flame in my head, a brief flash of thought, but then it went out. I sat up, pulled my legs to my chest. My head started to clear, just a little at first, then a bit more and a bit more. Had anyone at the camp noticed that I was gone? Surely Mary Lou did. But how would they know where I was? I hadn't designated anyone to be my support person, so there was no one to make sure I was okay, no one to come and bail me out. A slow awareness came to me at last, and I began to understand what had happened. I had lost touch with reality. I got so caught up in the death ritual that for a time I believed, really believed, we had all died. That it was over. I had lived the darkness of human nonexistence. That was how I'd ended up here. So now here I was, all alone and in trouble, and I had no clue how to get out of it.

I straightened my legs, pulled myself up to a standing position. I lifted one foot, then the other. Leaned backward, then forward. Jumped up and down. Someone must have heard me, because all of a sudden the door flew open. The overhead light came on. I squinted at an MP I hadn't seen before.

"My name is Sylvia Jensen," I said.

FIVE

2019

Corey's stony green eyes seem to demand a response, while my brain scrambles to decipher his words. *It's not over. Mark my words, Sylvia, it's not anywhere near over.*

"What?" His one sharp word slices into me like a teenager's whine.

"I'm sorry," I say. "I don't know what you're talking about."

He grins and seethes at the same time. "You'll find out." He pushes his shoulders back. "In due time."

His voice, eerily like Norton's, turns the lights in the diner suddenly too bright, its smells too greasy and sugary. "You remind me of your father," I say. Right away I regret it. Young people don't like it when someone says they're like their parents, and Norton didn't always sound like Corey sounds right now either.

Music blares from the jukebox. *Two hours of pushing broom buys an eight-by-twelve four-bit room.* Tension crawls across the Formica table. Corey's attitude, so much like Norton's during the summer and fall of 1984, leaves me nervous, uncertain about what and how to say something that won't alienate him.

After several seconds, he shakes his head. "Why are you looking at me like that?"

"I was remembering what your father said to me once, when I asked him what he was thinking."

I can't tell from his sideways look if he's irritated or curious. I decide to go with curious. "He said he couldn't tell me," I say, "so I asked him why not."

47

He raises his eyebrows.

"And he said . . ." I can hear Norton's exact words in my head. "He said, 'I can't tell you because I'm not as strong as you.' Then he said, 'I wish I were, Sylvia, but I'm not.'"

Corey's eyebrows are now scrunched together in a V. "Did you ever find out what it was he couldn't tell you?"

I study his face. Is he ready to hear the answer? Am I ready to tell him? "It's a long story," I say.

"What made him think you were strong?"

"I resisted arrest at a military base in New York where nuclear weapons were stored. I refused to give them my name."

His eyes widen. "Brave."

"No, it wasn't. It was stupid. I lost control. Your father thought I'd done what I had to do. He saw my action as something pure and unadulterated. But the truth is, I got overwhelmed and lost touch with reality. I didn't decide to do what I did. I was in no state of mind to decide anything."

"So what'd they do to you?"

"Held me in custody for twenty-four hours and then let me go. They made me sign an agreement that I'd appear in New York federal court to be arraigned on two charges—trespassing and resisting arrest. If I didn't show up, it would mean prison for six months and a thousand-dollar fine. I flew home filled with regret and shame."

Corey leans across the table, his eyes gleaming with interest, even excitement. "Why? You got people's attention, didn't you? I mean, you exposed our country's nuclear policy, right?"

I shake my head. "No. There never was an arraignment."

"Why not?"

"Who knows? There was no news coverage either, but that was a good thing. The media would have made me look deranged, and the Seneca Peace Camp, too. All I did was put the camp at risk and create dissension among the women there."

"But you tried. Isn't that what's important? To try?"

"Not if it means doing things without thinking them through."

48

"Still—"

"Not if it means losing control of your feelings and actions."

"What's wrong with that?"

"Nothing good came of it. That's what's wrong with it," I say, my final word on the subject. I don't want to argue with him like I did with Norton that summer. Those arguments always ended the same way, with him declaring me a heroine and with me angry and consuming more drinks, up until I blacked out. I finally grew tired of his stubbornness, and he became quiet and withholding, which led to me drinking more at home, alone, and many nights passing out on the couch cradling a bottle emptied of wine and filled with regrets about going to New York in the first place. As if redemption lay in doing good, I put in harder and longer hours at work placing children in foster homes and making sure they were safe. Too often, then, hangovers got in the way, until I feared collapsing from exhaustion, losing control again, and having another meltdown. Even losing my job.

"But . . . you don't . . ." Corey's argument is cut short when the waitress shows up with our order and plops it on the table. She tops off our coffees, again without asking, and trudges off without a word. Corey slathers his hash browns with ketchup, just like Norton did, then digs into his bacon and eggs. Just like Norton did.

"I remember when you were in preschool," I say. "And now here you are, a grown man. How old . . . ?"

His fork clanks on his plate. His body stiffens. "Thirty-nine. Old enough to know what I'm talking about."

I shake off his rebuke, try to smile, change the subject. "So, are you married? Any children?"

His eyes stare out the window like he's searching for something far away. I flip through the pages of songs on the jukebox.

"I'm married," he says at last. Then he turns away from the window and looks at me like he's made a decision. "Well, separated, but it's over with us. I don't want to talk about her. I have a son. Little Norton. He's four years old."

My throat swells. Norton lives on in a grandson he was robbed of ever knowing. "He's in preschool, then," I say.

Corey's eyes, suddenly consumed by a terrible sadness, stare down at his plate on the table. "When he can go," he whispers.

I lean forward. "When he can go?"

He sits back on the bench and averts his eyes. "Some days I have to pick him up early. We play video games and stuff until Rhonda gets home from work, and then I leave." He looks at me, a quick glance, turns away. "I got laid off from my job, so . . ."

"I'm sorry."

His shoulders go up and stay there when he says, "My fault," and then drop back down when he adds, "but it gives me time to be with Pickles."

"Pickles?"

For the first time, his lips make a smile and his eyes brighten. "Little Norton's nickname. It started when he was teething. Rhonda was . . ." His voice fades away, but when he jerks his head it comes back. "When my wife was pregnant, she had a craving for pickles and ice cream. One day Norton was fussing, and she had a pickle in her hand, so she stuck it in his mouth. He sure did love that pickle, sucked on it like you wouldn't believe. He still loves pickles." The brightness disappears from his eyes and he stares at the wall. "She had a miscarriage."

I reach across the table to touch his arm. He flinches and pulls away, sits farther back on the bench. "Did you know my mom, too?"

I wince. "Not well."

"She had to raise me alone."

I nod.

"She lied about my dad." He spits the words out through pursed lips. "She never told me the truth."

My tongue freezes in my mouth. What truth? What does he know?

"She should have told me." He tightens his jaw and shakes his head. "It could have made a difference." He stares down at the table again. "But now it's too late."

"It's never too late, Corey." It's a dumb thing to say. I don't know why I said it.

He jerks his head back, his eyes flare. "And maybe, Sylvia, sometimes it is too late." He jumps up, tosses a ten-dollar bill on the table. "Maybe sometimes it is."

He turns on his heel and stalks off, leaving me stunned and confused and holding my head in my hands, chastising myself for saying it. I don't know what he's talking about and I'm not sure I want to know. The truth is, I'm afraid to know.

"So this is where you're hiding out."

I look up at J. B. and smile. "You are a sight for sore eyes," I say, admiring his salon hairstyle, his clothes, worn to perfection like a model in *GQ* magazine. He grins and sits down across from me.

"Some guy almost knocked me over when I came in the door."

"He was with me."

"What'd you do to him to make him run out of here like a bat out of hell?"

I laugh. It feels good to laugh. "It's a long story," I say.

"I'll take the short version."

"His name is Corey Cramer. He's the son of a man I knew a long time ago. I just met him tonight."

J. B. raises his eyebrows. "And?"

"His father's name was Norton."

"And?"

"I was in love with him."

He grins.

"It's complicated. I'll tell you about it sometime. So, what happened? I saved you a seat at the memorial."

"Got caught up with another angle for my story."

"What story?"

"It's complicated. I'll tell you about it sometime." His back-at-you teasing makes me laugh again. "So what's with this Corey guy? Why's he so pissed off?"

"I don't know. I wish I did but I probably never will."

SIX

1984

For weeks, Norton and I stubbornly performed, like a memorized script, our different interpretations about what I'd done at the women's peace camp. We finally closed down the show when the fissure between us grew so wide we feared we'd never find our way back to each other. But that didn't mean the conflict was resolved, only that it went underground. Until the night of our affinity group meeting, when it bubbled to the surface and brought us another step closer to the end.

The seven of us met at my apartment to prepare for going on trial. All seventy-eight of the folks who were arrested at Nectaral headquarters on Good Friday had pleaded not guilty to trespassing and had requested trials, which would have jammed up the court docket for a year and a half. So the city attorney's office had agreed that we could go on trial in our affinity groups. Ours was scheduled for November, and this was our first planning meeting.

Norton came early. "I'm really looking forward to this," I said. Our trial was an opportunity for me to atone for losing control in New York, a chance to prove that I was able to channel my passion in a thoughtful way. But I didn't tell him that. I knew he still didn't think I had anything to atone for.

I hugged him, and felt his body pull away ever so slightly. "There's beer in the fridge. You can help me put out the snacks."

He seemed distracted and his feet dragged. I noticed a slight weave to his step as he headed for the kitchen. He grabbed a bottle of beer, then emptied a box of crackers into the basket on the table. Moving more slowly than usual, he tucked the bottle under his arm, picked up the basket and a plate of cheese slices, and went to the living room. I followed with a tray of wine, beer, and glasses and set them on my old chipped coffee table.

I patted the space next to me on my faux-leather couch. "A little snuggle before the others get here?"

He didn't answer, just walked over to the pulpit chair next to the couch. I didn't recall him ever sitting in it before. Nor had I ever seen him look this anguished. Tormented, actually. He lowered himself down on the red velvet cushion and pressed his back against the elaborately carved wood, gripping the left armrest with one hand, a bottle of beer with his right. Then he glanced at me from the corner of his eye.

"What's wrong, Norton?"

His eyes were moist and he attempted a smile, but it came out more like a grimace. Like he was in pain. Something was wrong, terribly wrong. I poured myself a glass of white zinfandel, raised it in a toast to him. He took a swig of beer without raising his bottle first. His hand was trembling. At the sound of a loud knock on the door, his bottle slipped onto his lap and splashed beer onto the red velvet cushion.

I invited the other five affinity group members into the living room, one eye welcoming them with a smile and the other eye watching Norton, my head running down a list of things that could be wrong. Number one on the list—that he was going to break up with me—I found unbearable to think about.

Madeline grabbed a napkin, half a dozen crackers and cheese slices, and a bottle of beer. "Too busy at work for lunch today, and I'm starving," she said. She had come straight from the office and was still in full-fledged work mode in a lawyerly black pantsuit and matching black thick-framed glasses.

Jim, who'd carried the cross with a nuclear bomb on his back at the Good Friday action, gave me a warm hug, his eyes twinkling with affection. Then he went over to Norton, talking to me over his shoulder. "What church did you get this beautiful chair from, Sylvia?"

"It was in the Bronx," I said. "My ex-husband did his seminary internship there, in the sixties."

His head tipped to the side with surprise. "You, a minister's wife?"

I laughed and said, "A lousy one."

He nodded like that was just what he expected and then reached down to shake Norton's limp hand. He gave it an extra squeeze, a kind of reassurance.

Katyna plopped down on the couch, ecstatic about being free of the demands of her kids for a few hours. "I love your apartment. It's outrageously unique, s-s-so much personality. S-s-suburban houses like mine are so sterile."

Jane, a mother and grandmother in her fifties, gave Katyna a sympathetic look. "I sure am glad I'm done with all that," she said. She held up her knitting bag as if to say the day would come when Katyna, too, would be able to enjoy making nice things for her family without having to cook for them every day. She poured herself a glass of wine and then looked from me to Norton. She was always good at picking up on emotions and could tell something was amiss right away. She'd probably suspected long ago that Norton and I were having an affair, but, thank goodness, she wasn't a gossip.

Tony trailed the others into the living room. He greeted Norton and me with eyes that melted into grandfatherly crinkles at the corners and then claimed my desk chair, just as I knew he would, so he could swivel around to face people when they were talking.

In the flurry of everyone arriving and getting settled, things almost seemed normal, but then I noticed the fixed smile on Norton's face, a look I'd never seen before. Instead of sitting next to Katyna on the couch as I'd planned, I sat on a wooden chair directly across from the pulpit chair so I could keep an eye on him.

There was no need for introductions or formalities at the beginning of the meeting. We all liked and trusted each other. We'd gone through several nonviolent training sessions together. We'd had each other's backs at several actions. We knew who wanted to be bailed out and when. Who planned to cooperate with the police and how. Whom to contact if someone was held in jail overnight. Who had special medical or other needs. Who wanted or needed a lawyer. All critical pieces of information that, to my shame, I'd failed to provide to anyone before I was arrested at the military depot in New York.

Logical, plainspoken Madeline took charge. She tucked in her chin and looked at us over the rims of her glasses. "Okay, our trial starts November seventh, only a month away, so let's get to it. Everyone ready?"

Jim gave her a thumbs-up. "You bet, boss." Madeline and Jim were night and day. She was an in-charge person, he was laid-back. She dressed in formal business attire, he in a gray hooded sweatshirt and faded jeans. She was a legal assistant in a high-powered corporate firm, he a former minister turned addictions counselor.

Everyone nodded that they were ready. Except Norton. Madeline either ignored him or didn't notice. "Before we get down to the nitty-gritty," she said, "a quick reminder about why we're going on trial instead of pleading guilty, okay?" She didn't wait for a response. "We're using the trials as educational tools. It's a way to get the message out that one of our local corporations is producing parts for nuclear weapons, including cruise missiles."

Tony raised his hand and swiveled his chair to face Madeline. "But it's not just information for information's sake." His voice was patient and paternalistic, honed through decades of working with people who have developmental disabilities. "We hope that, when people become aware of the danger of nuclear annihilation, they will *do* something about it."

"Yes," Madeline said. "That is our mission. Everyone agreed?"

"Agreed," everyone said. Everyone but Norton. He shrugged his shoulders and stared at the posters on my living room wall like he'd never seen them before.

"Okay, then," Madeline said. "Martin Lind gave all the affinity groups a sheet of instructions."

"I have it here," I said. "Want me to read them out loud?"

Everyone but Norton nodded.

"The first decision each affinity group needs to make is whether to request a trial by judge or by a jury of your peers." I heard Norton shuffle his feet. I stopped reading and looked at him. His hand dismissed me, so I continued. "The second decision each affinity group needs to make is if you want to have a coalition attorney assigned to your group as counsel or if you want to go pro se."

"Excuse me," Katyna said. "I don't know what pro s-s-se means."

Madeline eagerly jumped at the chance to explain things. She smiled indulgently at Katyna, our youngest member and a neophyte to the nuclear disarmament movement. "*Pro se* means we would represent ourselves without an attorney."

"Legalese," Norton grumbled under his breath.

Madeline either didn't hear him or decided to forge ahead anyway. "Okay, folks, you heard the instructions. First decision. What'll it be? Trial by judge or jury?"

"Jury," everyone said. Everyone but Norton, who sat still as a statue, his eyes downcast and his arms crossed over his chest.

Madeline laughed. "Well, that was easy! Let's move on then."

Jane put her knitting down, her face laden with concern. "A jury *is* a way to reach more people with our message, Norton, don't you agree?"

"I'm *sure* it is, Katyna." Norton's words dripped with sarcasm.

Jane's lips formed an O like she was going to correct him, tell him her name was Jane, not Katyna, but she furrowed her brow instead and picked up her knitting again.

Madeline clapped her hands. "Absolutely, Jane. A trial by jury is a way to reach more people. Okay, next decision. Do we ask for an attorney or do we represent ourselves?"

"Represent ourselves," everyone but Norton said.

"Hell yes!" Katyna's outburst was completely out of character. We all looked at her, bemused. "What?" Her cheeks flushed pink.

"Just agreeing with you," Jim said, with a kindness derived from decades of rough-and-tumble life experiences.

Tony rolled the desk chair over to Katyna and patted her hand. "We share your enthusiasm," he said.

Madeline slapped her knees. "Okay, pro se it is then."

Norton raised his hand, then dropped it onto his lap. I noted with alarm how bony it was. Jim slouched down in his chair like he'd noticed it, too, and it was weighing on him.

Jane put down the scarf she was knitting. "What is it, Norton?"

He didn't look at her, just shook his head. I caught myself biting at the cuticle on my thumbnail and quickly wrapped my hands in the soft cotton folds of my green peasant skirt. Something was wrong, and I didn't think it was just about our trial. Maybe something had happened at home. Maybe Chloe found out about us. I looked into Norton's eyes, but they offered up no clues.

After a few minutes, Madeline leaned forward with her hands out, palms up. "Okay, then, moving on to some of the other things we have to do." She reached in her purse and pulled out a notebook. "I made a list of five questions we should ask during voir dire." She paused and glanced around the circle, eyebrows raised. "Voir dire," she said, "is what jury selection is called, okay? In addition to deciding what questions to ask potential jurors, we have to decide who will make the opening and closing statements, too."

Norton held his face in his hands and moaned, so loud that even Madeline, despite her enthusiastic desire to keep things moving, couldn't ignore him anymore.

She crossed her arms. "What *is* it, Norton?"

He sat up rigid, his hands fisted on his lap, his knuckles white. He shook his head but said nothing.

Tony raised his hand like a student in school waiting to be called on. "I'm thinking that maybe." He paused, then started again, slow and patient. "I wonder if . . . I think each of us could maybe write out our testimony first? Maybe if we saw how they all fit together, it would be easier to make other decisions?"

Norton unclasped his hands, leaned forward and shouted, "No! We have to take more drastic action than any of you are talking about." His hands slapped the armrests of the chair. "We don't have a choice." The lines around his downturned lips were a mournful gray, an indication of pain or fear I couldn't tell which.

Katyna leaned forward. "I don't understand. Can you s-s-say more?"

Jim drew his legs in and pulled himself out of his slouch. "What are you suggesting, Norton?"

"We resist. Refuse to cooperate. Shut the system down."

I massaged my temples. *Please don't do this,* I silently begged him.

"Resist how?" Tony asked.

"We turn our faces *to,* I mean, we turn our backs *on* the judge." He shot me a quick look. I told him, with my eyes, that this argument was between him and me and that's where it should stay. But he ignored me and went on. "We refuse to give our names. We don't answer any questions."

Katyna fidgeted with the wedding band on her left hand. Madeline scowled. Mostly, the others gaped, baffled, confused. This wasn't the Norton they knew. They didn't understand what he was doing or why. But I did. He was saying we should all act in court like I had in New York. He was resurrecting our argument.

Jane cleared her throat. "What do you think we'd accomplish by doing that, Norton?"

Emboldened by the sincerity of her effort to understand, he leaned toward her. "We've been negotiating with the top folks at Nectaral for years, right? And where has that gotten us? The Department of Defense is literally throwing money at Nectaral, and it keeps developing and producing more and more weapons of mass destruction. Think about it. We've changed nothing. It's only gotten worse."

I had to admit he had a point. Despite all our efforts, all our protests and acts of civil disobedience, the war-making machine was thriving, and with almost no public notice, comment, or objection.

Norton leaned into the circle. "It's time to resist. Refuse to co-alesce . . . I mean . . . cooperate or negotiate. Shut the system down."

Madeline's eyes flashed like she'd reached the end of her tether. "We're *already* shutting the system down, Norton. It's going to take three or four months to get through all the trials."

Tony squinted and raised his hand again. "If we resisted, the judge would have no choice but to throw the book at us."

Katyna started wringing her hands. "I . . . can't go to prison. What would happen to my kids?"

Norton shot back, "Dangerous times! Drastic measures!"

Madeline gritted her teeth in a failed attempt to be patient. "We *already* took drastic action, Norton. Our trial is the part where we *educate* people about *why* we took drastic action."

Jim's face was strained. Conflict in the group was new, and he was clearly uncomfortable with it. "Our trial is a chance to *defend* ourselves and what we did, Norton."

Tony nodded. "The whole idea is to appeal to the consciences of the jurors and give them a chance to take action, too." He paused and smiled. "Preferably by finding us not guilty."

Jane looked at Norton like a mother sympathizing with a child who's being ganged up on. "You don't think that would be a good thing?"

Norton threw up his hands. "No, I don't!" He gripped the arms of the pulpit chair and pulled himself up. "I can't do this. I'm sorry. I can't." Then he walked out of the room, his steps slow and heavy. I heard the bathroom door slam behind him.

Madeline tried desperately to act calm and reasonable, but her eyes betrayed her. "I guess we might as well adjourn for now."

Katyna nodded. "S-s-should we meet again next week?"

Jane put her knitting away. "Maybe he just needs time to think about things."

"He needs to cool down," Madeline said.

Jane glanced over her shoulder as if looking to see if Norton overheard. "Do you think we should . . ." Her voice trailed off.

I interrupted her. "You all go. I'll talk to him. I'm sure everything will be all right."

SEVEN

2019

It's been five days since I met Norton's son Corey, and here I am, still ruminating about him. Why did he say *Sometimes it is too late*? What is it about his father that would have made a difference if he'd known about it in time? And what kind of difference would it have made? I want desperately to know what truth he discovered in Norton's journal.

Maybe I'll invite him to dinner. Maybe I can get him to open up to me. But who am I kidding? He doesn't want to see me, and it's not my place to determine what he needs, not my place to barge into his life uninvited. Besides, it's really me who needs to see him. It's me who needs to come to terms with his father.

But none of that matters. I don't even have his phone number.

I throw my untouched soggy Cheerios into the garbage disposal, pour my cold coffee down the drain, and refill my mug. It's time for the morning news. In the living room I reach for the remote control on the coffee table, then lower myself onto the couch. I close my eyes and fill my head with calming images. Only then do I press the power button and let my new flat-screen television hiss to life.

My favorite newscaster is on. "We start first this morning in the Midwest, where both resistance to and support of a government plan to store plutonium near Monrow City are growing. And clashing."

Juxtaposed in the background are sensationalized scenes from rallies in other places, images of protesters shouting at each other, fists raised, shoving, pushing. Then a commercial comes on about a prescription drug that's supposed to be the solution for some unspecified medical condition if all its side effects don't kill you.

I mute the sound and send a text to J. B. *What's happening out there? Are you watching NBC News?* To my surprise, he calls instead of texting back.

"People are getting violent," he says. "It's going on all around the country."

My head starts to feel like it's going to explode. Sometimes I have to work harder than others to stay calm. "Hold on a minute. The news is back on." I unmute the sound on my TV.

"Martin Lind, leader of the Monrow City Peace and Justice Coalition, insists that massive resistance there is growing. Here he is, pitching a rally to a riled-up crowd just last week." Martin's face appears on the screen in a video clip from the commemoration service for Bertha Pickering.

"Our leaders say they'll save us from North Korea's nuclear aggression with a Ground-based Midcourse Defense system that will knock their incoming missiles right out of the sky," Martin says. "Like hitting a bullet with another bullet, they say." He snorts derisively. "But we *only* have thirty-six GMDs, they say. We need more. Many, many more. So our very own Nectaral Corporation says it will produce those many, many more for them. And we know why, don't we?"

The camera shows the crowd in the sanctuary, all of us on our feet chanting *Mon-ey! Mon-ey!*

Martin nods, raises his hands. "And in exchange for tons of money, all Nectaral has to do is store the government's deadly plutonium. Here. Right here."

Hell no! Hell no!

The newscaster comes back on. "There are over ninety thousand metric tons of nuclear waste in the U.S. that need to be disposed of. The battle is on for whose backyard it will be stored in. As you can see, things are heating up, even in the heartland of our country."

I press the off button on the remote control. The veins in my neck are throbbing.

"Looks like the masses are rising up," J. B. says.

"Like in the eighties, I hope," I say. "The GMD program is just Reagan's Star Wars. History repeating itself."

"So I guess you and that angry dude who stormed out of the diner—Corey, right?—will both be going to the rally today."

"Not me. I'm speaking at an AA meeting tonight. I only have so much energy, you know." I prop a pillow behind my back and run my fingers along the black imitation-leather couch I got from the Salvation Army over forty years ago. "I doubt Corey will go, either. He thinks protests are a waste of time. Poor guy has other problems right now, too. He's unemployed, separated from his wife, and something else is troubling him." J. B. chuckles, and I know what he's thinking. "You're wrong if you think I can get him to open up to me," I say. "I'm pretty sure I'll never see him again."

"Never say never, Sylvia. You do have a way of getting in there with people."

"When are you coming to Monrow City again?"

"I'll be there on and off. I hear you're building up to a massive protest. I plan to come for that."

"So you're writing a story about *us*."

I hear his smile. See his brain scrambling to decide how much to tell me about his current project. "In part," he says at last.

I sigh. No use pushing. When J. B. keeps his investigations under wraps, it's for a reason. He'll tell me in due time. "Well, when you do come back," I say, "bring Mentayer with you." I smile. J. B. and Mentayer fell in love and got married after I introduced them to each other years ago. It's good to be reminded right now that sometimes good things can and do happen.

Our conversation is brought to an end by a little knock on my door. Four-year-old Annamarie from across the hall flies into my apartment. "Ms. Sylvia! Ms. Sylvia!" She throws her tiny arms around my legs. "We're baking cookies. We're going to la bodega for chocolate chips. Mamá wants to know if you need anything."

I tousle the dear child's curly black hair. "I don't, but it's very kind of you to ask."

She squirms away and peeks into my bedroom. "Your teddy bears aren't on the bed. Can I put them there?"

She knows in just what order to place my collection of stuffed bears. What she doesn't know is that, from left to right, each one represents a different stage of my life. The first one, my inner child, is the smallest. Each subsequent one increases in size. The biggest one goes in the middle, like the highest point on a bell curve. Then, in descending order to the right, each bear decreases in size again.

Annamarie stands back and admires the arrangement. "When I'm old like you, Ms. Sylvia, I'm going to have teddy bears just like these."

I put my arm around her. "You'll have just as many bears in your life, sweetie, maybe even more."

"Promesa?"

"I promise. But yours will be different."

She points to the last bear on the right, the one that symbolizes the person I am now. "Well, I *am* going to have one just like that, only mine will be at the *beginning* not at the end."

If only life worked that way, I think, as she skips down the hall and out the door.

I sit on my bed and look at each bear from left to right, me as a baby, teenager, student, wife, teacher, lover, social worker, activist. I pick up the last bear and run my fingers on the words embroidered in white on the red heart in its paws. *I am enough. I have enough. I do enough.* My final lesson. I hold the bear to my breast. All that is required of me today is to think about what to say at the AA meeting tonight and then to be the best speaker I can be. I put the little bear back in its place and lay my hand on its heart, knowing that for today, that is enough.

##

The AA meeting is in the basement of a Baptist church that I've never been to before. I get there early, while the coffee's still brewing, and two men half my age are unfolding and setting up metal chairs in rows. I sit off in the corner, out of the way, and watch as one hundred chairs fill with people I don't know. *Just tell your story. Just tell them what it was like before, what happened, and what it's like now. Just be yourself.*

A tall man with a protruding belly hanging over the belt around his nonexistent waist walks to the lectern. "Hello everyone, my name is Clarence and I'm an alcoholic."

"Hi, Clarence," everyone shouts back at him.

He clears his throat and smiles. Every meeting I've been to over the years has started the same way, so I know exactly what he's going to say next. "Is anyone here at their first meeting? If so, please introduce yourself by your first name only so we can get to know you."

A white-haired woman stands. Her voice shakes as she says, "My name is Sandy and I'm an alcoholic. This is my first meeting." Everyone claps, people shout "Welcome, Sandy" and "Keep coming back." Then a skinny man with the face of a teenager who doesn't have to shave more than once a week stands, his eyes glued to the floor as he mumbles, "I'm Teddy. Alcoholic." More clapping, even louder this time, as he slinks down in his chair. Clarence waits, his eyes roam the room. "Are there any other newcomers who would like to introduce themselves?"

A hand goes up in the very last row. I hear a metal chair scrape on the concrete floor, but I can't see who it is behind all the heads. Then I recognize his voice and my hands fly up, cover my mouth.

"My name's Corey." He hesitates. "I'm a . . . I'm a alcoholic." Then he plops back down.

Everyone shouts "Welcome, Corey," and I silently welcome Norton to the meeting. His presence in the room is as real to me as his son's, not just because Corey looks exactly like him but because of the central role alcohol played in our relationship. It was always with us, even during our most precious, most private moments. Even after Norton died, alcohol took his place as the love of my life for the next sixteen years. I wonder what would have happened if he had lived, if he would have claimed his seat in these rooms, too.

Once the preliminaries are over, Clarence introduces me as tonight's speaker. I place one shaky foot in front of the other and make my way to the lectern. The somersaults in my stomach disappear as soon as I look out at the sea of recovery, the faces of people I've never met but who are not strangers to me. I smile at Corey in the last row. He lowers his eyes.

"My name is Sylvia, and I am a grateful alcoholic."

Everyone shouts, "Hi, Sylvia."

"One night, over nineteen years ago, I got a DWI." I pause, surprised by what I just said. I've never started my story like this before, hadn't planned to start it like this tonight. "I thought it was the worst thing that ever happened to me and that my life was over. In these rooms people often say that everything happens for a reason. I don't always believe that." I pause as the thought goes through my head that maybe the reason I met Corey is because we're both alcoholics.

"But I do know there *was* a reason a cop stopped me that night," I say. "It got me into treatment. It gave me a new life. And it turned out to be the best thing that ever happened to me." Corey frowns. He doesn't believe me.

"My grandfather was a drunk. A binge drinker. He would disappear for weeks at a time. Then he'd come home, filthy and drunk, and my grandmother would clean him up. *After* he beat her." I shake my head, the stories my mother told me still as vivid and disgusting now as when I was a child. "Whenever I vowed not to drink and then drank anyway, I would pray, literally beg a God that I didn't even believe in, to please, please, not let me be an alcoholic like my grandfather. When I was in treatment, I told the counselor, and he said, 'Who prays like that, anyway? Even before you got that DWI, you knew you were an alcoholic.'"

People nod. They know. I nod back. "If you're worried enough to ask God to not let you be an alcoholic, there's a pretty good chance you are one, right?"

The laughter of my fellow alcoholics bounces off the basement walls. Oh my, how I love that sound. "But for years," I say after the room quiets, "I didn't know I had a problem.

"I actually got pulled over twice when I was driving drunk. The first time, I ignored the flashing red lights in my rearview mirror and smiled, feigned innocence, and out and out lied. 'Is there anything wrong, Officer? I'm the foster care supervisor at the Health Services Department, and I was just on my way home after dealing with a tough case at work. Did I run a stoplight or something? I'm afraid I must have been a bit distracted.' It worked. The cop thanked me for my service and let me go. After that, I promised myself I would quit drinking altogether.

"I tried to quit but I couldn't. That baffled me, but I still didn't think I needed help. Not when I threw up in my napkin at a fund-raising dinner. Not when I peed in the hotel bed at a conference. Not when I spilled a glass of wine on a case record on my desk at work. Not even . . ." I stop; this is a hard one to admit out loud. "Not even when I almost hit an elderly lady who was crossing the street. When I got out of the car to see if she was okay, I fell. Oh God. Not even then did I think I had a problem. My denial was that strong."

I pause to signal that I've ended the part of my story about what things were like when I was drinking and get ready to move on to the part about how I got into recovery.

"The second time I was pulled over was a year later. I had been at a reception at work, and, despite knowing the city streets as well as I know the veins on the backs of my hands, I was lost and couldn't find my way home. This time, when the police officer asked, 'How much have you had to drink, ma'am,' I collapsed on the seat. I knew it was over.

"I spent that night in jail and the next morning pleaded guilty to a charge of driving while intoxicated. It turned out that I hadn't kept my alcoholic face as much of a secret at work as I thought I had. I was given a choice, either go into treatment or lose my job. I took a month's leave of absence and checked myself into a treatment center two hours north of here."

I go on to talk about how things changed after I got into recovery and conclude with my heart filled with gratitude. "I no longer regret the past." I pause, look at Corey. "The promises can come true for you, too, just as they have for me."

After the meeting ends, I see Corey getting his court slip signed by Clarence, which means he was ordered to go to AA meetings. Now I know why I started my story the way I did. I go over to him.

"So." I glance down at the slip in his hand.

"DWI," he says in a sheepish voice.

I nod. "Something else we have in common. Want to go somewhere for coffee?"

"I'm not allowed to drive." He rolls his eyes and does an angry flick of his ponytail.

"My car's out back."

We walk to the parking lot in silence. I point to my old faded red 1985 Toyota, unlock the passenger side door for him, then walk around the car to the other side.

"Are there any coffee shops nearby?"

He shakes his head. "I don't know this part of town. I took the bus."

I put the key in the ignition. "I'll drive you home and we'll find something on the way." But instead of starting the engine right away, I sit back in my seat and say, "The first meeting's always the hardest."

He swipes at one cheek and then the other with the back of his hand. I wish I could rescue him, take away his pain. But of course, that's not the way this works.

He turns to me after a long silence and says, "I screwed up." He stares out the passenger window. "I really screwed up."

"That's what alcohol makes us do," I say. "But you're here now and that's what counts. You came to the meeting. You took the first step."

I feel the heat of his shame and remember back to the time when I too believed I was bad, immoral, defective. Stupid and unlovable.

"When I went into treatment," I say, "one of the first things my counselor told me was that I'm not a bad person. He said I had a disease, that's all. Like diabetes. But it's a disease that will kill us if we don't stop drinking."

All of a sudden he slams his hands on the dashboard. "It's not fair! Pickles needs me . . . and now I can't even drive him to preschool or . . ."

I feel confused and, strangely, impatient. Getting his son to and from preschool is *not* the most insurmountable problem Corey is going to have in recovery. "Can't you and Pickles take the bus? How far is the school from your apartment? Maybe you could walk. Maybe there's a regular bus you and your son could take every day."

He jerks forward in his seat, twists toward me, and screams in my face, "He can't! Don't you understand? He can't." He stops, glares at me, his eyes icy.

I feel my body shriveling. "I'm sorry, Corey. Can you help me understand?" My voice is soft, contrite.

His eyes well up. "He's so little . . . he shouldn't . . . he's so precious." He chokes on the words. "You can't understand. Nobody can. There's nothing I can do . . . there's no money . . . I don't have a job . . . and now I can't even drive him . . ."

He covers his face with his hands and gasps, wheezes, struggles for breath. Then he lets out a howl, a long, mournful sound. People passing by jump, then turn their curious eyes away out of respect for the newcomer.

I reach out and put my hand on his back, and he collapses, lays his head in my lap. He grips my legs like so many terrified children have in the past when their lives were falling apart. "It's going to be okay, Corey. I promise."

"No, it's *not* going to be okay. It's too late. It doesn't matter anymore. That's why I have to . . ." His words trail off, and that's when I hear Norton's voice from all those years ago when he finally broke down and told me his secret. *It doesn't matter anymore. I have to do what I have to do.*

EIGHT

1984

The other affinity group members left, but Norton didn't come out of the bathroom. I paced the living room floor. Thirteen steps from one end to the other. Fifteen seconds. Over and over, the same number of steps, the same amount of time. After a while the counting got lost and a soft breeze wafting through the patio doors lured me outside. I rested my elbows on the metal railing. Some windows on the apartment building across the street were open, people inside fixing dinner, watching their favorite detective show, reading a bedtime story to their kids. Other windows were closed, curtains drawn, people either out for the evening, not yet home from work, or already in bed. Normal people living normal lives. Things will fall apart for them, too, as they do for all of us. Fortunately, they don't fall apart for everyone at the same time. Personal crises are passed around like a dish around the dinner table. Whatever was happening to Norton, to us, would pass. It was just our turn.

It was unusually warm for the beginning of October, so I hadn't brought the cushions in yet for the winter. I sat on the bench and looked up at the stars. Five more minutes, I told myself. Then I'm going in to get him.

"I didn't know where you were." I turned, startled. Norton stood in the doorway looking wasted. His voice was timid, childlike, frightened. Not his. "You didn't leave me," he said.

I patted the cushion next to me. "I would never leave you, Norton."

He sat on a sliver of the bench, on just enough of the edge so he wouldn't slide off. He ran his fingers through his beard, then twisted his whiskers into a knot. My hands pressed into the seat of the bench to hold me up.

"Are you breaking up with me?" The words squeaked through my lips like a soft whistle.

Norton almost fell off the bench; the blood drained from his face. "No! Oh my God, no!" His hollowed-out eyes were wet. "I love you, Sylvia. I need you. You're the only person who can understand."

I swallowed my relief, but right away, anxiety moved in to take its place. "Understand what, Norton?"

He made a low choking sound, and then the dam broke. I drew him to me, felt the sharpness of his ribs, his bony shoulders poking into me. The tips of my fingers stroked away the deep creases in his forehead, but the rest of his body stayed rigid. "I can't keep the secret any longer." His lip curled up. He jerked his head from side to side. "I *won't*."

The flash of anger fizzled out as if he'd spent all the courage he had and now there was nothing left but fear. He gasped, sobbed, took in deep breaths, let them out, and sobbed some more. He was like a terrified child begging to be reassured that he wasn't alone even though he was going to live with foster parents he didn't know and there was no way he could not help but feel abandoned because the truth was, his life was falling apart. He gripped my hand like his spirit was broken and he was grasping at the shards left behind. I sheltered him in my arms and tried to soothe his fears while fighting off my own fears at the same time.

It started to rain, a gentle shower. The drops, friendly and cooling, shimmered on the concrete patio and blended with the scent of his aftershave lotion. I longed for the touch of his fingers on my skin, light as a feather at first, then intensified and urgent until my body ached with desire then tingled with the joy of fulfillment. But when Norton pulled away from me I was ashamed. This was not the time for such feelings.

My lips planted a chaste kiss on his wet cheeks. "I love you, Norton, no matter what it is. I love you."

He shivered. He wrinkled his brow. He studied his hands. His throat cleared, then seemed to have second thoughts and cleared again. He stared back down at his lap. It looked like his cheeks were being sucked

72

into his face.

"Have you been ill, Norton?"

He let out a little gasp. "What makes you think that?"

"You look . . . tired . . . and you're not yourself."

He lowered his head.

"Have you seen a doctor?"

He didn't answer. Didn't look at me. My mouth and throat went dry. My shoulders dug into the back of the bench as if that would give me courage.

"What did the doctor say, Norton?"

Another tear escaped from the corner of his eye and slowly made its way down his cheek. "He's waiting for the test results." He pursed his lips. "But I know what happened to me, Sylvia. I know it's bad."

I held my breath and waited for him to tell me more, but he didn't. I was losing him. Maybe I already had.

He rubbed the back of his neck as if rubbing away his regret. "I'm sorry, Sylvia. I couldn't tell anyone. I took an oath."

"You took an oath not to tell anyone you were ill? Who would ever ask you to take such an oath, and why?"

He swiped at the wetness on his face as if slapping away a black fly before it could bite him. His eyes turned dark and his eyebrows scrunched together in a V in the middle of his forehead. "I was poisoned."

"Poisoned?"

"That's all I can tell you."

"The hell it is!" I jump up from the bench, fists clenched. Enough is enough.

"It's against the law." His hands were wringing. He was worried that he'd already said too much.

"What law? What are you talking about?"

"The hell with it. The hell with the law." His hands balled into fists and he pounded them into the cushions. "I'm an atomic veteran, Sylvia."

I shook my head. Nothing was making sense. I didn't even know what questions to ask.

He sucked in air then pushed it out through his mouth. "There are *hundreds of thousands* of us. We didn't know we were poisoned. They lied to us."

I listened to the words spewing from his mouth, a torrent of staccato accusations filled with bitterness. I'd never heard about atomic veterans before. And now Norton was saying he was one of them. How could no one know that hundreds of thousands of men had been poisoned? How could I not have known?

Norton's eyes drilled into my head as if reading what was inside. "I didn't know either, Sylvia." His eyes flashed. "How could I? I was just out of high school. I signed up for the military right after graduation and was shipped off to this godforsaken island in the South Pacific." His eyes left me and stared off into the distance. "But now the veterans are organizing, and that's helping me piece together what happened. They tested nuclear bombs. They wanted to see what the blasts would do to us." He sucked in air, then speeded up, his speech animated by anger. "I thought I was a soldier, but I was nothing but a guinea pig."

He took a deep breath. I held mine. Then his lips pursed and his fist punched the air. "They knew about the risks and they didn't give a damn. They knew about the increased cancers among the Hiroshima and Nagasaki survivors, their children born with smaller heads and physical disabilities. They knew, Sylvia, and they didn't even warn us. They didn't care what happened to us. They still don't. Well, it doesn't matter anymore."

His body deflated like the poison was pulling in his skin. But then, all of a sudden, he grabbed my hand. "You know what gets me more than anything, Sylvia?"

I shake my head.

"When they forced me to secrecy," he said, "they forced me to collude with the very nuclear program I oppose."

My hand stroked his cheek. "We'll wait for the test results, Norton. Then we'll know what to do."

He jumped up, his feet apart and his hands in the air like a boxer in the ring. "No, Sylvia. No waiting. It's time for me to do what I should have done a long time ago. It's time for drastic action."

"Like what?"

"It's best if you don't know."

I stood up with my face inches from his and drilled my intent into him. "No, it's not, Norton. It's best that I *do* know. You already broke your oath. Tell me."

He took my hands in his and pressed them against his chest. "Leave it alone, Sylvia. I've already said too much."

"Tell me," I said. "I'm in this with you."

He shook his head. "Don't ask me again," he said. "Please promise you won't."

He couldn't expect me to do that. Everything was different now. The crusade to which we'd both been committed had suddenly taken a personal turn, a life and death turn. How could he tell me what was going on and then not tell me what he was going to do about it?

"Please."

Through his pleading eyes I saw the radiation invading his body, coursing through his veins, attacking his muscles, ligaments, nerves, organs, bones . . . and because he was all of life there was for me and I couldn't bear the thought of losing him and living without him, I said, "I promise." I didn't know I had already lost him.

NINE

2019

The moonless sky stares black through the windshield. It's cooler than normal for an early summer night, the temperature in the low sixties. The cars belonging to the meeting regulars are gone now and mine is the only one left in the church parking lot. Corey is curled up in a fetal position, his head next to my lap, his hair brushing against my leg. He whimpers and hiccups like a child after a good cry. Even his silence moans with despair, tender and burning to the touch. The raw red soreness of it settles in the pit of my stomach. Finally he turns onto his back, knees bent, feet resting against the passenger side door. A little whoosh of self-consciousness escapes his lips.

I offer a sympathetic smile. "It's okay, Corey."

He sits up, runs his hands up and down his bare arms. "Why's it so cold in here?" His arms wrap around his chest and his shoulder presses against the door, as far away from me now as possible.

I turn the key in the ignition. "The heat'll kick in soon."

"You mean the heater in this old rattletrap still works? What year is this piece of garbage anyway?"

I chuckle at the derision in his voice, his embarrassment talking. "It's your lucky day. I just got it fixed last week, though I didn't think I'd need it until the fall."

He sniffs and fumbles in his jacket pocket. I reach in my purse for a tissue and hand it to him. His nose honks into it while his eyes stare at his reflection in the side window. "I'm sorry."

"Pain is nothing to be sorry for," I say.

The heat vent starts warming the air. I turn the fan on full blast and the car turns into a sauna, so I switch it down to low, but he doesn't seem to notice. I stare up at the sky and listen to his breathing.

"Time for coffee," I say at last.

His face turns toward me. His jaw tightens. I wonder if I've offended him.

"I'm not the only one who screwed up, you know. Mom lied. She said Dad died of a heart attack."

"But . . ." I bite my tongue. Norton *did* die of a heart attack, but the wise part of me tells me not to correct him.

"If she had told me the truth, maybe I wouldn't have had children. But then . . ." He turns and looks at his face in the window as if talking to himself. "No, no, not that." He chokes up, moves his stare down to his lap. "But there must have been something we could have done. Before Pickles was born, even after he was born. I don't know. Mom should have told me. There might have been some tests. Some treatment. *Something.* She should have told me."

I hear Norton's voice inside me. *I was poisoned. It's bad, Sylvia.* I put my hand on Corey's shoulder. He flicks it away with a sharp jerk of his eyes, Norton's eyes. "Corey." I wait for him to look at me. "What's wrong with Pickles?"

His lips purse and he spits out the words. "Dad's cancer is in him. *That's* what's wrong, okay? You satisfied? I want to go home now." He tucks in his chin and slumps down in the seat.

"Oh, Corey . . . I'm sorry."

He reaches for the door handle. "I'll take the bus."

"No. Stay. I'll drive you."

He slouches back in the seat. My eyebrows point to his seat belt until, finally, with an exaggerated movement, he sits up and buckles it. His lips mumble his address and then don't move again for the next twenty minutes. Anguish consumes the silence, so palpable it hurts, so powerful it draws into his personal grief a grief for others. For the children and grandchildren of atomic veterans with cancer, birth defects, other diseases. For the Marshall Islands people who suffer devastating hardships from

U.S. nuclear weapons testing. For the babies on Pine Ridge Reservation with respiratory or liver or kidney ailments. For the poisoned Native people who have been dying ever since corporations started mining uranium deposits on their land. So much grief. Too much grief. It demands answers. It screams for release. It requires accountability, attention. That's what Corey meant at Nick's Diner last week when he said *We have to make 'em listen. It's not anywhere near over.*

"This is it." His voice brings me back to an awareness of the road, other cars, stoplights. "Stop. There. In front of that building."

I pull up to the curb, and he reaches for the door handle, ready to bolt.

I quickly write my phone number on a packet of AA literature and shove it in his hand. He jumps out of the car. I roll down the window. "My regular meeting is tomorrow night. Want me to pick you up?"

"I'll call you," he says and then walks away.

Much to my surprise, he calls the next day to apologize and to thank me. I take him to my regular AA meeting, and this time we go out for coffee afterward. I encourage him to get a sponsor and he says he will. I tell him it's important for his sobriety to deal with his anger toward his mother and he agrees. He admits it's a struggle for him and tries to justify her secrecy, worries that he's being unfair to her. He knows it must have been hard for her to cope after being left alone to raise him with no compensation from the VA for what happened to her husband. He talks about Pickles, a lot, shows me pictures of the kid with hair before the chemo took it, the two of them at the zoo and museums, Little Norton as a wrinkly newborn. He talks about how, every day, cancer sucks away more and more of his son's curiosity and energy. He says he knows it's good for his recovery to talk about it.

I drop him off at the curb in front of his building, feeling encouraged. He leans into my open window. "See you next week at the protest?"

I blurt out the first thing that comes to mind. "You don't have to go, Corey." The truth is, I don't want him to go. It will only inflame his anger. He's too new in recovery to risk that.

"Yes, I do need to go." His voice is tight, determined.

"You don't need any more stress, Corey. You have enough to deal with right now."

"This *is* what I have to deal with right now." He jabs his finger in my face. "And so do *you*."

I give myself time to think about how to respond and then make my voice calm and reasonable. "I don't think I'll go to the rally. I know it's important, but I haven't decided yet what I need to do, what I *choose* to do. I think you should give yourself time to decide what's best for you right now, too."

He pivots on his heels and storms off, a clear reminder that giving unwanted advice is almost always a bad idea. I listen to the angry thump of his footsteps until the sound fades away and he disappears into his building. Then I drive away.

TEN

1984

On November 6, after the polls closed and Reagan was re-elected president, the temperature in Monrow City plunged to below freezing with fifteen-mile-per-hour winds. I drank bourbon in bed until I passed out.

The next morning I woke up, still shivering. It was the day our trial was to begin. With a giant mug of hot coffee radiating heat into my hands and my mother's crocheted afghan warming the rest of me, I went over my testimony at the kitchen table until it was time to leave for City Hall. Then I put on my warmest turtleneck sweater and lined wool slacks and, on my way out the door, grabbed the ankle-length quilted coat I usually dug out of the closet only when the temperature dipped lower than twenty degrees below zero.

Tony, Madeline, Jim, Katyna, and Jane were already in the courtroom, standing in a clump by the defendants' table in the front. "Good morning, Sylvia," they all said in unison.

"We're moaning about the election," Tony said. "I hope it's not a bad omen for our trial."

Just then Norton walked in, and the sight of him was a sucker punch into my already chilling malaise. His cheeks were sunken into deep dimples, which he didn't have, and he looked like he was dying, which he was, and to top it all off, he was dressed like a damn corporate executive. Totally not like him.

"Great look, man," Tony said. The wrinkles around his eyes cancelled out his attempt at a smile.

81

Madeline looked over her black glasses frames. "Hey, how about giving me the name of your hairdresser," she said with a forced laugh.

"S-s-sweet." Katyna's hand stroked the soft gray fabric of his jacket sleeve.

Everyone was putting on a happy face. Norton had told them about his diagnosis just a week ago, and it was obvious that they hadn't yet absorbed the news. There were still times I didn't want to believe it myself.

Jim tugged awkwardly at the stretched-out neck of his gray hooded sweatshirt. "Hey, how come I didn't get the memo that it was three-piece-suit-and-tie day?"

When Norton grinned, his sunken cheeks widened at the base and the dimples disappeared. "We do what we have to do," he said.

My thoughts went back to the moment when he first told me about his diagnosis, before his cheeks started caving in. "I'm not afraid of dying," he'd said, "but it's eating me alive to think that I might die before they're held accountable. It's going to take something big to get their attention. Something they can't ignore. Something that will scream their guilt to the world." Then he'd paused before adding, "I have an inoperable brain tumor, Sylvia, so what do I have to lose?"

Was this it, then? Was Norton going to do something drastic during our trial? I wanted to ask him, but I'd promised I wouldn't. His eyes flitted now in my direction and then moved to the podium from which the judge would preside. His grin faded when he looked at the witness stand from which we would deliver our testimony. Then the lines on his forehead deepened and his head moved up and down as if counting to make sure there were enough chairs in the jury box for those who would decide our fate.

The heavy courtroom door creaked, and in walked a woman in a red wool coat with a multicolored scarf around her neck. Thin worry lines crisscrossed her forehead. Her gaze flitted across the room until she spotted Norton and then her shoulders relaxed. She flicked her thick brown curls and rushed toward him. As if sensing his wife's presence, Norton turned and smiled. I could feel the tenderness of his lips on her cheek, hear the kindness in his voice as he introduced her to the other members of our affinity group.

Then it was my turn. "And this is Sylvia Jensen," Norton said. "Sylvia, this is my wife, Chloe."

Chloe's smile was unsuspecting, her handshake warm and sincere. "Ah, my husband's soul mate. It's very nice to meet you, Sylvia. I've heard so much about you."

My throat swelled. "And I you, Chloe."

Norton cupped his wife's elbow in his hand. "Come on, hon, you can sit on the bench in the front row, right behind me." Then he led her away. The hole in my heart burned.

I took in a deep breath. It was right and good that Chloe didn't know her husband had been having an affair. There'd already been so much for her to absorb, so much she hadn't known before about Norton's past and his demons. And then there'd been the diagnosis, of course. I understood Norton's need to cling to his wife and son in the days or weeks or months he had left, understood that there were different kinds of love and that in the face of death, a rank ordering was required. But damn it, my heart was bleeding. Right or wrong, he was the love of my life, and the pain of losing him, of having already lost him, was worse than the guilt I'd felt when we were still seeing each other.

I tried to focus on other things. Like the defendants' table, long enough to accommodate all seven of us. Like the hard wood I was sitting on, my chair the last one at the far end of our table. Like the much shorter table to the left of ours for the assistant city attorney. Like Prosecutor Kenneth Vendenal, short in stature, his black eyes close together, his hair combed straight back.

"Sylvia?"

Norton looked down at me, his hands flat on the tabletop between us. I worried that the sudden wetness under my armpits would make my wool sweater smell like wet socks drying by the fire.

"I changed some of my testimony," he said.

"Oh?" I wondered if he'd decided to keep some of the angry and threatening parts that I thought were self-defeating. I couldn't blame him if he did. I was angry, too. Big-time angry. The kind of beside-yourself rage that could only be safely expressed in private. But I wasn't as worried about Norton's anger as I was about him feeling helpless. Helplessness made people do destructive things. It led them to conjure up all kinds of ways to retaliate.

"The best revenge," I'd told him, "is to be the most credible and effective witness you can be. People are turned off by anger."

For a long time he'd resisted my advice, insisted that anger was exactly what got people's attention. I kept pushing back until he finally surrendered, and the last I knew, he had incorporated all my suggestions into his testimony. So what had he changed? And why now? Had something happened?

"I just wanted to tell you," he said. "So you won't be surprised."

"Okay." My tongue felt too thick for my mouth.

He held up several pages of testimony in his small, tight handwriting. "Would you like to read it?"

"No need," I said. I wanted to trust him, wanted him to think I trusted him, didn't want him to know I was worried.

He smiled at me with a tenderness that melted my heart and pushed back my concern, at least temporarily. With long, confident strides and his arms hanging relaxed at his sides, he went back to his seat at the opposite end of the table.

I saw Chloe put her hand on his shoulder and whisper in his ear. I heard his low chuckle, saw him pat his wife's hand. I fought back tears.

"How am I to live, Sylvia, when I'm dying," he had asked me right after he was diagnosed.

"Living is loving, Norton," I'd answered. "Living is doing the things you must do."

Maybe changing his testimony was one of those things.

At nine o'clock a side door at the front opened and a smartly dressed court reporter walked in and went over to her workplace. A few minutes later Judge Cheryl Sundquist came through the same door. We all stood, but she quickly instructed us with the palms of her hands to sit back down. Based on the grandmotherly mound of silver-white hair in a swirl on top of her head I assumed she was in her late fifties, maybe early sixties.

The judge scrutinized the seven of us from her podium, starting with me at the end of the defendants' table and moving to Norton at the beginning. She gave Mr. Vendenal a curt nod and did a quick scan of the faces of the dozens of coalition members who'd come to observe our trial. Once her assessment of the kingdom over which she ruled was complete, she turned back to us.

"I understand," she said with a smile, "that you will be defending yourselves." We all nodded. "Please let me know if there's anything you don't understand and I'll explain it to you." A little insulted huff, too soft for anyone but those closest to hear, escaped from Madeline's mouth.

With impressive efficiency, Judge Sundquist moved us through the morning proceedings, showing amazing patience during the voir dire process when we took turns asking potential jurors detailed questions and then huddled together to decide whether to strike or accept each one. By noon, despite our slow deliberations, six jurors and two alternates had been sworn in, and the judge called an hour and a half recess.

We stayed in the courtroom to debrief in our affinity group circle before going to lunch. Chloe pressed her shoulder into Norton and clung to his arm like an insecure outsider. Only I knew she was an insider where it counted most, in her husband's life. I also knew a little resentment toward her could give me relief from the pain that was burning the back of my eyes, but it would come with a price I wasn't willing to pay.

"I'm sorry about the way I behaved," Norton said. "You know, when I blew up at all of you."

Tony shrugged, gave him a friendly smile. "Grain of salt, man. I know you might think it's selling out, but in my testimony, I'm going to give the jury a hook to hang an acquittal on. I'm going to argue that because we pay for Nectaral's military work with our taxes, we have a right, as public citizens, to stand for a few hours on the property that we're paying for."

Everyone waited for Norton to object. Katyna sat like a bird frozen on a wire. Jane looked like she expected him go off again like he had at the meeting when Tony first suggested this. "See? See how it works?"

Norton had yelled. "You compromise with the system long enough and you end up being a whore to it. Give them a hook and you end up being nothing but a hooker."

But today Norton was calm. "I was a jerk," he said. "I'm sorry."

Then everyone, like the snap of a rubber band, started talking at once.

"Hey, man, no problem."

"No need to apologize, Norton."

"We understand."

"That's right, don't give it a s-s-second thought."

"We all know it was . . ."

That last, unfinished comment shut down all protestations. Jane and Katyna's eyes focused on their watches, Madeline's at the clock on the wall. Jim's sideways glance landed briefly on Norton and Chloe and then fell down to his lap. No one wanted to think about the elephant in the middle of the room, and no one was capable of thinking about anything else.

At long last, Madeline cut through the silent circle of grief. "Okay. Good job this morning, everyone."

After that, we talked about how long the trial might last, what we would do if we were found guilty and had to serve prison time, what our families thought about what we were doing. We talked and talked, about everything except what was right in front of us—a wife smiling bravely and clinging to her dying husband, and his best friend, me, acting strangely detached.

"So," Tony said, "is everyone ready with their testimony?"

That set off another round of talking over our fears and excitement about speaking from the witness stand. Norton smiled and nodded but said nothing. Everyone turned to him. Still, he said nothing.

"Well?" Madeline said at last.

"You're in for a surprise." That was all he said.

"It's too late to refuse to give your name," Tony said, laughing.

Nervous glances were passed around the circle, memories of our first planning meeting silently handed from person to person. Norton blowing up. Insisting we do something drastic. Like refusing to cooperate. Like turning our backs on the judge. And, finally, him storming out of the room.

Tony raised his palms and his shoulders. "Sorry, man, I couldn't resist."

Norton laughed. "Yeah, I know, that was stupid of me."

Everyone but me laughed along with him. I knew things the others didn't know. Things that sometimes happened, since the diagnosis, when he raged or lost control, when he said and did things he would not normally say or do, some of them downright scary.

"So, man," Tony said. "What about your testimony? What's the surprise?"

"You'll see," Norton said. He looked and sounded calm, much too calm.

Chloe looked down at her lap. She already knew.

Tony joked, "Just don't go giving that prosecutor an apoplectic fit."

Norton's diminished belly shook. "That wouldn't take much."

Again everyone laughed but me. If I'd read his changed testimony when I had the chance, I would know if I was overreacting or if there really was something to worry about. I did know that Norton wouldn't do anything to hurt us. He didn't do stupid things. Not normally. But then normally there wasn't something growing in his brain and interfering with his judgment. Still, he was on medicine to control that now, wasn't he? The doctors knew what to do with brain tumors. Didn't they?

ELEVEN

2019

I'm sitting at my kitchen table with my coffee thinking about Corey. It seems to have become part of my morning routine. I haven't seen him for three weeks now. Not since the night I tried to talk him out of going to the Nectaral rally. I've called him several times to apologize for giving him unsolicited advice, left texts, offered to pick him up for meetings, and nothing. Not a word. It's like he just disappeared. Nothing I can do. I pick up the newspaper and turn to the obituary section, always the last part I read in the morning.

"Norton Cramer Jr. died five days ago. He was four years old."

The words sting my eyes. There's a picture of Pickles, little bald head, sweet smile. I reach for the phone.

"This is Sylvia," I say to Corey's answering machine. "I am so sorry. I didn't know Pickles was . . . well, it's so sudden . . . I mean . . . I'm coming over this afternoon . . . I'm bringing some food . . . oh, today's Wednesday . . . I'll come after I finish delivering Meals on Wheels . . . I'll keep those visits short and get to your place as soon as I can . . . I'm so sorry . . . so very sorry." The machine cuts me off with a long beep as if disgusted by my rambling.

I make split pea soup with a bag of peas from the cupboard and some leftover ham, an onion, and a bag of carrots from the fridge and leave it simmering on the stove while I shower and dress and then go to the corner bakery for a fresh loaf of whole wheat bread. When it's time to leave, I put the pot of soup and the bread in an insulated basket to keep them warm.

I finish my Meals on Wheels deliveries early and get to Corey's shortly after lunchtime. There's no space to park in front of his building so I have to carry the heavy basket a block and a half. When I get to the front door I set it down on the ground and ring the bell. No answer. I ring again. Hold the button down. Push it in and out several times. Either he's not home or he's not answering.

Just as I turn to leave, I spot him in the distance, heading toward me with his head down, his steps uneven. He trips on the corner curb and flails his arms, almost falls. When he's a few feet from me, he tips forward, his eyes narrowed. He reeks of alcohol. I reach out to hug him, and his arms hang limp at his sides.

"I brought you some soup," I say.

He reaches in his pocket and a ring of keys falls to the ground. When he bends over to pick it up, he loses his balance and his shoulder crashes into the door. I bend down and pick up the keys, hand them to him. He fumbles and tries to put a key in the lock, then gives up and flings them all into a bush. Pepto-Bismol splotches run up his neck and cover his face. "Damn it, damn it, damn it!"

I pull the key ring from the bush and unlock the door. He staggers inside and up the stairs as if I'm not there. Three flights of steps later, the basket feels like a bowling ball and my shoulder a throbbing hot iron. Wheezing and coughing, I let the basket drop to my feet in front of Corey's door. I hold the key ring out to him. He stares at it, puzzled, then at me like he's trying to figure out who I am. He turns the knob, opens the unlocked door, and goes inside.

His apartment, if you can even call it that, is two hundred square feet of stinky wet socks, dirty underwear, stale beer, and mildew. The only furniture is a lumpy mattress in the middle of the floor on top of which is a tangle of dingy gray sheets. My feet kick at empty cans and bottles and clothes on the way to a counter along the wall that's holding up a microwave. I have to push aside several greasy cartons of leftover takeout food to make room for my basket.

Corey sits on the edge of the mattress while I wash out a bowl in a freestanding sink next to the counter. I fill the bowl with soup, and then bring it and two thick pieces of buttered bread to him. "Let's get some food in you. It'll make you feel better."

He slurps the soup and shoves the bread into his mouth with his fists like he hasn't eaten in days. He mumbles something, maybe thank you, maybe my name, maybe just a groan, I can't tell.

I smile down at him and reach for the empty bowl. "I'll get you some more." But instead of giving it to me, he snatches the bowl from my hands and hugs it tight to his chest. I step back. "I'm so sorry about Pickles."

He presses his brows together in a deep groove and then, without warning, he hurls the empty bowl at the window frame, sending fragments of shattered bowl everywhere. He jumps to his feet, thrashes his arms in the air. "I'm not gonna let them get away with this! I'm gonna make them pay! Mark my words! They're gonna be sorry!" His body sways. His stomping feet grind shards of the bowl into the linoleum floor. I press my back against the wall and protect my face with my arms. "They poisoned Pickles and Dad. They killed my unborn baby. They're not gonna get away with it. They're gonna pay for it. They're gonna pay for *all* of it."

Finally he stops and stands in front of me with a look of helplessness on his face. "No one knows the truth. No one knows. No one knows."

I open my arms to him, but he twists away and throws himself face down on the mattress. I sit next to him, place the palm of my hand gently on his back, and listen to the muffled sound of him sobbing into the crumpled-up pillow.

"I know, Corey. I know." I wish I could tell him there was a shortcut through grief. I wish there was one. "But you *will* be okay. You will."

He thrusts the upper part of his body up and takes a swing at me. I duck. Just in time. *Stupid. Stupid. Stupid.* What was I thinking, anyway? I should know that until he can believe he's going to be okay himself, all I can do is believe it for him—silently.

"Sylvia!" He shouts my name as if I've just appeared and he's surprised to see me. He leans over the edge of the mattress and reaches under it, pulls out a notebook. Its pages are yellowed and frayed at the edges.

I take in a sharp breath. "Is that . . . ?"

"Dad's journal," he says. A conspiratorial whisper seeps out of the thin opening between his lips. "He wrote it all down. Everything." His fingers fumble with the pages. "Here it is. Listen." His finger follows Norton's familiar handwriting on the page, his speech slurry as he reads the words.

I'll never forget it. At first, there was this buzzing noise and then a wave of intense heat, hotter and brighter than anything you can imagine. It went into my arms, my eyelids. The light burned. I put my hands over my eyes and opened them in little slits. I saw all the bones in my fingers. I saw the bones in the back of the guy in front of me.

Corey stops, sucks in a lungful of rage, and then continues reading.

When we were allowed to turn around, I was blinded at first, but then my sight came back and I saw this mushroom cloud. Reds, oranges, purples, lavender, black. A molten fire inside a cloud. I heard a distant rumble like thunder, then a huge roar. The island shook. It felt like something slamming into me and I could hardly keep my balance. All of us were terrified. Someone called out for his mother. I hummed a hymn and prayed.

Corey stops and blows out his breath. "Keep reading," I say. He rolls his eyes up toward the ceiling. "Please."

He looks at me, his eyes misty. "This is why Pickles . . ." He chokes on his son's name.

I nod. "I know," I say. "I know."

He squints at his father's small, tight handwriting and reads more.

The mushroom cloud started moving. It was drifting toward the island, toward us, but then it headed north. When it was over, none of us moved. Then Trayne said company dismissed and we all just walked away. Like sleepwalkers.

Corey stops reading, puts the journal down. "Go on," I say.

He sighs but picks it up again.

In the mess hall at dinner that night, the radio was blaring and we were laughing and calling out to each other, bragging, pumping hands. I didn't know what had happened. I didn't even know what Operation Redwing—that's what the test was called—was about. All I knew was this. That morning I was scared I was going to die, and that night I was still alive. I thought I was invulnerable. We all did.

The journal slams shut, drops onto the dirty mattress. I reach for it and Corey pushes me away.

"Don't you see, Sylvia? You see how shrewd they were? They made sure there was no evidence, nothing in his military record about the hydrogen bomb tests, nothing about him being exposed to radiation. Nothing about what it could do to him. To Pickles." He picks the journal up, thrusts it inches in front of my face. "But Dad wrote it all down. Everything he tried. It's all here. Every rock he turned over and looked under. That's how I know what they did. And what they're doing now." He stops and gives me a piercing look that sees right through me. "And you know, too, don't you, Sylvia?"

I nod. "Yes. I do."

He drops the journal back on the mattress with a dark, ominous expression that makes goose bumps spring up on my arms. "And soon the whole damn world is gonna know it, too. We're gonna make sure of that." His words slur and fade away as he falls back on the bed. He stares at the ceiling with a cold rage in his eyes.

I whisper. "What are you going to do?" The same question I asked his father so many years ago.

"Not just me," he mumbles. "I'm not alone. There are . . ." His voice trails off. His eyelids droop.

"What do you mean, Corey? Who?" But his eyes close and his mouth goes slack. He's either asleep or passed out.

I pick up the journal and drag myself up from the mattress. I brush away the slivers of the shattered bowl from the windowsill, sit on its edge, and read Norton's handwriting until the clock on the church across the street strikes. Then I tear myself away and check on Corey. Despite a beard that needs trimming and long hair that needs a good shampoo, in sleep he looks like the sad and confused four-year-old boy I first saw at his father's funeral, the boy whose father's death was as quick and unexpected to him then as Pickles's death is to me now. He rolls over onto his side with his hand tucked under his cheek and becomes the child who lost his father and later his mother. But when he moans, he becomes the father who lost his son, the husband who lost his wife, the man with nothing left to live for but vengeance.

TWELVE

1984

We ate lunch in the City Hall cafeteria, and when we got back to the courtroom, there was a man waiting outside the door. It was his clothes that first set off alarm bells in me, the black all-weather topcoat hanging lopsided under his shiny, shoulder-length black hair, the unevenly knit bright orange scarf around his neck that was strangely at odds with his boyish pink cheeks.

"Mr. Cramer?" His eyes darted from Jim to Tony and then settled on Norton. "Norton? Norton Cramer?" I was unsettled by the hungry look on his face.

Norton beamed. He squeezed his wife's shoulder. "You go on ahead, hon. I'll be there in a minute."

Chloe's left foot gave way to her right as her eyes moved back and forth between her husband and the suspicious-looking man. Then she nodded and went into the courtroom. She knew who he was. A dark wave of loneliness came over me and washed away all the late-night talks and intimate moments that had once given me special access to Norton. I squared my shoulders, walked into the courtroom, and made my way to the defendants' table at the front.

A few minutes later, Norton and the strange man sauntered in. Norton was excited. He winked at Chloe, but she looked worried. The other man sat in the second row and started digging into a faded cloth bag, searching for something deep in the bottom. I slumped down in my seat with my head throbbing, the hangover from last night not yet finished with me, my worries magnified.

Judge Sundquist walked in, waved for everyone to remain seated, and then quickly moved our trial along. The accusations against us were read first. "'These are the matters of the State versus the following defendants, a charge of trespassing from April 20, 1984.'" The court reporter's voice droned on as she read, for each of us in turn, our name and file number, and then repeated the same specific charge.

After that, Mr. Vendenal, the prosecutor, made his opening statement. I massaged my temples and allowed in only bits and pieces of it. "On Good Friday, about three hundred people approached Nectaral headquarters . . . Roughly half of them left the premises voluntarily subsequent to a warning . . . but these defendants stayed . . . they *intended* to trespass." My eyes wandered to the strange man in the second row, writing on a yellow legal pad. To Norton, leaning back in his chair with his hands behind his head. To Chloe, the shreds of tissue on her lap and beads of sweat on her forehead.

Madeline gave our opening statement next. First she summarized what we would cover in our testimony—a bit of information about each of us, what we had done at Nectaral headquarters on Good Friday, why we did it, and why we had a right to do it. When she concluded, she looked directly into the jurors' eyes. "We know that the prosecutor must prove us guilty beyond a reasonable doubt. We believe, after you have heard our testimony and weighed the evidence, that you, as the *conscience* of the community, will find us innocent of a criminal act, and on that basis will find us not guilty."

"Good job," we all whispered to her as she sat down.

Next, the prosecutor made his case against us in mind-numbing and repetitive detail, with photos, fingerprints, and the testimony of two corporate security guards and two police officers. It was a waste of time, completely irrelevant, for him to make the case that we'd trespassed when we had already admitted that we had. We were there to make the case that we didn't trespass with criminal intent, but he didn't even address that. Jane poked me and rolled her eyes. I rolled mine back.

At five o'clock, Mr. Vendenal finally rested his case, and Judge Sundquist announced that court would be adjourned until tomorrow. Norton grabbed Chloe's hand and rushed out the door, probably to pick Corey up from preschool. He would be spending the evening with his family, and I would be spending the evening alone with the wine I planned to buy at the liquor store on my way home.

##

The next morning I woke up on the couch, still dressed in yesterday's clothes, my head pounding, an empty wine bottle on the floor, and no recollection of the night before. Mission accomplished. But now, in the light of day, the loneliness and dread that had stalked me in court yesterday were back with a vengeance, along with another hangover, this one undaunted by a pot of coffee and several aspirins.

I used an extra measure of makeup to cover the puffiness in my face and wore a bright magenta silk blouse to disguise my gloominess. But there was nothing to be done with the pounding in my head but endure it.

Madeline, hands on her hips, greeted me at the front of the courtroom. "Where have you been? Didn't you get my messages?"

My mind was blank. I hadn't heard the phone ring. I wondered if I'd turned off the ringer last night while I was drunk.

"Well," she said in a disapproving tone. "We had to go ahead and meet without you. Everyone else agrees."

"Agrees about what?"

"Norton was supposed to give his testimony first." She leaned into me and lowered her voice. "But he asked if he could be last. So we talked about it, and in the end we all agreed that it would be okay if he testified for all of us."

I glanced over at Norton. He was wearing the same three-piece suit as yesterday, only this time with a bright red shirt open at the collar, a bold casual look. He was talking to the strange man, who was back again, only this morning his lopsided coat and orange scarf were gone, replaced by a wrinkled white shirt that was dingy to the point of gray.

Norton glanced at me with a smile that matched the worry-free expression on his face. I bit my bottom lip and looked back at Madeline. "Why? I mean, we spent a lot of time talking about this and we've each prepared our own testimony. Why such a huge change at the last minute?"

She brushed a piece of lint from her black wool slacks. "I know it's a big deal, Sylvia, and I wish you'd been here to hear why Norton wanted to do it this way. He was very convincing and in the end we decided it would actually be a lot more effective this way." I closed my eyes and blew air through my lips. She lowered her voice a bit more. "And under the circumstances . . . we think it would do him good . . . don't you think?"

"I don't know," I said. "Maybe."

"If you'd been here I think you would have agreed with the rest of us," she said. "We all hoped you'd be okay with it." Her fingers fluttered like they were dismissing any concerns I might have as nothing to worry about. Then she scurried off to confer with Katyna and Jane. I sat down at my place at the table with my hands holding up my pounding head, not knowing what to think.

At the sound of Norton's voice, I looked up. "Everything's going to be fine, Sylvia. It'll be over soon." A whiff of Aqua Velva pinched my nostrils and the feel of his thin hand on my shoulder squeezed my heart.

"What's going on, Norton? Who's that man you've been talking to?"

Before he had a chance to answer, Judge Sundquist came in and took her place. Out of habit, we all stood up, and then sat back down again at her command. Norton rushed back to his place at the other end of the table.

The judge looked at each of us in turn, with a kindly smile on her face. "Now then, folks, the State rested its case against you yesterday. It's your turn to defend yourselves. Who wants to go first?"

Norton stood. "I'll be testifying on behalf of all of us, Your Honor." With strong confident steps, he strode up to the witness stand and raised his right hand.

"Do you swear to tell the truth, the whole truth and nothing but the truth?"

"You bet!" His words bounced like a beach ball over all the heads in the room. I'd never seen him so determined. He sat down and scanned the courtroom with his lips curled up, twitching like a dog on a hunt, a man on a mission. He tipped his head at the strange man in the second row, who was holding his cloth bag in his lap with his hand in it. Then he smiled at Chloe, who looked like she was about to have a nervous breakdown.

"My name is Norton. N-O-R-T-O-N. Cramer. C-R-A-M-E-R." His voice echoed through the room. "I want to first apologize to my fellow defendants. I'm sorry I didn't tell you what I'm about to do."

His eyes fixed on me, pleading with me to see and hear what was going on with him as separate from what was going on with me. I smiled to let him know I wanted to do that more than anything, and hid my fears in my clenched fists under the table.

"Ladies and gentlemen." He turned to the jurors with a smile. "I am forty-eight years old. I'm married, I have a four-year-old son, and I have worked for the U.S. postal service for twenty years. I've been protesting nuclear weapons for a long time. I've read the research, and I know that if we ever have a nuclear war, none of us will survive."

Mr. Vendenal's greasy head popped up. "Objection, Your Honor. Hearsay. Lack of foundation. Mr. Cramer is not an expert witness."

"Overruled," the judge said. "It speaks to the defendant's motivation. I'll allow it."

The prosecutor went back to scribbling on a piece of paper as Norton continued.

"It's common knowledge that we wouldn't survive a nuclear war. But few people know that we aren't surviving the *preparations* for nuclear war either."

He paused to let that sink in. My foot started tapping. I'd warned him not to reveal too much personal information. *You don't know what the jury will do,* I'd advised. But this part of his testimony was new to me. I didn't know what he was going to say next, and now there was nothing I could do but hope for the best.

The jurors' inquisitive faces clung to Norton's words. "We haven't just *produced* weapons of mass destruction," he said, "we've *exploded hundreds* of them . . . in the atmosphere . . . in the ocean . . . in the ground. Bombs that are *at least* seventy-five times, even up to one thousand times, the power of the ones that killed hundreds of thousands of people in Hiroshima and Nagasaki in 1945."

He paused and then asked, "So how many people do you think died from those explosions?" He paused again, raised his eyebrows. "The answer is that nobody knows. And that, ladies and gentlemen, is no accident."

"Objection!"

"Mr. Cramer," the judge said, "you can go ahead if what you're speaking to is your motivation, not fact."

"I am, Your Honor." His eyes roamed from one juror to another. "I'm going to tell you my story now. And by doing so, I will be committing a crime against my country."

There it was. He was going all the way. He was going to blow the whistle. No matter what that might mean. He was going to do it. On the record. My heart raced. My head was ready to explode. I couldn't stop him, and, strangely, I was no longer sure I wanted to.

"I joined the army when I was eighteen. I was just a pimply-faced kid with nothing but little wisps of beard on my face and a desire to serve my country." He bounced a smile at the jurors, and they bounced nervous half smiles back at him. "I was sent to the South Pacific." He leaned so far forward he was now teetering on the edge of his seat. "I witnessed eleven nuclear explosions there . . . with no goggles or special clothing for protection, only instructions to turn away and cover my face. No one mentioned the danger of radioactivity." He waited a few seconds before continuing. "It isn't that they didn't know. Scientists knew the risks, from the earliest days of Los Alamos. They knew our military personnel got blistered and scarred after the bombings in Japan . . . they knew their hair fell out . . . they knew they had convulsions. They knew they had radiation poisoning . . . but they never told them. They never told us either. They wanted to see how we would react, what the blasts would do to us, whether our equipment would function." Norton's voice

100

expanded and contracted, expanded again, and finally rose to a crescendo. "We were their guinea pigs. Nothing. But. GUINEA PIGS." His voice shot up in the air then fell to the floor. "And then they dropped us like hot potatoes."

His hands crashed down on the wooden railing in front of him.

Silence descended. Chloe smiled and nodded. Observers in the courtroom shook their heads. The man in the second row scribbled, his pencil digging holes in the paper. The jurors looked stunned. *I* was stunned.

Norton raised his hands, palms facing the jurors. "It's not your fault you didn't know. It's been a very carefully kept secret. It's true. By telling you, I have just violated the Nuclear Radiation and Secrecy Agreements Act. I have just committed treason. I can cite the law for you if you'd like." His back stiffened and his chin jutted out. "Well, today the jig is up." The words spilled from his mouth. "The secrecy ends now. Right here. Right now."

Light and shadow roiled in front of my eyes like a burst blood vessel had just released dozens of competing thoughts and feelings in my head all at once. My chest swelled with pride and admiration for Norton's courage. It constricted with fear about what was going to happen to him. It shriveled with guilt for having doubted him. It made me want to protect him with my life.

But Norton wasn't finished. "Ladies and gentlemen." His shoulders sagged. "I have an inoperable brain tumor. I'm dying."

Jane put her arm around me. Audible gasps found their way up and down the jury box.

"Please." Norton raised his hands and shook his head. "Please don't feel sorry for me. That's not why I told you. I told you because I want you to know why I can no longer, why I *will* no longer, collude with the very nuclear program that I oppose. I told you because you need to know that four hundred thousand others like me were exposed. Many have already died . . . we don't know yet what will happen to our children and grandchildren. Maybe your grandfather or father is an atomic veteran, and you don't know that because he took an oath not to tell you. Maybe he got sick, like I did, but couldn't tell his doctor he'd been exposed to radiation. Maybe, like me, he was denied compensation because there was nothing in his military record about the tests."

He stopped, out of breath. The seconds ticked by. "Ladies and gentlemen of the jury," he said at last. "We ask you to be the conscience of the community and to join us. We ask you to refuse to collude with the death machine. We ask you to answer one question and one question only. Which should be the criminal act: our trespassing, or Nectaral producing weapons of mass destruction that have already caused the deaths of thousands of patriotic Americans and their families? If your answer is the former, you will find us guilty. If your answer is the latter, you must find us not guilty. The decision is yours."

Threads of feelings inside me wove themselves into a tapestry of love for Norton, awe at the strength of his endurance and the power of his spirit over his damaged body, anger for his wronged soul, admiration for the revolutionary ire that had arisen from a human need deep within him, sadness at the reality of his impending death. He had insisted on doing something drastic, and indeed he had. But it would not be without consequence.

THIRTEEN

2019

The wind howls through the gaps between the window frame and the wall, a storm moving in to break the high humidity that starts around here just before the Fourth of July and continues through August. A street lamp outside casts a shadowy ray of light on the dingy mattress on which Corey lies, still passed out. Alcohol has given him a temporary reprieve from the pain of losing his son, but when he comes to, the pain will be back, and even more alcohol will be required to make it go away. That's how alcohol works. That's its job, to make you need it more and more. I sit on the windowsill and think about what I just read in Norton's journal. About his many efforts, all futile, to get compensation for Corey and Chloe. I imagine him, now, looking down at his son's motionless body. I imagine his heart breaking to see his son living like this.

Drops of rain seep through a crack in the window frame and land on my neck. My back and every other joint in my body are stiff and cramped up from sitting in one position so long. And for what purpose, I ask myself. How does my sitting here help Corey? How does it help me?

I get up and stretch, lean forward and backward, bring blood back into my limbs. My feet kick their way through the debris on the floor and my fingers search along the plasterboard for a light switch. When I find one and flick it on, a bare bulb in the middle of the ceiling spotlights the wreckage below and produces a rustling sound from the rumpled pile of filthy sheets on the mattress.

"Corey?" No response. "Corey, are you all right? Can I get you anything?" He turns over onto his side, eyes closed, lips a tight, thin line.

My first impulse is to turn the light off, go home, let him sleep, call him in the morning. But I can't leave him like this, not when I can see how far alcohol has brought him down. I don't want him to be alone like I was when I woke up to the reality of what alcohol had reduced me to. I need to do something. But what?

I pull a large garbage bag from a box under the counter and start stuffing all the clothes scattered about on the floor in it. Soft snoring sounds from Corey's open mouth echo his father, bring him into the room. *It's okay, Norton. I'll take care of your child. I'll protect him.*

I pull two more garbage bags from the box, put all the cans and bottles in one and bits of dried-up food, greasy takeout cartons, paper, and other rubbish in another. I stop to catch my breath and hear Norton breathing with me, see his grateful smile. I open the fridge in the kitchen area and see that the only thing inside is a half-full bottle of red wine. I pour the rest of the wine down the sink and throw the empty bottle in the recyclable bag with a loud clang. Corey doesn't stir.

I dig through the laundry bag and pull out a threadbare T-shirt to use as a cleaning rag. Seeing that it's the old Star Wars Is a Hoax shirt that Norton used to wear brings me back to the day Chloe called to tell me Norton was dead. I quickly stuff the T-shirt back in the laundry bag and pull out a towel instead.

The past gradually recedes with each particle of food and stain the towel wipes away, with each stuck-on fragment my fingernails scrape off. I scrub the inside of the fridge until it's an almost blinding white and put the pot of soup and bread inside. Then I wipe down the counter, wash the dirty dishes in the sink, and dry them on my skirt. I sweep the floor with an old worn-out broom I find in the closet. I scrub the toilet, sink, and tub with a can of Comet and a grimy sponge I find in the corner of the bathroom. On my hands and knees I wipe the floor with the sponge, first the bathroom, then the other room. The sponge disintegrates in my hand and I throw its remains in the trash.

I drag two plastic bags of garbage and recyclables down the stairs to the basement and toss them in the garbage bins. Then I go back upstairs to get the bag of dirty laundry to take home with me.

Before leaving, I take one last look at Corey. What will he think, I wonder, when he wakes up and sees that everything is clean? Will he think he's hallucinating? What if he's been in a blackout this whole time and doesn't even remember I was here? Maybe he'll worry that he's lost his mind. I pull out a piece of paper and pen from my purse and write a note.

Dear Corey, I cleaned your room because I want you to know you're not alone and that I care. Love, Sylvia.

I shake my head. No, that's not right. That's not what I want to say. I scratch it out and start again.

Dear Corey, I'm so sorry about Pickles.

No. I shove the note in the pocket of my skirt. What I'm feeling is too complicated for words. And how can I explain why I cleaned his place when I don't even know why I did it myself? Anyway, no matter what I say, he's going to think I found it so filthy and disgusting that I just couldn't stand it. And maybe that's the truth, I don't know. I turn off the light and leave.

I get home sore and exhausted, still second-guessing myself and worrying about Corey. I wonder if he'll sleep through the night or if I should have stayed until he woke up. Maybe I should have at least left a note saying that I'd been there and that I'd call him in the morning. I thought bringing him soup would be helpful, but if it was, then why did he smash the bowl?

I do his laundry with a vague sense that I'm crossing a line but I don't know why, only that I'm driven to do it just like I was driven to clean his place.

Finally, after the laundry is finished and I've worn myself out completely, I go to bed, and before turning off the light read the message for the day in my meditation book. "To be modest is to be able to see that we are not in a position to change the whole world."

I read it to myself again, only this time I change the last part. *To be modest is to be able to see that I am not in a position to change Corey.*

Now I get it. Now I know why I was driven to clean his room and do his laundry. It was because I secretly believed, or at least hoped, that then he'd be okay. I didn't do it for Norton. I didn't even really do it for Corey. The truth is, the reason behind my doing it, behind what many of us do at times like this, resides within me, in what I need to do for myself. And for that we can all be forgiven. I turn off the light and slip easily into a deep and gratifying sleep.

The next morning my iPhone rings me awake. "It's about my clothes, Sylvia. I don't suppose you know where they are."

I glance through the door at his neatly folded laundry on the living room couch. "I'm sorry. I should have asked if you wanted help. I'll bring them to you."

He snorts.

"There's soup and bread in the refrigerator. You should eat something."

"I just want my damn clothes, Sylvia." The phone clicks off.

I call him right back. I may not be able to change him or make things okay for him, but there is something I can do, even if it's only because it's something I need to do for myself.

"What?" he yells in my ear.

"I'll be there tonight at six with your clothes," I say, "and then we're going to a meeting."

FOURTEEN

1984

Norton's testimony left the courtroom stunned. Its inspiration was handed from person to person through nods and smiles, its honest courage through the fluttering of hearts. But its power was limited; it could only influence, not determine our guilt or innocence. Judge Sundquist placed that power in the hands of the jurors when she gave them instructions and sent them to another room to begin their deliberations. If they found us guilty, the power to determine our punishment would then be placed in the hands of the judge. There was nothing left for us to do but wait.

Peace and Justice Coalition members rushed to the front of the courtroom, shouting "Fantastic job, guys!" and "Good luck!" and practically suffocating us with hugs. "It won't take the jury long to reach a decision," Martin Lind predicted. I pushed my way through the crowd to get to Norton. I wanted to tell him how proud of him I was. But he had already left.

I went home, threw off my clothes, and even though it was only midafternoon, put on my pajamas. I poured myself a glass of wine and thought about how brave Norton was, how he was facing death with such incredible courage. After a second, or was it a third, glass of wine, I thought about how much I loved him. Missed him. Feared for him. A few more glasses and I thought about how he had left without even saying good-bye. And after pouring the last drop of wine from the bottle, I didn't think at all.

And then it was the next morning and my head was throbbing. I went down to the lobby to get the paper. Several copies of the *Monrow*

City Tribune were, as usual, in a stack on the small table next to the mailboxes. I grabbed one from the top of the pile, and the front-page headline—"Atomic Veteran Exposes Government's Nuclear Secrets in Court"—hit me right me between the eyes.

No, it couldn't be. It had to be a story about someone else. I brought the paper closer and read the headline again. Then I kept reading. "Yesterday, during one of the Nectaral trespassing trials that have been taking place for weeks in Monrow City Municipal Court, Norton Cramer, one of the defendants, divulged classified information about nuclear bomb tests in the South Pacific. In his testimony, Mr. Cramer broke an oath of secrecy he'd made to the U.S. government and violated the . . ." I read on, gripping the paper with clammy hands and racing for the elevator. ". . . violated the Nuclear Radiation and Secrecy Agreements Act, which is a federal offense."

I couldn't believe it. I had been worried enough about Norton breaking his silence to fewer than a hundred people in the courtroom, and now here it was splashed all over the front page of a large city newspaper for thousands to read. This was worse than I'd thought. He was in more trouble, much deeper trouble, than I'd feared. Maybe he'd already read the paper and gone into hiding. But what if he hadn't? I had to warn him.

I pushed the elevator button and kept on reading. "When interviewed later about his testimony, Mr. Cramer indicated that . . ." Wait! He was interviewed? Outside of the courtroom? When? Why didn't he tell me?

I stubbed my toe getting off the elevator and limped down the hall to my apartment. Once inside, I slammed the paper on the kitchen table, grabbed the phone, and dialed his number.

After several rings, Chloe answered, out of breath. "Oh, Sylvia, it's just you. I was about to take the phone off the hook. It's been ringing nonstop since early this morning. Everyone wants to talk to Norton. They're calling him a whistleblower . . . they want to know when he decided . . . even someone from the *Washington Post* called . . . they want to know if he's going to prison. I thought it was only going to be a short article, if any, maybe just a paragraph or two in the local paper. I told him he was taking a big risk. He wouldn't listen." I heard the sound of scuffling on the other end of the line. "Just a minute. He wants to talk to you."

"Hey, Sylvia." Norton sounded upbeat, victorious, the exact opposite of how Chloe sounded and how I felt.

"Norton, are you okay?"

"Are you kidding? I'm more than okay!"

"What the hell were you thinking?" I said. "Damn it, Norton. It's a good thing Chloe and I are worried about you, because it doesn't sound like you have enough sense to worry about yourself."

"Tom did a great job, don't you think?" He went on, exuberant, not even hearing me. "I wasn't sure about him. He's brand-new at the paper, pretty green. But he came through, didn't he?"

I glanced down at the byline, the tiny photo next to it. Tom Strickland, Staff Reporter. "So that's who that strange man was in the courtroom," I mutter.

"Yeah, funny-looking guy, huh? I called to thank him. I told him he's going to make a name for himself. He was pretty happy about getting an exclusive. I didn't tell him he was the only one interested. Bet all those other reporters who thought there'd already been enough coverage of the Nectaral trials are sorry now."

I gritted my teeth. "You didn't tell me."

"I didn't want you to worry. Chloe was worried enough for both of you."

I swallowed the hurt in my mouth and it moved down my throat and into my stomach.

"I can't tell you how free I feel, Sylvia. I feel whole for the first time."

"Your testimony *was* incredible, Norton." That was all I could say.

The volume of his voice dropped. "I did what I had to do, Sylvia."

"I know. I know. But what happens now? I mean, it's all over the news."

"I guess that all depends." He sounded resigned.

"On what?"

"On the verdict."

"The verdict? What difference does the verdict make, Norton? Whether we're found guilty or not, either way, you broke the law, and you know I'm not talking about trespassing. Don't you realize how serious this is? Do you think the FBI's just going to look the other way?"

"It doesn't matter what the FBI does or doesn't do. It's what *I* do that matters."

"What the hell does that mean, Norton? Is there something else you haven't told me?"

"I'm sorry, I should have. I mean, I would have told you, but . . ." His words were cut off by a child's voice in the background, the muffled sound of Chloe saying something I couldn't make out. "Sorry, Sylvia, I gotta run. I'll see you back in court. I bet the jury will be back with a verdict by this afternoon."

I paced all morning, back and forth from one end of my apartment to the other. I chewed my nails and drank enough coffee to sink a ship. *I would have told you, Sylvia, but . . .* But what? Finish the damn sentence, Norton. But I didn't get a chance? But I was protecting you? But I thought you'd try to talk me out of it? But I only told my wife? But you and I don't share secrets anymore, and now I'm going to get off the phone fast because I don't want you to know what I plan to do next?

Noon came and went with no verdict. Why was it taking the jury so long? Were they having trouble reaching a consensus? Or were they just taking their sweet time making a decision? My head was spinning out of control until, all of a sudden, a voice wormed its way into my brain and stepped on the brakes. *For heaven's sake, Sylvia, would you please stop making yourself crazy. Go to work or something.*

So that's what I did. I spent the rest of the afternoon at my office, pretending to do paperwork.

FIFTEEN

2019

At six o'clock sharp that night I'm at Corey's with a plastic bag filled with his clothes, clean and neatly folded, in my arms. I don't expect him to be there, and if he is, I won't be surprised if he's still drunk or working on getting drunk again. I ring the doorbell and wait.

Several minutes pass. Looks like I'll be going to the AA meeting alone. He never did say he'd go with me. One more ring and I'm going to give up. But then the door flings open and a stone-faced Corey, wearing the same clothes he wore yesterday, motions with a flick of his head for me to come inside. "I'll be right back," he says, his voice flat, unreadable.

He bounds up the stairs two at a time with the plastic bag hitting each step behind him. The entryway reeks of mold; the floor is littered with candy wrappers, cigarette butts, and something that looks like dried-up dog poop. The door to the building opens again and an elderly woman totters in, a firm grip on a bag of groceries in one hand and a cane in the other. "Would you like help?" I ask.

She shakes her head and with a toothless smile says, "No, thank you, dearie. I'm fine. I'm just one floor up." I watch her pull herself up one slow, painful step at a time, hoping her apartment is bigger and nicer than Corey's one room on the third floor. Based on the condition of the foyer, though, it's more likely that all five units in the building are equally cheap and below standard.

After several minutes, Corey reappears wearing a bright blue T-shirt and jeans. He smells of Aqua Velva and clean clothes, and his wet hair is

111

pulled back in a neat ponytail.

"You look good," I say.

His eyes give up nothing, not even a blink or a thank-you. He holds the door open for me, not out of respect, more like a little boy who's been told it would be rude not to. He heads for my car with angry steps that pound into the pavement, then fastens his seat belt without being prompted. When I say, "I found a meeting not far from here, in a Congregational church," he glues his eyes on the road as if he's the one driving, not me, and he's telling me not to distract him.

In the church basement, we sit in folding chairs in a tight circle with twenty others. "Are there any newcomers to the meeting who would like to introduce themselves?"

I raise my hand. "My name is Sylvia and I'm an alcoholic. I've never been to this meeting before."

"Welcome, Sylvia!"

I poke Corey with my elbow.

"Um, I'm Corey." He folds his arms and tucks his chin into his chest and stretches his legs out, then doesn't move for the next hour. I smell alcohol on his breath. At the end of the meeting, after we stand, hold hands, and say the Serenity Prayer, he speaks to no one and instead bolts for the door and waits for me outside.

On the way back to his place, I spot a lopsided neon sign over the door of a café in a tiny strip mall. I park in front and pull on the emergency brake.

"Okay, Corey, time to talk."

He pushes the car door open with his shoulder, kicks an empty beer can down the sidewalk, and follows me inside. We sit in a booth in the back corner on maroon plastic seats mended with strips of gray duct tape. A waitress my age, probably working to pay her health care expenses, drags herself over to us with an order pad in one blue-veined hand, a shaky pen in the other. Her name tag says Maggie.

"Just coffee with cream for me," I say. Maggie draws in her breath like someone who doesn't mind waiting, or is maybe just resigned to life. "Make that two coffees," I say.

112

"Black," Corey mumbles without looking up. Maggie gives me a sympathetic look and limps away.

"Corey . . ."

The veins in his neck bulge. The palms of his hands push against the air between us. "Who are you, Sylvia Jensen? Why are you messing with my life?"

The profound sadness in his eyes is more deafening than his angry words. I want to grab his hand and say, *Because you need me, because I'm your only connection to your father, because I need you, because you're my only connection to Norton.*

"Maybe we need each other, Corey," I say.

He's annoyed, turns his face away from me and toward the wall.

"I'd like to get to know you," I say, "and I'd like you to know me." He shoots me a sideways glance, suspicious, but perhaps in spite of himself also curious.

"But that can't happen," I add, "if there are secrets between us."

His hands grip the edge of the table. "I hope you don't expect me to bare my soul to you." He starts to stand up.

I reach out to him, my hands pleading, palms up on the table. "I want to tell you the truth about *me*," I say. "About my relationship with your father."

He squints and lowers himself back down in the booth.

"We were very close." A spasm squeezes my throat and forces me to swallow before I can go on. "We were in love."

Sharp sarcasm escapes his puckered lips. "Well, just another lovely thing for me to know about dear old Dad. Is that supposed to make me feel, oh, I don't know, what? Better? Connected to you? What?"

I take a sip of coffee. Tell myself this is not about me, or my longing for Norton, or the pain I still carry about how I lost him. This is about Corey. I've just dropped a bombshell on him, and now I need to help him deal with it. I let his anger wash over me.

His lip curls up. "Just something else my mom lied about."

I shake my head. How easy it is to blame mothers for everything. "No, Corey," I say. "Your mom didn't know." But then I remember how

113

cold Chloe was to me at the end. "I mean, I don't think she knew," I add. "I hope she didn't."

"Cut the sympathy, Sylvia. I'm sure Mom didn't want it. Neither do I."

"I just thought . . . I'm sorry, Corey."

"Doesn't matter. The only thing that matters is getting justice for Pickles."

I nod. I get it. I truly do get it. "If your dad were here today, his heart would be breaking for you and what you're going through."

His face turns beet red and he leans forward, his hands flat on the table. "I don't care. The *only* thing I need is justice for my son." His voice quiets but his lips clench even tighter. "And I will do *whatever* I have to do to get it."

A chill runs through me. "I understand," I say, even though I don't.

He makes his hands into fists. "It took Pickles a long time to be born . . . twenty hours . . . he worked so hard to get here . . . so hard." He collapses back on the bench.

"I'll never know what it's like to lose a child of my own, Corey. But I do know what it's like to be willing to go to any lengths to get justice when a child I care about has been harmed."

His jaw tightens. "Do you? Do you really? And what if getting justice means some people get hurt or killed? Do you still understand?"

No, I don't. I can't. "You're scaring me, Corey."

He glares at me, his eyes icy. "I will do whatever it takes." He drops his chin and mumbles, "Unlike my dad."

Loyalty pumps hot through my veins. "Your father risked going to prison, Corey. He could have died there."

"And who, pray tell, would have noticed if he *had*? Who would have even cared?"

"A lot of people," I say. "Your father did what *he* believed was right. That's what's most important."

He tucks in his chin. "Then he'd understand why I have to do what I have to do."

"And what is it that you think you have to do, Corey?"

114

"What *we* . . ." His eyes drop. "Something that will get their attention."

"We? Who?"

He turns his face to the wall and goes mute.

I lean into the courage all of a sudden surging through my veins. "Your father would never support . . . would never approve of . . . hurting people, Corey. He would understand your need for vengeance, but he wouldn't want you to resort to violence."

Corey's fists hit the table. The saltshaker flies up in the air and lands on its side with a thud. "Did you ever think, Sylvia, that maybe no one listened to him because he didn't make them listen? Did you ever think that's why they never admitted they poisoned him? Well, believe me, they're gonna admit they killed Pickles. Mark my words, Sylvia, they're gonna listen this time."

"People listened to your dad, Corey. He made a difference."

He lets out a snort. "You're kidding me, right? If he made such a big difference, then why is Nectaral plotting to store poison in our own back yard now?"

"If your dad were here, Corey, he would be doing whatever he could to stop them. But he would never resort to violence. He never hurt anyone, despite the injustice done to him, not even when he was dying."

"Yeah, he'd probably be going to meaningless rallies and signing petitions and doing other useless stuff like that." His chin juts out like an accusing finger pointing at me. "But I s'pose that's better than not caring at all and sitting on your duff like *some* people."

"That's a low blow, Corey."

"Face it, Sylvia, if you fuss around much longer about what you think you should do about it, it'll be too late." His shoulders go up then plummet down in defeat. "Probably already too late."

"It's never too late," I say.

He rolls his eyes, and we slip into a deadlocked silence. At least this time he doesn't storm off.

"Do you really think," he says at last, "that your affair with Dad didn't hurt my mom?"

I cringe. My folded hands turn clammy with old guilt, useless regrets. "Your father loved her," I say. "He proved that to her in the end."

The roll of his eyes says it all. He doesn't believe me. I had an affair with his father and kept it a secret, which isn't exactly a ringing endorsement of my credibility. If he is ever to be persuaded to follow in his father's nonviolent footsteps, it's going to take more concrete and substantive evidence about who Norton was than the opinion of his lover.

"Are we done now," Corey says, "or is there something else you want to tell me."

"Another time," I say.

SIXTEEN

1984

When I got home from work, there was a message on my answering machine from Norton.

"Hey, Sylvia. Chloe and I are taking Corey camping up north for two days. I'm leaving the number where I can be reached in case they call. And don't worry. Whatever happens, happens. I'm prepared. The number is . . ."

My finger punched the button and erased Norton's cheery voice. No need to write down the number. Nothing was going to happen over the weekend. The jury hadn't reached a verdict by six o'clock, and today was Friday, so the judge would have sent the jurors home with instructions to come back and resume their deliberations on Monday morning.

I bundled up in my afghan and looked out the sliding glass door at the snow accumulating on my patio railing. It was coming down harder now than when I left my office, with three inches predicted, and even more north of the city. Norton said he was taking Corey camping? The second week of November? Hardly. More like skiing. Or sledding. He was mixing up his words again. I pictured the three of them, wherever they were, shoulder to shoulder on a couch in front of a fireplace, drinking hot chocolate, maybe roasting marshmallows. Cozy. Together. If I knew, truly knew, how to love, I would be happy for him and sadness wouldn't be heating up the backs of my eyes.

I went into the kitchen, grabbed an almost empty bottle of wine, and took a swig. Norton had said that no matter what happened, he was prepared. I'd ruminated about that all afternoon and still didn't know what he meant. Maybe it was just that he was prepared to go to prison if we were found guilty. I gulped down the last of the wine. Maybe it meant he was prepared for whatever consequences he'd have to face for exposing nuclear secrets. I tossed the empty wine bottle in my metal garbage can and it cracked in half. Or maybe, just maybe, Norton meant something else entirely. Maybe he was prepared to take yet another action that he wasn't going to tell me about.

I sat down at the table and laid my head in my arms. I wanted Norton to be with his family in the time he had left. I wanted him to have a good time this weekend. I wanted him to feel good about what he'd done. But I didn't want to feel sad for myself. I didn't want to feel so desperately lonely. I didn't want to worry. I didn't want to do anything. I didn't want to feel anything.

So I did what I always did. I grabbed my purse, threw on my coat, and slammed the door behind me. I pushed the elevator button over and over, swearing, berating it for not responding quickly enough. Once outside, my feet slid like runners on a sled across three blocks of slippery sidewalk to the liquor store. *My* liquor store, the one I stopped at almost every day on my way home from work to make sure I had enough white zinfandel to last the night. The whole way there I berated myself for not stopping on my way home earlier. Breathless, I yanked open the door and stood before all the rows of bottles that promised relief, escape, oblivion.

I came home with five bottles, two of white zinfandel, two of gin, one of tonic. My loneliness soaked into the lime being sliced. Dripped onto the ice clinking in the glass. Mingled with the gin and tonic splashing in the tumbler. Added salt to the taste of the first drink going down my throat. And to the second. Maybe the third, I didn't remember, because after that, everything was a blur. Mission accomplished.

SEVENTEEN

2019

Bitter coffee and the debris from last night's disastrous talk with Corey leave a foul taste in my mouth, like sour milk churned into watery butter. Why did he go to the AA meeting with me in the first place? All he did was sulk, and it was obvious he'd been drinking. And whatever made me think it was a good idea to try to have a personal talk with him? Why did I tell him about my affair with his father? Everything that could go wrong had gone wrong, and it was no wonder. I'd asked for it, after all.

I'm pretty far down the path of self-deprecation when I'm forced into a time-out by the ring of my iPhone.

"Good morning, Sylvia. My plane just landed."

"J. B., you're here? Why didn't you tell me you were coming?"

"I'm here to cover today's rally. It was a last-minute decision," he says. "Should I meet you there?"

I scratch my neck. "Well . . . I wasn't planning to go, but . . . maybe I should." It suddenly occurs to me that maybe I should ask Corey if he'd like to go with me. Maybe it would provide an outlet for his anger and grief. And since J.B. is going to cover it for the *New York Times,* maybe that would get Corey to change his mind about protests being a waste of time. Maybe it would help him realize that you don't have to do something violent to get people's attention.

"It *is* a hot issue right now. No pun intended." J. B. chuckles. "No one knows what to do with nuclear waste except that they don't want it in their own back yard."

I think about what Corey said last night. *If you keep fussing about what you're gonna do, Sylvia, it'll be too late.* "Okay, I'll go," I say. "I've been mulling what to do for long enough, ever since Bertha's memorial service."

J. B. laughs. He probably thinks he's convinced me to go because I can never say no to him. "Eleven o'clock?"

"Meet me at the bus stop at the corner of Sixth and Nectaral Plaza Place," I say.

"Okay, we'll go find trouble together."

I groan. "Uh-uh. If there's any trouble, J. B., I will be leaving. Just so you know." I hang up before he has a chance to say, *You and trouble are joined at the hip, Sylvia,* or some other wisecrack.

Before showering and getting dressed, I pour myself another cup of coffee. It feels right for me to stop vacillating and go today. But it doesn't feel right to ask Corey to go with me. It's too risky. With him so torn up, and on the verge of ruining his life already, if something happened at the rally it could push him right over the edge.

J. B. is standing under the bus stop sign when I get there. He takes my hand and helps me down the steps like I'm an old lady. He's the only one who can get away with that without annoying me.

"Well, aren't you a fish out of water," I say with a shake of my head. He smiles, accustomed to me teasing him about his fancy clothes. Without my having to say it, he knows I'm telling him he could have dressed down a bit for a protest.

"Look who's talking." He glances at my faded ankle-length jean skirt and bright pink T-shirt with a black peace sign on it. His smile tells me what I already know, that he admires me for not dressing appropriately for my age.

There are only about two hundred protesters at Nectaral Plaza when we get there. "I hope the heat isn't scaring people away," I say. Midwest summers have always been hot and humid, but the temperature has risen in July a few more soggy degrees for each of the last several years. It's already in the nineties and expected to top one hundred by noon.

J. B. points to several national television news trucks. Some photographers are setting up tripods on a hill. "The media's out in force. Guess they're expecting a good turnout."

We position ourselves at the top of an incline near the plaza gate so we have a good view. From there we watch as more and more people spill into the plaza by the minute. They carry umbrellas to protect themselves from the brutal midday sun and banners to identify where they've come from (as far away as Massachusetts to the east and California to the west) and whom they represent (environmentalists, people of various faiths, pacifists, activists, organizations of all stripes). By noon there are at least two thousand people packed in the plaza—the entire spectrum of humanity from pregnant women to infants in their mothers' arms to children gripping their parents' hands to people in their nineties and every age in between, from youthful strong people to older frail people in wheelchairs, and all races and ethnicities.

"Corey thinks no one pays any attention to rallies," I say to J. B. "Looks like he's wrong about this one."

J. B.'s curious right eyebrow shoots up. "So you're still hanging out with that guy."

I shrug. "Look at all these people," I say. "They're trampling the flower gardens. And, over there. Some are even up in the branches of that tree."

People start chanting. *Get up, get down, we'll have no poison in this town.* Their voices get louder and louder, closing in on a fever pitch. *Hey hey, ho ho, your plutonium has got to go.* Swarms of local and national reporters and camera crews search for what they consider the most newsworthy coverage. They converge on a group of young, long-haired white men, fists raised, anarchist labels pinned to the backs of their black shirts, who are facing off with another group of white men, clean-cut, crew-cut, and tattoo types waving American flags and sporting Nazi symbols on their signs.

I point them out to J. B. and shout over the clamor. "I hate it when the media focuses on extremists like that. It scares people."

"People should be afraid," J. B. says.

"Not of the protesters."

"No." He looks down, writes something on his little notepad, and then adds, "Not usually."

"Why do you say that? Do you think some of those anarchists are government plants? I'm sure the Nazi sympathizers are. Is that something you're investigating?"

"In part . . ." He slips the notepad back in his pocket with a shake of his head and a look in his eyes that says, *I'm sorry, Sylvia, but I'm not at liberty to say anything more at this time.*

By one o'clock, the time the rally was set to begin, people are packed together like sardines, heaving and sweating under a 102-degree sun. Skirmishes break out, a shove here, a shout there. A young man waves a Confederate flag in the face of a gray-haired woman and screams at her to go back to the nursing home. "Stop that," I yell, but of course no one hears me.

Nazi-type counterprotesters shout *Keep America safe* at the top of their lungs, their eyes spewing hate as they push their way through the crowd, always checking to be sure the swarms of local and national reporters and camera crews are focusing on them.

"The media is eating this up," I shout to J. B.

More fights break out, a shouting altercation in one spot, a push and shove in another. Martin Lind calls into a megaphone for order, but the ear-splitting fervor of the crowd swallows up his voice. Peacekeepers in orange vests trying to calm people are ignored. A mother with a little girl, frantic to get out of the way, turns her stroller too sharp, and it tips over with the child still in it. The mother lets out a blood-curdling shriek, the child a high-pitched scream. I yell for help and start to run toward them, but J. B. grabs me and pulls me back. "You'll get hurt," he says. Shielded and masked officers, covered in military-grade riot gear, stream out of the entrance to the main Nectaral headquarters building. Cars flash blue and screech to a stop at the plaza entrance, and police spill out, clubs in hands, guns at the ready. An ambulance, its siren blaring and lights flashing, drives down the sidewalk.

I watch with my fists clenched, my blood boiling. Why is this happening? We've been protesting at Nectaral Plaza since the 1980s, and our rallies have always been peaceful and respectful. It's not that there weren't any agitators back then—there were always a few people who called themselves anarchists or patriots and tried to stir up trouble—but it was nothing like this.

"This is ugly," I say to J. B. He grunts and nods, keeps writing on his notepad.

An agitator wearing a Guy Fawkes mask walks slowly around the outside perimeter of the crowd. It looks like he's drawing something on a piece of paper. He stops about six feet away from me, folds up the paper, and shoves it in the back pocket of his jeans. I arch my shoulders, ready to do something, I don't know what, if he tries to stir up more trouble. Then he takes off the mask and my legs start to give out under me. It's Corey.

J. B. grabs me so I don't fall. "What's wrong, Sylvia? You look like you've seen a ghost."

I want more than anything else to shake Corey's shoulders and shout *What the hell is wrong with you?* in his face, but after what he said last night—*Whatever it takes*—I know something big is up and I have to keep my head about me, have to get away, think things through before deciding what to do.

"I'm leaving," I say to J. B. "Don't worry, I'm fine. This is just . . . it's just too much."

I turn away from him and head toward the gate. A policeman runs by, and his billy club grazes my elbow, right in the funny bone. I press my lips into a silent scream and stumble away from the plaza.

On the number 33 bus, I look in the driver's rearview mirror at a wrinkled, pink face that doesn't look like mine staring back at me. A hand that doesn't feel like mine brushes wisps of sticky gray hair from my sweaty cheeks. I look out the window at the people we pass, normal people living normal lives—going in and out of a department store, a florist shop, a corner grocery store, a pharmacy—in a surreal Walt Disney–style family movie set in perfect contrast to the scene I just left.

What happened at Nectaral Plaza was inevitable. Too many people in a small space. A relentless igniting of heated passions and divisions. Agitators itching for a fight. Agitators like Corey, I think with a shudder as the door of the bus hisses open and deposits me at my stop.

The air in my apartment is hot and stuffy and infused with the thick, spicy smells of Mexican cooking from next door. I open the windows and patio door and fix myself a jumbo glass of ice water. It's dangerous for old people like me to get dehydrated. I pry off my sandals and prop my swollen feet up on the coffee table. Then I turn on the TV and watch the rally being reduced to news as entertainment, sensationalism for ratings.

"We're reporting live from the plaza outside Nectaral headquarters, where a protest turned violent this afternoon." The camera cuts away to the sights and sounds of people pushing, running, shouting. Then the newscaster comes back on screen. "A child was injured in the riot and was taken from the scene by ambulance." The camera flashes on a pink blanket lying on the ground. "We go now to the Monrow City Hospital for an update on the child's condition."

A different reporter stands in front of the emergency entrance to the hospital. I turn up the volume. "We just received word that the two-year-old girl rushed here by ambulance from the rally at Nectaral Plaza was pronounced dead on arrival. Her name has not yet been released." My knuckles turn white from gripping the remote control so tight. The newscaster's voice fades in and out in my head. "Organizers say . . . outside agitators . . . conflicting eyewitness reports . . . fell from her stroller and landed on her head . . . pulled down . . . trampled to death . . . calls for an investigation."

I press the off button and hurl the remote control at the TV. *Why? Why? Why?* I clutch my chest, then curl up in a ball on the couch. *No, no, not another innocent child. What is happening to us?* Time passes, the seconds and minutes and hours moving forward as if the world hadn't stopped for a little girl and her mother. A fiery orange-red sun outside keeps moving, too, creeps behind the building across the street like it does every day. It keeps moving until it's gone and the room goes dark.

Someone knocks on the door. I don't answer. It's just a neighbor. They'll come back. But then there's another knock. I sit up. The next knock is louder, more insistent. I turn on the lamp next to the couch, and the knock turns into a pound followed by a voice that makes my heart stop.

"Sylvia? It's me. Corey. Let me in."

EIGHTEEN

1984

The court called, finally, when I was in the middle of an alcohol-induced dream that was as vivid and real as the time it really happened, when I was a toddler. I'm rattling the bars of my crib. Then the door to the house slams shut. I listen to the silence outside my bedroom door, longing to hear voices, the slightest of movements, any sound at all. But everyone has gone, and they're never coming back. Why cry when no one is there to hear? Why howl when no one cares? My arms aren't long enough to reach the light switch and my legs aren't long enough to get over the side of the crib. I lie down and the darkness takes me.

The phone by my bed rang and rang until finally my head woke up enough to tell my hand to pick up the receiver. "Hello," I mumbled through my cotton-filled mouth. I looked at the clock. It was three o'clock in the afternoon. Must be Monday.

"Sylvia Jensen?" It was a woman's voice, businesslike and very real.

I sat up in bed. "Yes."

"I'm calling from the Monrow City Municipal Court. The jury has reached a verdict. The judge wants you back in the courtroom in one hour."

My legs hauled the rest of me over the side of the bed. My fingers massaged my throbbing head. My purse was on top of the dresser where I vaguely remembered putting it when I returned from the liquor store on Friday night. I reached inside. The keys were still in it, which meant I hadn't left my apartment all weekend or, if I had, at least I didn't drive. I didn't recall having seen or talked to anyone. As far as I knew, no one had witnessed my red eyes, puffy cheeks, tangled hair; no one heard me slur my words; no one saw me trip on the edge of the couch and fall in a heap on the floor.

I took a freezing cold shower to tighten the skin on my face and neck, but all it did was render the shampoo sudsless and leave me shivering. I put on the brightest sweater I had, rich red with a bit of orange in it, almost scarlet—the blood of life, the color of power—and topped it off with vermilion-red lipstick and a touch of rouge. The outside of me looked almost human, but my insides were wretched.

I was unprepared for the atmosphere in the courtroom when I got there. The air was filled, like a balloon about to burst, with nervous anticipation and the chatter of dozens of coalition supporters. Tom Strickland, Norton's fledgling reporter, was back, but not alone this time. He was surrounded by at least ten other journalists who were clearly much more seasoned than he. Chloe, her body stiff and her hands clasped tight on her lap, stared at the back of her husband's head as if nothing existed in the world but him. Norton, who by contrast looked relaxed and at peace, leaned back in his chair and gave me a little wave as I passed his place at the table.

Jim, Tony, Jane, Katyna, and Madeline were staring at the door through which the jurors would come taking a break from their vigil just long enough to give me a nod. Barely seconds after I sat down, the six jurors walked in, single file, and took their seats. They were ordinary people, as familiar as my neighbors next door—an accountant, a housewife, a retired high school teacher, a secretary, a manager at a grocery store chain, an engineer. Each one looked solemn and studiously avoided making eye contact with any of us.

Judge Sundquist came in, this time waving us back down before we even had a chance to stand up. "Good afternoon," she said. Then she turned to the jury. "Ladies and gentlemen, I understand you have reached a verdict."

The foreman was an engineer, a nondescript middle-aged white man whom I hadn't paid much attention to during the trial. "We have, Your Honor."

He handed the verdict form to the bailiff. Who passed it to the judge. Who read it to herself with no visible expression on her face. Jane grabbed my hand and squeezed it. Jim crossed himself, so small a gesture that I may have been the only one to notice. Katyna held a tissue over her mouth.

Norton looked composed, almost bored, as if after he'd put his life on the line, the verdict was, if not irrelevant to him, at least anticlimactic.

It seemed to take forever for Judge Sundquist to pass the form back to the foreman, who read the verdict out loud. "We, the jury, find the defendants not guilty of trespassing on April 20, 1984, at a place known as Nectaral Plaza in Monrow City." Gasps rippled through the courtroom, followed by an eruption of cheers and applause.

Prosecutor Vendenal looked stunned. He stumbled to his feet. "Your Honor, I request that the jury be polled."

Judge Sundquist's eyes rolled ever so slightly. She nodded to the court reporter, who then ordered the jurors to stand, one at a time, and answer the question "Do you agree with the verdict as so stated?" Each one, looking directly at us this time and smiling, affirmed the verdict in a firm and unwavering voice.

"Members of the jury," Judge Sundquist said after the last juror had been polled, "this court dismisses you and thanks you for a job well done. Court is now adjourned." Then she looked at us with a smile and said, "You are free to go," to roars of approval and gratitude from the crowd.

People rushed to the front to congratulate us, their eyes brimming with excitement. Everyone hugged everyone. Norton looked vindicated. Like he believed the jurors had reached their verdict not because they'd found some loophole or hook on which to hang it, but because they actually shared our concerns.

"Hey, you coming?" Jim said.

"Come on, S-S-Sylvia," Katyna said. "We're all going to the Boom Boom Room to celebrate."

I told them to go on ahead and then sat down to wait for Norton.

NINETEEN

2019

Corey keeps pounding on the door. I square my shoulders and wipe the beads of sweat from my brow and only then pull it open. He charges in and skids to a halt in front of me, jaw clenched and lips pursed. His white-knuckled fingers press the Guy Fawkes mask against his chest like a badge of honor.

"*Now* do you see, Sylvia? Now do you understand?" His eyes drill into me with the force of an electric screwdriver.

"How did you find out where I live?"

When he doesn't answer, I will myself to stay calm. He must have searched for my address, must have come to me for a reason. I touch his shoulder, ever so gently. "I'm glad you're here." He pivots his upper body away, and I drop my hand.

"You heard what happened? A baby died! A little girl!"

I nod. I bite my lower lip. "I saw it on the news. Come in and sit down." My voice is soft, almost a whisper, a parent soothing a child in distress. "I'm here, Corey."

Words tumble out of him, somersaulting over each other. "I was there. I saw what happened. We have to do something. You *have* to see that now."

He holds the image of Guy Fawkes like an adoring lover and runs his fingers over its strange mustache and pointy beard. Once again I want to shake some sense into him, but instead I say, "I'll make us some coffee."

His head snaps up. I hear the bones in his neck crack. "*This* is the only way to stop them." He brandishes the mask, like a weapon, in front of my face. "After what happened today, you *have* to understand that."

I step back and he lowers the mask. He doesn't intend to hurt me. "I *do*, Corey. I do understand."

His shoulders sag, his back starts sliding down the wall. This is why he's come to me. This is what he needed to hear. I reach for his hands and pull him up. "Come. We'll talk." I take the mask from him and leave it dangling on the doorknob.

The living room is dim, the small lamp by my couch only as bright as the flame of a candle. I switch the desk lamp on. Corey turns in circles in the middle of the room like someone disoriented after waking from a deep sleep. His eyes move from one poster on the wall to another and another and finally settle on the one made by the Black Panther Party.

"What the . . . ?"

I stand next to him and look at it with him for a few seconds. "I got it in 1968 when I lived in the Bronx." He lets out a muted *harrumph* and turns his attention to the poster next to it, a black-and-white photograph of an American Indian Movement demonstration. His lips part and his eyebrows go up. "Have I surprised you?" I ask. He places his palm on his cheek, and I smile at him, but he doesn't smile back. He's turned his attention to my new flat-screen television and his brows are scrunched together. I shrug. "My old one died."

He reaches into his pocket and pulls out Pickles's obituary. "I'm doing it for him."

He sits down in my pulpit chair with the obituary on his lap. I pick up a twelve-by-fifteen-inch framed collage of children's photographs that I keep on my end table and hand it over. Then I sit adjacent to him on the couch, our knees touching. "These are some of the children I've cherished over the years," I say. His fingertips touch their little faces, one by one. "They're the reason I can no longer sit back and do nothing."

"I'm doing it for *justice*," he says through pursed lips. "Justice for Pickles."

I place my hand on his and whisper, "Yes, I know."

He looks at me sideways like maybe he's half trusting me?

"Let me in, Corey. Please. I want—"

His raised hand cuts me off. "You don't know what I'm . . . what we're doing."

"It doesn't matter what it is. You can tell me."

"No. I can't."

"I want to help."

His eyes flash in warning. "We don't . . . you don't want to know. You really don't want to know."

"Want something cold to drink? I have some lemonade in the fridge."

"Just water." It's obvious he's relieved that I've changed the subject.

He sits at the kitchen table with his arms crossed over his chest while I run water over an ice cube tray at the sink. I fear for him, but it's different from the fear I once had for his father. My fear for Norton was that, because of what he'd done, he'd end up dying alone in a federal prison cell. With Corey I fear that because of what he might do, others may be injured, even killed.

I hand him a glass of water and sit across from him. I know he's angry, but I believe it's his ambivalence that led him to me. A tiny glimmer of trust floats around the edges of his eyes, and in it I see a reflection of Norton, and he's slipping a metal key into my hand. He's telling me what to do to help Corey.

I lean forward and look him in the eye. "There's something else I want to tell you about your father."

He rolls his eyes and pushes the chair back. "Please. I don't want to hear any more about what *you* think Dad would tell me to do if he were here."

"I want to tell you . . . I want you to know." I stumble over the words, start again. "I have something to show you. His briefcase."

His eyes widen. "His briefcase? What's in it?"

"I don't know."

"You don't *know*?"

"It's locked."

He crosses his arms and shakes his head. He's not buying it. "So why'd you keep it? Why didn't you give it to my mom?"

131

"It was a promise I made to your dad. I honestly don't know why I kept it all these years, though. It's not like I forgot about it. Not like some old school memento I kept in storage for decades and never had any need for. I never forgot it. It's on the top shelf of my closet, way in the back corner."

He tilts his head to one side like he's intrigued, and then rolls his eyes. Maybe he thinks I've been waiting for Norton's ghost to come back for it.

"So you don't know why you kept it," he says, "and you don't know what's in it."

"Maybe, without realizing it, I was waiting for the right time."

"Aha. And now there's something inside you want *me* to see."

"I don't know what's inside, Corey. Honest."

He nods like maybe he believes me, then shakes his head like he doesn't. "Do you think there's something valuable in it?"

Something healing, I hope, but I don't say that out loud. "Maybe we should open it and find out."

"Why not," he says with a shrug. "There won't be anything in it to make me change my mind, though. I know what I have to do."

TWENTY

1984

The emptied courtroom was as surreal as a theater after a performance, the only sound left on the stage the low buzz of reporters' voices
mingling with the muted rush hour sounds that drifted in from outside—screeching brakes, humming engines, a siren in the distance. I sat
alone at the defendants' table and waited for the reporters to run out of
questions to ask Norton. It seemed to me there could be only so many.
Obvious ones, like, How do you feel about the not-guilty verdict? When
did you decide to break the law? Do you think you'll be charged and
tried in federal court? What if you have to go to prison? Will it be worth
it to you?

Chloe stood by her husband's side, clutching his arm like a shield,
her eyes unfocused, a brave smile frozen on her face. She saw me watching and tucked her head in the groove between Norton's neck and shoulder. I looked away.

The courtroom door opened, and in stepped two men wearing
identical navy blue jackets with FBI emblazoned in gold on the front.
They flanked the door, to the left a tall, muscular one with no hair on his
head, and to the right a shorter, more compact one with curly black hair.
Both pairs of eyes targeted Norton with razor-sharp focus.

I jumped to my feet. "Norton!" My knees locked and sent me reel-
ing. I grabbed onto the edge of the table. Norton glanced at me, and I
pointed at the door, frantic, my lips mouthing *FBI! FBI!*

He smiled and nodded, then whispered something in Chloe's ear and
headed my way. The reporters started to follow but held back when he

raised his palms to stop them. His arms swung at his sides like he didn't have a care in the world. As soon as he reached me, I grabbed his upper arm with both hands and squeezed it so hard he winced.

"The FBI's here! They've come to arrest you."

He took my hands in his and then, with a half smile, gathered me in his arms. This was more than I'd been waiting for. More than I'd ever hoped to get. I would have waited hours, even days, for just a smile from him. As I clung to him, I felt the bony ribs he'd kept so well hidden under layers of clothing and was alarmed by how much weight he'd lost.

"I knew they were coming, Sylvia," he whispered in my ear. "They're taking me in for questioning, that's all." Then he released his grip on me and took a step back.

I shook my head and my voice trembled. "How can you be sure? Do you *have* to go with them?"

He turned our bodies around so his back faced the agents, which prevented them from reading his lips. Then he slipped something into my hand. "Don't look at it," he said, his voice urgent and yet too soft for anyone but me to hear. He closed my hand, then placed his over it and gave it a squeeze. "It's a key to a locker at the downtown bus station. My briefcase is in it. Go get it. Hide it on the top left shelf of your bedroom closet, in the back, behind a pile of clothes. That way I'll know where to find it. In case you're not home when I come to get it. Don't tell anyone. Ever. Not a soul."

I flicked my eyes in Chloe's direction.

He shook his head. "No one. No matter what happens."

Then he reached out to hug me one last time. His lips brushed my ear as he whispered, "I still have the key to your apartment." Then he pulled away, patted my hand, and in a loud voice intended for others, said, "Don't worry, Sylvia, everything's going to be okay."

I slid my hand into the pocket of my slacks and felt the warmth of the key radiating from my hand up through my arm and into my chest, filling the hole in my heart. Norton still loved me. He chose me. He trusted me above all others. And in that moment, nothing else mattered. In that moment, everything was already okay.

Chloe left through a back door. With the reporters hovering behind and scribbling on their notepads, Norton and the two FBI agents walked out of the main courtroom door. For a long time I stared at the closed door, not realizing that I had just seen Norton for the last time.

TWENTY-ONE

2019

Corey and I sit next to each other on my couch, half of Norton's briefcase on my leg, the other half on his. His eyes glow with anticipation. "Ready?" he says. He wants to find proof that his father's attempts to get justice were misguided, weak, not drastic enough. He wants confirmation that what he plans to do is right and what his father did was wrong. I'm concerned about what he'll do when the briefcase doesn't give him what he's hoping for.

He nudges me with his elbow. "What are we waiting for?"

Two broken parts of the briefcase lock stare at me like accusing eyes from the coffee table. I stare back. I am *not* violating Norton's privacy. I'm giving him a chance in death to tell his son what he couldn't tell him in life.

"Well?" Corey taps his fingers on the handle.

"Okay. I'm ready."

"One, two . . ." On the count of three, he pops the lid open.

I blink and let out my breath, give myself a minute before looking inside. But Corey digs right in, rifles though the contents of the briefcase like a boy searching through a box of toys. I scoot back on the couch and clasp my hands on my lap, brace myself to weather the storm of his disappointment.

"Hah!" He pulls something from the briefcase. "Hah!"

I lean forward and look at what appears to be a stack of mimeographed sheets of paper stapled together. My first thought is that it's a collection of writings, maybe by famous peacemakers like Gandhi and the Reverend Martin Luther King Jr. My second thought is that it could be a history of the Nectaral Corporation. But then, why would any of that need to be kept secret?

"I can't believe this!" Corey waves the booklet in the air. His laughter is more sinister than joyous, and there's a gleam in his eyes that makes me flinch. He reads the title out loud. "*Radical's Guide to Homemade Bombs and Improvised Explosives.* Woooo-eeee!"

My body collapses into itself. I'd heard about these kinds of underground publications but I'd never actually seen one. I can understand why Norton wouldn't want subversive material like this to fall into the hands of the FBI. What I can't understand is why he had it in the first place. Corey flips through the mimeographed pages with one delighted "Hah" after another escaping his lips, each one like a hammer pounding into my heart. I cover my ears. I don't understand. I don't understand. I don't understand.

"Look at this, Sylvia. Here's a section about all the basic equipment you need to make a bomb in your own kitchen." He flips through several more pages. "And, look at this, the essential elements of chemistry, all the ingredients you need, recipes, even schematics. Instructions for making all kinds of bombs!" He pushes the page closer to my face, a blur of diagrams and lists, scribbled notes in pencil in the margins. I shove it away. Finally, he closes the booklet, placing it on my coffee table with the same reverence he'd bestowed on the Guy Fawkes mask.

He turns to me with a big smile and grasps my shoulders. "You were right, Sylvia. I underestimated my dad. Boy, did I!" His eyes are so wide the rings of white around his irises are glowing.

I open my mouth and try to say *Your father was not violent,* but there's a strange taste of lead on my tongue that blocks the words. Could there have been a side to Norton I never knew? Had I been right, during our trial, to worry? Had he planned to do something violent after all?

Corey's hands are back in the briefcase. "There's more stuff in here." He pulls out a yellowed copy of our local newspaper. My voice finds its courage when I see the front-page headline. "Atomic Veteran Exposes Government's Nuclear Secrets."

"Your father was noble, brave, and heroic," I say.

He shrugs and tosses the newspaper to the side like it's irrelevant. Then he pulls out two more newspaper articles. "'Father Daniel Berrigan and the Catonsville Nine Arrested for Burning Draft Records.' Hmm, that's interesting," he says. His eyes skim the second article. "'Plowshares Protesters Take Hammers to Missile Warheads in King of Prussia, Pennsylvania.' So is this." He lays the three articles on top of the booklet, then pulls a book from the briefcase. *1984* by George Orwell. "Even more curious," he says as he drops it with a thud on top of the pile. One more search of his fingers yields a small statue, about two and a half inches tall.

"Sure is heavy for something this tiny," he says as he hands it to me. "What is it?"

"The Infant Jesus of Prague," I say. "A friend of mine says they sell these statues everywhere over there." I study the slender figure: left foot barely visible under a long tunic, royal robe with a large cross on the front, left hand encircling a globe and right hand extended in blessing, the first two fingers upraised, thumb folded and touching the last two fingers.

"Why do you think Dad had *that* in the briefcase?"

I shake my head. The statue's face is that of an infant but not yet infant, his outward expression more like a little king. It silences me, a silence both confusing and calming. The mystery of God become child, the child of God, we're all children of God, protected and cared for by God, a God who holds us all in the palm of His hand, the protector of the whole world. It isn't until I hear Corey singing *He's Got the Whole World In His Hands* that I realize I've been humming the tune.

"That's it," he says, laughing and clapping. "Dad knew God was on his side. That's the message he got from the statue. And now he's telling me that God is on my side, too."

The light of dusk forms an arc over the statue of the Infant Jesus of Prague still perched in the palm of my hand. Is the infant's message that violence is sometimes necessary to save the world, as Corey would like to believe? Or is his message a warning *not* to use the bomb-making booklet, as I would like to believe? Or was his message something else for

Norton, some in-between truth?

Corey falls back onto the couch, arms outstretched, palms up like he's blessing the items on the coffee table. "Thank you, Dad, thank you," he says.

My fingers tighten around the Infant Jesus as I wonder how well I really knew Norton.

TWENTY-TWO

1984

I left the courtroom and walked to the bus station around the corner. The temperature had dropped to below zero, November weather typically unpredictable in this part of the country, where it can be warm and balmy with stragglers of colorful leaves still on the trees one day and then white sloppy snow on them the next. The sidewalks were treacherous from a weekend of snow accumulation that had started to melt but then froze into icy clumps. After I retrieved the briefcase from the locker, I took a taxi home instead of the bus to get there quicker in case Norton stopped by for it on his way home from meeting with the FBI agents. Secretly hoping he'd come to my place *instead* of going home, I fixed my hair and put on fresh makeup, changed into jeans and the bright pink sweatshirt he loved.

But he didn't come or call that night. Or the next day. I didn't go to work, instead waited by the phone with the briefcase next to me, stuffing potato chips and other junk food into my mouth and chewing on ice cubes. My liquor supply was depleted from the weekend's binge, but I couldn't leave my apartment and risk missing Norton when he came.

That night I slept on the couch, but only intermittently, because I feared if I slept too deeply I'd miss the knock on my door, the ring of my phone. The day after that, with still no word from Norton, I called in sick, started having panic attacks, with shortness of breath on and off, that I kept under control by staring at mindless television programs. The morning of the third day, just as I was on the verge of hysteria, the phone finally rang.

I grabbed the receiver and cried into it. "Norton? Oh thank God.

Where have you been?"

After a long silence, there was an audible sigh.

"Norton? Are you okay?"

"This is Chloe."

A sharp cramp moved from my stomach up to my throat and paralyzed my tongue. I knew the FBI was going to take him into custody. I just knew it. All that would come out of my mouth was "N-...N-...?"

It sounded like Chloe was blowing air into the phone. "I'm calling to tell you that Norton is . . ." A deep intake of breath stopped her.

"Where is he," I managed to say. "Where are they keeping him?"

"Norton is dead, Sylvia."

I covered my mouth.

She let out a long sigh. "At least . . . at least . . . he didn't linger like I . . . like we . . . At least he didn't have to suffer a slow, painful death." She was crying openly now.

I dropped onto the couch, clutching my chest.

"He went in his sleep." She paused like the words had gotten caught in her throat. "They think it was either a heart attack or a stroke, but I think it was the pressure. It was just all too much for him." I heard her blow her nose.

"Did the FBI hurt him?"

"They came this morning to arrest him." She paused, made a harsh sound like air was being forced from her throat. "Hah! But they were too late. At least he was spared *that* ordeal."

The blame in her voice stirred in me irrational and almost overwhelming feelings of regret. If only I could go back and change things. I should have tried to stop him from going with the FBI. If I had only done . . . something . . . then maybe, then maybe . . . maybe what?

"I'm sorry, Chloe. I am so sorry."

"The funeral is Monday. Tell the other defendants. Norton would want them to be there."

"Of course." My response was automatic. But how was I to tell the others something I couldn't grasp myself?

Chloe's voice shifted from sad to angry. "*Don't* talk to the press, Sylvia. And, if it's not *too* much to ask, there isn't going to be room for extra people at the service. Just you and the other defendants, okay?"

My heart opened to absorb her rebuke. "Okay. Let me know if there's anything I can do to help."

"There's nothing else." Her rejection was brusque, the unspoken words—*You've done enough already*—more biting than those spoken, the click of the phone more cutting than a knife.

I let the receiver dangle from the cord wrapped around my hand. I stared into space with no idea how long it was before I was finally able to move. Norton wasn't supposed to die like this, without warning, without a chance for me to say good-bye. I couldn't accept it. I wouldn't.

"No! Just no!" I shouted. I grabbed his briefcase and ran into the bedroom. Climbed onto a chair. Pulled out two shoeboxes of old family photos from the top left shelf of my closet. Dropped them onto the floor. Shoved the briefcase in their place. Threw a stack of sweaters on top of it. Out of breath, I got down, satisfied that now Norton would know where to find it when I was gone. Then I grabbed my purse, put my coat on, and headed for the liquor store.

Hours later, sufficiently fortified by several glasses of gin and tonic, I phoned the members of our affinity group. No one was home, so I left the same message for each one, speaking slowly and trying not to slur my words. "Norton would want *us* to be there. But Chloe says there won't be room for anybody else from the coalition." The phone calls completed, I went back to my alcohol, my rescuer, my pain medication.

When the others called back, I let the answering machine take their messages. Jane was the only one who kept calling, several times over the next few days, to see if I was okay. Sometimes I didn't answer the phone, and when I did, I told her I was fine. She was right not to believe me. She insisted on taking me to the funeral service. On the way to the Greenwood Mortuary, when I moaned and rubbed my throbbing head, she handed me two aspirins and a bottle of water. When she said "I can't believe he's gone" and I said, "I can't believe it's over," she patted my leg like she knew that what I meant was very different from what she meant.

The service was in one of the mortuary's larger reception rooms. It was decorated in quiet creamy colors that Norton would have considered too subdued and comfortable, and it had intricately woven oriental rugs that he would have detested. When Jane and I got there, all one hundred seats were already filled, but the others in our affinity group had saved two places for us. We sat in the last row, way in the back, like inconspicuous ghosts, intruders grieving the loss of a hero whose cause had no significance and was of no consequence to the other mourners in the room.

The coffin at the front was closed and covered with flowers. On an easel next to it was a giant photograph of Norton and his wife taken shortly after their son was born. Norton was smiling, his arm around Chloe, their baby in her arms, good days, happy times.

Katyna whispered in my ear. "S-s-so I guess they only do open casket for the family." I turned away from her.

Chloe walked down the aisle to the front of the room with an older man, maybe her father, holding her up. Her four-year-old son, Corey, clung to her skirt, his eyes filled with the kind of confused innocence that saves children from the sadness adults experience at times like this. Chloe pressed her forehead on top of the coffin and then she kissed it. My lungs constricted and cut off the air so I couldn't breathe. I leaned forward with my face between my knees, felt Jane's hand on my back.

People I didn't know and had never heard of—co-workers from the post office, family members as close as a Nebraska farmer brother and as distant as a second cousin from Alaska, even old friends from elementary school—took turns telling stories about Norton. To them, he was the boy next door who cried when his dog was hit by a car, the teenager who was the first in his class to get his driver's license, the co-worker who ate tuna salad sandwiches for lunch every day. But to those of us in the last row, Norton was a man who, despite facing a premature and unjust death, had channeled his rage and desire for revenge into positive action, a man committed to the truth regardless of the consequences. To me, Norton was the only man I had loved and the only man I had ever felt loved by, the man who'd entrusted his briefcase to me and only me, the man who had left to me a secret that I would hug for the next thirty-five years as tightly as I held it in that moment.

TWENTY-THREE

2019

A bright sun and warm breeze stream through my windows, the promise of another hot summer day, a fleeting hope that all will be right with the world. But after sleeping with the statue of the Infant Jesus of Prague in my hand, the piercing deep grooves in my palm are a vivid reminder that nothing is right with *my* world this morning. Last night I tried to help Corey and failed. Not only that, what I had accomplished was just the opposite of what I'd hoped to achieve. Instead of being a source of healing, the items in his father's briefcase reinforced Corey's need for vengeance and left me racked with doubts about how well I really knew Norton.

A corner of the mimeographed booklet on explosive devices peeks out at me from the bottom of the stack of briefcase contents still on my coffee table. I slide it out and flip through the pages of instructions, hand-drawn diagrams, lists of ingredients. A diagram numbered 6.6 on page six chills me, reminds me of the minister in church when I was a kid talking about 6-6-6—the number of the beast, Revelations, the last chapter of the Bible, the end times, the Antichrist rising up to oppose God and God's people, the faithful rising up to heaven, the damned descending into hell. I cradle the little statue in my hands. What the hell was Norton doing with this booklet?

The question demands a deeper look. I start with the booklet's table of contents and find it curious that after each set of instructions about how to make an explosive device, there are also instructions about how to defuse and deactivate that same device. I turn to the first section and notice that some sentences are underlined and there's a note scribbled in the margin. *What if it's trip-wired?* It's written in light pencil, easy to miss. A note on another page says *Good info*. I recognize the tiny, hard-to-read handwriting. Several pages and several notes later—*Learn more about this, Remove this first, Hard to improvise, No to this one*—and there is no doubt in my mind that Norton wrote all these notes.

I glance down at the little statue in my hand and it reveals the truth to me now. Just as the Infant Jesus was called to protect all people, so are we. Then more truths start wafting in on a warm breeze through my open patio door. I breathe them in, one after another.

Norton was *not* learning how to make bombs. He was learning how to disable them. He hid the booklet so no one, especially the FBI, could misinterpret his intentions. The newspaper articles show that he'd grasped the difference between taking a hammer to the head of a missile and taking a hammer to the head of a person. For him, the little statue symbolized miracles and healing, not death and destruction.

I step out onto the patio. The city looks clean and shiny. People on the sidewalk below hustle off to work. Children skip their way to school. Proof that all is, indeed, right with the world. The garden-fresh smell of the muggy summer air brings Norton back to me—the tip of his head, the velvet softness of his fingers on my neck, the compassion in his voice—and wraps my heart in a hope that comes only from loving and being loved.

With my body warmed by a gentle flow of certainty, I'm ready to tell Corey what I've discovered. But as soon as I pick up the phone, reality intrudes and I hesitate. Corey doesn't *want*, won't be *able*, to hear anything that threatens his newfound connection to Norton, his firm belief that he has his father's blessing. Instead of listening to me, he'll assume I'm trying to manipulate him. He might even stop talking to me, and then I'd lose any chance of influencing him; as a result, people's lives could be lost. It's possible, of course, that whatever Corey is talking about will never come to anything. But it's also possible that what he's involved in could end up being a life and death situation. I can't take the chance. I have to do something. I have to at least find out what he's up to.

Another truth, the final and most difficult one, then reveals itself to me. I will have to lie to Corey. If I want to learn about the group and their plans, I will have to convince him that I agree with him.

I punch in his phone number, and he answers on the first ring like he's been expecting my call. He sounds revved up like he's ready for something, something big.

"I couldn't sleep last night," I say. "I kept thinking about your dad. I kept thinking that if he was willing to do something as drastic as making bombs . . ." I pause and silently ask Norton to forgive me. Corey, too, if it turns out that I'm overreacting. "If your dad was willing to do whatever he had to do to stop the madness, then I should be willing to do whatever it takes, too. So, Corey, I support whatever it is you're planning to do. I agree that we have to do whatever is necessary."

When he doesn't say anything, my pulse thunders in my ears. I swallow down a lump of guilt-infused panic, think about whether I should continue or not, whether or not I'm not doing the right thing, and then decide that doing nothing is not an option.

"All night," I say, "I kept seeing you at your dad's funeral. You were so little and confused. You didn't know where your dad had gone. He'd always been at your side, and all of a sudden he wasn't." I clear my throat and steady my voice. "But *I'm* here now, Corey. *I'm* at your side. Whatever you're planning to do, I want to be part of it. Please let me."

Endless seconds pass before he finally says, "It's not up to me, Sylvia. I'll let you know." He hangs up before I have a chance to say anything else. I think he might believe me, maybe even want to include me, but now I know it's not his decision to make. He has to convince the others first.

After waiting for two days for him to call back, though, I start to doubt myself. Maybe I was wrong in the first place, or maybe Corey's having second thoughts. Maybe I was right that he believed me, but he hasn't had a chance to talk to the others yet. Whoever they are. Maybe they have to meet first to discuss whether or not to include me. I'm just about ready to call and ask him what's going on when the phone rings.

"Hey, Corey," I say.

"I thought you always picked up when I called because you were glad to hear from me," J. B. says with a chuckle. "Now I see that you just don't check to see who's calling before you answer. What a blow to a guy's ego."

I shift gears, adjust my expectations. "I *am* glad to hear from you, J. B.," I say. "Where are you?"

"I'm back in New York and busier than hell. I'm calling to apologize for not saying good-bye before I left."

"I thought you came to cover the rally. Why didn't you write anything about it in the *New York Times?*"

"Something else came up, so we just ran with the AP story."

"You mean you came out here for nothing?"

"Not at all." There's a pause, a short intake of breath, that moment when I know he's about to change the subject. "But what about you? Sounds like you were expecting a call from that Corey guy. What's up with him now?"

"I'm worried about him. He's really broken up about his son's death."

"And?"

"I'm just watching out for him, that's all."

"Of course you are," he says.

My phone beeps, and I see Corey's name on the ID. "Sorry, J. B. Another call. I have to take it. I'll talk to you later."

Corey starts talking before I even say hello. "We'll meet with you tonight, Sylvia."

"Really? So does that mean—"

He cuts me off. "I'll pick you up at eight. Be out front." Then he hangs up.

TWENTY-FOUR

At eight o'clock sharp Corey pulls up to the curb. He's driving a truck with a boat on a trailer attached to it. He nods but says nothing, lets me open the door for myself. I hoist myself up into the passenger seat, which is no easy feat for someone my age who's holding up the hem of a long dress with one hand and gripping the side of the door with the other.

I fasten my seat belt, try to both breathe and sound normal. "So why the boat?"

He presses the turn signal, looks in the rearview mirror, and very slowly pulls away from the curb. "We'll be needing it."

I smooth the wrinkles in my dress, a light blue A-line wash-and-wear cotton I bought at the thrift store for a dollar. I spent hours thinking about the impact my appearance could have on people about whom I know nothing before I finally decided what to wear tonight. I never thought to factor a boat into my decision, and if I'd known I might be getting in and out of one, I certainly wouldn't have chosen a dress that comes down to my ankles. T-shirts and boats go together well, but the only ones I own are political and I'd ruled them out because I didn't want to risk offending anyone. My most comfortable clothes, a pair of faded and worn bell-bottom blue jeans and the thirty-year-old peasant blouse I bought in Mexico had been my first choice and probably would have been the best outfit for being in a boat, although some might judge it as inappropriate for someone my age. Like most of my clothes are, if I'm honest. I pull down the windshield visor and check my hair in the mirror—bland, combed back in a simple ponytail above the slightly scooped neckline of my simple cotton dress. But enough about how I look. I've done what I can to not stir negative reactions from those who will be meeting me for the first time tonight.

Corey hasn't said a word for the past twenty minutes. His anxious eyes are glued to the road, which means his DWI is still in force, so he can't afford even a minor traffic violation. I'd offer to drive but I know what he'd say.

Finally I can no longer stand the silence in the truck or the noisy thoughts in my head. "So, where are we going," I ask.

"Two more hours."

"Oh? What's two hours from here?" I speak in a pleasant tone that masks my irritation. Maybe he can't tell me where he's taking me, but couldn't he have at least told me the meeting wouldn't start until ten o'clock?

His fingers tap tap tap on the steering wheel and his eyes steal quick glances at me. "I'm not sure you realize what a big deal this is," he says. "We're not just talking about another protest or march or any of those other namby-pamby things you do."

I blow air through my lips and focus on what's in front of the windshield, the dusk moving in and turning the pine trees along the two-lane road into shadows.

"It's our private meeting spot. That's all you need to know."

No, that isn't all I need to know. I need to know a whole lot more than that. Like, for starters, whose truck is this? Why the boat? And why does everything have to be such a big secret? But my teeth tighten in my mouth and my throat swallows the questions. No point in asking. He won't answer because he doesn't fully trust me. And that means I can expect the others to not trust me at all. I close my eyes and practice the script I'd put in writing that afternoon and then memorized, everything I want them to know—the true, the embellished, the outright lies.

It's dark outside when the truck comes to a stop, turns around, and slowly moves backward down a steep, rut-filled dirt road. At the bottom of the hill, the sliver of a moon and a multitude of stars cast a dim light on the shore of a lake. When half of the boat is in the water, Corey pulls up on the emergency brake.

"What lake is this?" I ask.

He doesn't answer.

"I probably never heard of it," I say. "I don't know where we are anyway."

He grips the steering wheel and stares out at the darkness. "I don't think you know what a big risk I'm taking, Sylvia."

The knobs of my arthritic fingers throb, a warning that I may be heading down a rabbit hole I may not be able to climb out of.

The truck door on the driver's side opens, and a light pops on inside the cab. Corey's lips curl up in a worried grimace, or maybe his attempt at a smile. "Sylvia." He stops, thinks better of whatever it was he was going to say, and gets out of the truck.

My ankle twists when I jump to the ground. Nothing serious, which is good, because Corey's too busy releasing the boat from the trailer to notice. He grabs hold of the bow with one hand and reaches out with the other to help me over the side of the boat. I plop down on the front seat and squeeze the water out of the bottom half of my dress. "You know," I say, "if I'd known we were going in a boat, I wouldn't have worn this."

Either he doesn't hear or he doesn't care. He pushes the boat farther into the water, then jumps in and lands with a thud on the middle seat. The boat rocks back and forth as he staggers back to the stern.

I grip the sides of my seat. "Life vests," I call out. "There aren't any life vests?"

He's too busy to answer. He keeps pulling the starter cord on the outboard motor, and swearing under his breath each time it doesn't catch. After several attempts, he throws up his hands. Maybe he's giving up, maybe it's a sign that I'm not supposed to do this. But then he gives the starter cord one more yank, and the motor sputters, then roars, to life.

With me hanging on and swearing under my breath, we zip across the choppy water. Ahead of us, a bolt of lightning splits the fabric of the night sky into jagged pieces. I count up to forty. "There's no thunder," I

151

call out to Corey. "That means the storm is far away." He doesn't hear me.

When he finally cuts the motor, the wind has subsided and the moon and stars have disappeared behind a yellowish-brown blanket of clouds. It's eerily quiet, the kind of calm before a tornado, but fortunately most tornadoes strike around here between March and June, not this late in July. Corey turns on a flashlight and points it at a hill of trees and rocks, a miniature island. The boat drifts over and tucks itself into a secluded pond of water between two boulders.

"I'll tie the boat to that tree and then help you out."

He helps me lift my leg over the side of the boat, and my foot lands on something soft and furry-like. I stifle a scream and whisper, "I think I just stepped on an animal or something."

"Probably just moss." Corey's voice sounds like a shout in the stillness. "There's a steep incline here. I'll help you over some of the bigger rocks and tree roots. Watch out for branches."

He leads the way up the hill, turning around and pointing his flashlight at the ground in front of me every few seconds to make sure I'm okay. I hold up the hem of my dress with one hand and swat at the mosquitoes buzzing around my ears with the other. Tiny thistles prick my toes and legs as my feet search for solid ground before taking each step.

"This is it." Without warning, Corey stops, and I smash into his back. I grab the tail of his shirt to keep from falling.

He points the beam of his flashlight at a clearing that's completely hidden, even from above, by a forest of huge pine, white birch, and other trees and is surrounded by hot, humid air and the overwhelming smell of pine and mold. An A-frame cabin in the middle is roughly built and slapped together with odd-shaped pieces of wood, branches, and tree trunks. Corey leads me to a deck in front, three feet above the ground.

"I can't step up that high," I whisper.

He gets up on the deck and lays his flashlight down, then takes both my hands and pulls me up. An ancient-looking potbelly stove stands in the middle of the deck. Four or five sleeping bags scattered around it. A candle flickers in an open window. The soft murmur of voices inside the cabin.

Corey turns his flashlight off and places his hand on my shoulder.

Then he whistles, first a low long whistle and then two short ones. The same long and two short whistles come back from inside the cabin. I hang onto Corey's arm and silently count our steps to the door. One, two, three. We reach the door at twelve, an easy number to remember.

"Ready?" Corey says.

I hold back. My legs start to tremble. What have I gotten myself into? And whatever made me think I could do this by myself?

"What?" His voice is tense, impatient.

"Are there any women in there?"

He sighs.

"Tell me or I don't go in. Yes or no."

"Yes. Geez, Sylvia."

"Okay, then."

The door opens, and he nudges me inside with his hand cupping my elbow. Four silent silhouettes stand before us, their faces concealed in the shadow of the light from one dim candle. I feel their eyes on me as Corey guides me to a lopsided stool in the middle of the room. A nail or sliver of wood punctures my left toe and I wince. I lower myself onto the seat of the stool, a slice of tree trunk, and plant my feet on the floor to keep its legs, three thick, unevenly cut branches, from wobbling and tipping me over.

Now five shadows are sitting on wooden crates three feet away—two women and three men, one of them Corey. One of the women stands up and approaches me. She pulls a match several inches long from a wooden box. She drags its head against the side, and in the flash, I catch a glimpse of pink cheeks, bangs of black hair, a smooth-skinned brow. She turns away and uses the match to light an ornate brass candelabrum on the crate next to me. In the blaze of seven candles I can see the anguish in her eyes as she lets the match sizzle out between her thumb and forefinger. Then she goes back to sit with the others.

The spotlight is now on me as I face the five-person inquisition, or was it a firing squad. I fold my hands on my lap and wait for my interrogators, whose facial expressions I cannot see, to begin.

"Sylvia Jensen." The man's voice is cold. "That *is* your name, is it not?"

My stomach sucks itself in and my head orders me to buck up, tells me there's no turning back now. "Yes, that's my name." I'm surprised at how calm I sound.

"Begin."

"Don't be rude, Vince." It's the woman who lit the candles. "Don't you think we should introduce ourselves first?"

"And let her know who we are?" the man says. "Really?"

"By first names only then," she says.

"Nicknames."

"Okay, fine," she agrees. "I'm Bunny."

"Well, thanks to *Bunny*," Vince spits her name out like an olive pit, "you already know my *real* name."

"I'm Nicole. I'm too old for nicknames." Bossiness around the edges of the second woman's voice.

"Freddie here." The slight tremble of an older man's voice.

Corey says nothing.

"Begin." Vince's voice is cold and detached, almost robotic. The others at least sound human.

I vacillate between telling them what *I'd* like them to know and asking them what *they'd* like to know. Maybe I should ask them what Corey already told them.

"Well? You're the one who asked to meet with us, did you not?"

"Yes, I did."

"So?"

Corey's shadow shifts position, his legs cross and uncross. It's as if he wants to tell me but wouldn't be comfortable saying out loud, under the circumstances, that I'm on my own, that he did his part by getting me here, and now the rest is up to me.

"Why don't you start with why you're here, Sylvia?"

I'm encouraged by the hint of kindness in Nicole's voice.

"I . . . I need to be with people who . . . who not only understand what's going on but are willing to *do* something about it." I take in a deep breath and let it out. "I'm sure you already know that Corey's father was an atomic veteran. But what you may not know is that Norton Cramer was the only man I ever loved. I still love him." I swallow hard, slide the backs of my hands over my eyes.

"He was your husband then?" Vince sneers. He already knows the answer. "Or would you rather not admit you had an *affair* with a married man who had a son."

"Come on, Vince," Nicole chides. "That's irrelevant. None of our business."

I keep the focus on my script. "Norton died when he was in his late forties. Corey was only four. None of us knew he was an atomic veteran. None of us knew there were hundreds of thousands of others like him who were sick and dying from radiation poisoning. None of us knew their children and grandchildren would . . ." Without my permission, a tear escapes the corner of my eye and slips down my cheek. I wipe it away. "They made sure we didn't know."

"That's right." Nicole leans forward and raises her hand as if we're in church and she's saying amen to my testimony.

"Uh-huh," Bunny adds.

"But before he died, the man I *loved* . . ." I dangle the word in front of Vince. "The man I loved exposed their dirty little secret. Norton Cramer was a whistleblower." I lean forward and tuck my hands under my thighs, hide my crossed fingers. "That's why the FBI took him away. That's why they killed him."

A gasp shoots up to the ceiling. Bunny's hand follows it, then covers her mouth.

"No!" It's the man named Freddie, no tremble in his voice now.

"Oh my God, how . . . ?" Nicole shakes her head.

Vince leers. "Yeah. How, *exactly*, did they kill him?"

"Do you really think the FBI would tell us that? Do you think they'd even admit it? All I know is that they took him in for questioning, and two days later, he was dead of a supposed heart attack. *You* figure it out." I cross my arms over my chest in a dare. I think he knows I'm lying, but I'm picking up sympathy from the others.

"And now," I say, "Corey's son Pickles is dead, from the same poison that his grandfather was exposed to. I am so sorry, Corey. I know how badly you want justice for Pickles. It was wrong of me to try to talk you out of it."

Vince claps his hands with an *aha* sound that shatters the darkness around him. "You did *what*?"

I sit back and close my eyes, take in deep breaths, the way my therapist taught me. When my eyes open again, they automatically land on Corey.

"When your dad died, I was angry like you are. But, unlike you, I held my anger inside for thirty-five years, and it grew into a monster that was terrifying. I was afraid of your anger because I was afraid of my own." I blow air out through my lips. "You helped me face the truth, Corey. That I want revenge, too. For Norton and Pickles and you. And, yes, me."

"But we're not after revenge," Bunny starts to say. She stops, and starts again. "I mean, yes, we're all plenty angry, too. But what we want, at least what I want, is to hold the government accountable for what it did."

"And for what it's doing now," Freddie says with a nod.

"And to stop them," Nicole adds.

"Yes, and we all agree, do we not," Vince says, "that the only way to stop them is by getting people to rise up and force the government to get rid of its nuclear program."

Nicole leans forward. "You see, Sylvia. This isn't about revenge. This is about saving the world."

I practically shout, off script now. "That's what I want, too."

Corey clears his throat, then coughs, clears his throat again. "*I* want revenge."

I lean toward him. "I know you need to avenge Pickles."

His body backs away, but I feel his eyes burn into me. "But . . .?"

"No, no buts, Corey."

He stamps his foot, his hot fury taking over. "They didn't just kill Pickles and my dad. They're killing other children, too. Other grandchildren. We're gonna make them pay. *Whatever it takes.*"

"That's what your father would want, Corey. He would want us to

156

do whatever it takes. Whatever that has to be." The heaviness of deception heaves in my chest, but Norton is whispering in my ear, saying, *Do what you have to do, Sylvia, and know that you are right.*

Vince snorts. "Come on. You don't *really* think that."

I make my back as straight as I can. "You're right, Vince. I didn't always think that. But then I discovered that Norton was learning how to make bombs, and that changed everything. Now I believe, like he did, that violence is sometimes necessary, when it's for the greater good."

"Oh, so it's the greater good now? I thought it was revenge."

His suspicions cut into my skin. "I do want revenge." I lean forward, my arms and hands outstretched in a kind of prayer. The devil's prayer. "But isn't it also for the greater good if we ensure that not one more child like Pickles has to die? Isn't it for the greater good if not one more parent like Corey has to watch his beautiful child shorn of hair, laid low, robbed of his childhood and stolen from him?" I look from one shadowy person to the other, then drop my face down into my hands.

"I had cancer," Bunny blurts out. "And now my daughter is sick."

"My father was an atomic veteran," Nicole says. "No one's ever apologized, never even admitted what happened to him. And now my—"

Vince stomps his foot on the floor. The cabin shakes. "Enough! This is *not* the time."

The others fall silent. They shuffle their feet. They shift positions on their crates. After a few interminable seconds, Vince jumps to his feet. He points at me. "You. Don't move." Then he waves his hands in the air. "Everybody else. Outside. Now."

157

TWENTY-FIVE

They're out on the deck now, deciding my fate. I strain to hear what they're saying but can't make out the words. Meanwhile, I struggle to keep my balance on the wobbly stool, with every joint in my body—hips, knees, hands, knuckles, neck—resisting the effort.

The voices aren't arguing, at least not loudly. Nicole and Bunny believe I'm sincere. I don't think Corey would have brought me here if he didn't at least want to believe me. It's hard to tell if Freddie is neutral or of two minds, only that he very much seems to be his own person. Then there's Vince, and he's going to be a problem, a very big one.

When I decided to infiltrate Corey's group, I knew, of course, that rejection was a possibility, but I hadn't anticipated being taken to a deserted island out in the middle of nowhere and out of cell phone range. So what will happen if they say no? How do I get away from here if I have to? My eyes search the room, but the stingy light from the candelabrum gives up no clues, only the shadow of a ladder leading up to what looks like a sleeping loft and a bucket and some dishes on a shelf along the wall. No escape hatch.

The voices on the deck go silent, replaced by a soft shuffling sound, maybe a mouse inside or some kind of animal scampering by outside the door. Now the shuffling is replaced by the sound of feet stomping. They're coming back in. If they've made a decision this fast, the odds are in my favor that it's a yes, but then, oh my God, what happens next? What have I gotten myself into?

They arrange themselves in a semicircle in front of me. A flash of lightning outside the window makes the hairs on the back of my neck sit up.

Vince steps forward, close enough that I can see his face for the first time. His squinting eyes and droopy eyebrows are only inches from my face as he curls his gaunt frame over me. "We need one more thing from you," he says.

"What is that?"

"Proof of your commitment."

I fix my eyes on him. "I *am* committed."

He stands back and claps his hands. "Let's set things up then."

Everyone jumps into action—Corey unfolds the legs of a rectangular white plastic table and sets it up with me sitting at the head; Freddie places the wooden crates around it, two on each long side and one across from me; Vince drags a large white cooler from the corner, then plops six glass canning jars of varying sizes on the table. Nicole places the candelabrum in the middle of the table, and Bunny takes one of its candles and uses it to light the kerosene lanterns hanging at three-foot intervals along the cabin walls. All their scurrying comes to a halt as abruptly as it began.

Vince moves his crate close to my stool and sits down. He smells of shoe polish and leather with a hint of sawdust and charcoal, a strange and confusing, but not terribly unpleasant, combination of body odors that don't match his woodsy flannel plaid shirt and jeans. He gestures for the others to sit down.

The cabin is now aglow with tiny moons of light, enough for me to see what everyone looks like. Bunny's eyes are dark brown, almost black, and knit together in a knot of worry and anguish that makes her appear older than her white tank top, jean shorts, and youthful smart glasses suggest she is. When Vince leans closer to me, she gives him an eager-to-please smile. She seems to be nervous around him.

Unlike Nicole, who mumbles, "Give her some space, for God's sake, Vince." Nicole's a lot older than Bunny, with wrinkle lines in the corners of her matronly eyes and small, grandmotherly arthritic bumps on the knuckles of her fingers. When Vince responds by moving his crate even

160

closer to me, she shows her displeasure with a flick of her hand.

Freddie is hard to read; he seems oblivious, preoccupied, in his own world—maybe more than one world, judging by the way the blue jacket covered with military patches, the American flag tattoo on his neck, and the wild, frizzy hair contradict his trim gray mustache, sage green eyes, and classic British cane.

Corey, at the foot of the table, looks back and forth from Vince to me. His fingers move up and down his arm like he's either nervous or self-conscious. I wonder if he regrets, or is maybe having second thoughts about, bringing me here.

Vince leans down, reaches into the cooler. He keeps his eyes on me as he places two bottles of wine on the table. He grins and raises his eyebrows, then reaches for one of the jars. I shake my head, and he pulls his hand back with a shrug. He reaches down to pull something from a paper bag on the floor, and a bottle of Kentucky Straight Bourbon lands with a thud inches in front of me. He reaches for the largest quart-sized jar on the table and, with it in one hand and the bottle of bourbon in the other, raises his eyebrows again.

"This is your most favorite thing in the world, is it not?" he says.

I move back, too fast, and lose my balance, manage to grab the edge of the table just as the stool disappears from under me. Bunny jumps up to right it and helps me sit back down. A sinister laugh erupts from Vince's throat. Nicole shoots a little "tsk-tsk" at him like a spitball, and I glance at Corey. He averts his eyes, pretends to scratch an itch under his beard. How could he betray me like this?

Vince fills the jar halfway, then holds it up to the light, swirls the honey-colored liquid in front of me. I shake my head, try to turn away, but the amber glow draws me in, tightens around my eyes like an elastic band that leaves a buildup of salty tears behind it. Vince waves the jar under his own nose and then, with a menacing smile, under mine. The sweet aroma of vanilla, caramel, honey, and butterscotch transport me back to the Bronx, over fifty years ago, when those same smells first enticed me with a promise of relief, only to later kidnap my life.

Vince fills the jar up to the top and holds it out to me. "May I?"

161

"No," I say. "Thank you."

"You sure?"

"Yes, I'm sure, thank you." I glance at the candelabrum, up at the ceiling, at the kerosene lanterns along the walls.

With an exaggerated motion, he shoves the drink closer to me. "Drink it."

"I can't," I say. I squeeze my eyes tight and run to safety, to my favorite church basement, where the furnace, with an odd *tut-tut-tut* sound, keeps time with the seconds ticking their way around the face of the oversized clock on the wall. Where the hooks lined up like soldiers next to the door sag under layers of coats, scarves, and gloves in the winter. Where old-timers, newcomers, and in-betweeners rub shoulders and balance Styrofoam cups of coffee on their laps. Where the laughter of alcoholics in recovery echoes through the overhead pipes and bounces into my brain, then and now.

Something brushes against my arm and my eyes pop open. It's Corey, and he's grabbing the jar from the table. He hesitates, then slowly downs a bit of bourbon, slams the jar on the table, and says, "I believe her." Then he walks back to his place at the foot of the table.

Nicole reaches for the jar and drinks the rest of the bourbon. She tips her head toward Vince and says, "I believe her, too." I wonder how much she knows about what taking a drink would mean to me. Does she know I'm in recovery or does she just think I can't drink for some other reason?

Bunny takes the bottle and pours herself a shot next, downs it, and tips her chin up and then down. Then Freddie pours a double shot in a jar, downs half of it, and pours himself some more—like he could care less whether I drank or not—before passing the bottle to Corey.

Corey stares at it, too preoccupied now with his own demons to worry about mine. After several excruciating seconds, he pours a pinch, at most a tablespoon, of bourbon into a jar. He downs it quick and then plunks the jar down as if saying, *See, Sylvia, a sip doesn't count, a sip isn't a slip.* Then he sends the bottle back to Vince at my end of the table.

He holds it up in front of my face. "Change your mind?"

Droplets of sweat escape from the pores in my temples. Maybe

Corey's right. I mean, if this was a test, if I took just one tiny sip to prove my commitment, would it really do any harm? Even if I drank a whole glass—that would be a slip, but if lives were saved as a result, well, wouldn't I have done it for a higher good? What's more important, after all, my recovery or people's lives? If I fell off the wagon, I'd have a chance to get back on, but if people died there'd be no more chances for them. Then again, I didn't even know whether these people were planning to hurt anyone. What if they weren't, and I took a drink for nothing?

"For heaven's sake, Vince." Nicole's voice has all the charm of a mother scolding her children from the end of her rope. "Can we please get on with it already?"

Vince pours himself a shot of bourbon and downs it. "Just having a little fun." The jar hits the table with a hollow plunk.

"He doesn't mean anything by it," Bunny says with a nervous laugh.

Nicole rolls her eyes. "He likes to play with people."

Vince jumps back in. "You're not off the hook. We still need proof of your commitment." He slaps a piece of paper on the table. It looks like a pledge for me to sign, my name already written at the top. "A guarantee that you will keep everything we say and do secret."

I start to read it and am reassured. Is this all they need from me? It's a good statement, one I could have written myself.

"Of course," I say.

But then I read farther, and the last three sentences drain every ounce of blood from my face and make my hands go clammy. Vince scowls and his chin juts out. "*We* have already proven *our* trustworthiness. Now it's your turn." He reaches into his shirt pocket and pulls out a phone, the disposable kind I've seen in stores. He taps his forefinger on the paper. "Read it out loud."

I search for help from the others, but all I see are Nicole's shifting eyes, Freddie's flushing cheeks, and Bunny's wringing hands. Corey won't even look at me. His beard hugs his chest like a life jacket.

Vince pushes the record button. "Okay. Ready. Go."

I have no choice. I square my shoulders, tuck a stray strand of hair back into my ponytail, and read.

"My name is Sylvia Jensen, and I am here to declare that I cannot remain silent and do nothing while we face the end of life on this planet as we know it. The world is at greater risk of being destroyed than ever before. North Korea holds its nuclear weapons system like a cocked gun to the head of our country. Other countries are modernizing their arsenals, and there is a real danger that more countries like Iran will procure nuclear weapons as well. Yet, despite the threat of death and destruction at an unbearable level of horror, a lot of people don't know or understand how powerful these weapons are. We can't afford to wait for a disastrous event to convince them that nuclear war is unacceptable. The atomic bombing of Hiroshima and Nagasaki should already have convinced us of that. But it has not."

I stop reading. Vince makes an impatient motion with his hand.

"I take sole responsibility . . ." I swallow, then start again. "I take sole responsibility for planning and carrying out today's action." My fingers drop the paper onto the table. Vince picks it up and holds it for me. "My intention has been to wake the American people up to the dangers we face. I hope it is not too late to save us. May God bless and protect us all."

Then Vince pushes the button on the burner phone and slips it back in his pocket.

TWENTY-SIX

A blinding light flashes through the window just as I finish reading the statement. There's an ear-splitting crack of thunder, then a deafening roar—the wind howling through the cracks in the walls, sheets of rain slamming against the window and pounding the roof with the force of a million hammers.

"Quick, shut the windows!"

"Bring everything in!"

Wooden crates scrape, feet pound, the door opens, sleeping bags are tossed in, the door slams shut.

Once the rush is over, Corey squats down next to my stool and squeezes my shoulder. "Looks like we'll be sleeping here tonight." He's relieved. He took a chance on me and it worked out. I look away from his trusting eyes.

"So . . . you okay?" he asks.

"I'm fine."

He stands, smiles down at me. "This means a lot to me, you know."

I can't look at him. I hate deceiving him like this.

Everyone sits down, ready to ride out the storm with the table now loaded with an impressive array of food—two chunks of cheese, a box of crackers, peanut butter and jelly sandwiches, a bag of tortilla chips, cut-up celery and carrots, a bunch of red grapes.

Nicole holds up the two bottles of wine. "Red or white? Pass your jars."

Corey reaches into the cooler, pulls out a Diet Coke, and slips it into my hand. My eyes sting as I watch him walk away.

Bunny clears her throat. "If everyone has their drinks, I'd like to go first." She raises her jar of wine—white zinfandel, my favorite. "I'm doing this for my dad and for Princess, my baby."

My ears grab onto the word *this*, the only word that counts, the word whose meaning I'm here to find out. This. This still unknown action for which, on the record, I will be held solely responsible unless . . . unless what?

A toast is raised. "For Bunny's dad and Princess."

Bunny focuses on me, the only person here who doesn't already know her story. "My dad died when I was a teenager," she says. I nod, an automatic response. "Mom and Grandma were always hush-hush about Pop's sickness. It was a secret, something they were ashamed of. Whenever I asked if Pop had done something wrong, they were quick to say no, but their eyes always said yes. So I had this horrible shame and guilt about my family. I never told anyone, not even my husband."

She stops and guzzles some wine, sets the jar down. "When Mom was dying, she finally told me why Pop was so ashamed. It was because he put animals—sheep, monkeys, pigs, horses, goats, guinea pigs—into trenches just before the nuclear bomb tests and then dumped dirt over their charred carcasses after the blasts. Mom said he cried when he told her, that he thought his sickness was God's punishment for what he'd done.

"Once I knew the truth, I was able to stop dwelling on the past. My husband and I had a baby. A girl. Princess. She was born with . . ." She looks down at the table. "Something's wrong with her autoimmune system. I don't know what's going to . . ." She picks up her wine, unable to go on.

Freddie lifts his jar. "To Princess."

Nicole pats Bunny's hand and then looks at me. "I'll go next," she says. "In 1957, my husband, Pete, witnessed a hydrogen bomb test from a trench in the Nevada desert. In 2000, he was diagnosed with lung cancer. He applied for compensation, but lung cancer wasn't one of the presumptive illnesses. He appealed and was denied again. Two years later, lung cancer was added to the list." She balls her hands into fists. "By then Pete was dead." She raises her jar. "I'm doing this for my husband and all the other atomic veterans like him who were denied justice."

"To Pete and all atomic veterans." I join the toast with my Diet Coke, and when I take a sip, I taste Bunny's and Nicole's pain on my tongue. Their verbal expressions of anguish and anger are so similar to those I read in Norton's journal when he wrote about his many failed attempts to get reparations for Chloe and Corey that I have to be careful not to let myself get swallowed up in their misery and lose my focus. I have to think clearly, strategically. Everything depends on it.

Freddie studies his hands, opens his mouth in a bid to go next, but instead finishes off all the wine in his jar. Then he tries again. "I witnessed the largest aboveground nuclear explosion on U.S. soil." He takes a deep breath like he's just taken a step toward the edge of a cliff, and if he isn't careful, he could easily fall off. "It was Shot Hood, a seventy-four-kiloton blast in the Nevada desert. I was only about three thousand yards away. When the flash came, I saw all the bones in my hands." He studies his hands like he's seeing the bones in them again, right now. "After the blast, we played war games right up to ground zero, where the sand had melted into glass. We didn't know."

My anger pushes me to the edge of the stool. I want to jump up and shout. *Norton saw the bones in his hands, too. He didn't know either. No one knew. People still don't know.* Instead I shove my hands under my thighs and tighten my lips over my teeth.

"I've had a heart attack, three strokes, and an aneurysm," Freddie says. "An abdominal aneurysm operation gave me trouble in my feet so I couldn't walk for two years. I didn't apply for compensation. My conditions weren't on the list."

My hands escape from under my thighs and fly up to hit the table. "They *are* on the list. Radiation exposure has been linked to heart attacks and strokes. I've read the research."

Freddie shrugs. "My oldest daughter, Denise, was diagnosed with a malignant brain tumor a couple years ago. I did apply for her. It was denied just before she died."

My blood is boiling now. I want to scream. I want Freddie to scream. I can't understand why he doesn't. "There's something wrong with all my children," he says. He looks down and starts counting on his fingers. "Mildred has endocrine problems. Her daughter Shari, my granddaughter, was born with a deformed foot. My son Jimmy has bipolar disorder. My other son, Tommy, has a rare adrenal condition called Addison's disease." He stops, holds up four fingers. "The thing is, there's no history of any of those conditions in my family."

Nicole leans forward. "They're finally studying the effects of radiation exposure on our offspring now. We had to pressure them for years to do it, but they *are* doing it now."

Freddie blows out a long, tired stream of air. "I know. But the thing is, I'm not qualified to be in any studies. There's no evidence in my military record that I was exposed." He pours more wine in his jar and finishes it off in one loud gulp.

Bunny's hands, palms up, reach across the table to him. "But you're not giving up."

"No. I promised Denise I wouldn't." He closes his eyes. "But I'm running out of time."

A roll of thunder outside makes me flinch. I'm having trouble breathing. It's as though the oxygen's been sucked out of the room from all of us having to carry Freddie's pain and anger, because the load is too heavy for him to carry alone.

"I'm doing this for my son and father." Corey blurts out the words. His load is too heavy for him, too. "Sylvia already knows my story." He slumps over the table, lays his head down on his arms.

Vince is the only one left to tell his story. His words are pared, tidy, staccato. "I did cleanup in the Marshall Islands. In the 1970s. In T-shirts and shorts. We scraped up radioactive dirt and debris. One of my buddies got lung cancer. Others got sick with different kinds of things. Skin rashes. Stuff like that."

Like a robot whose switch has been turned off, his voice goes silent. It's not like he's trying to control his emotions like Freddie did. It's more like there are no feelings there. Something's wrong with him, something's off. I don't believe him.

They're all looking at me now, their eyes like empty buckets waiting to be filled. I want to tell them what they want to hear. I want to be honest with them like they've been honest with me. But how can I be?

"Thank you for sharing," I say. My voice sounds weak, timid, apologetic.

Nicole's furrowed brow registers disappointment. Bunny tips her head like she's waiting for more. I hear their rebuke as if they're saying it out loud. *So, we let you into our pain and anger, and all you have to say is 'thank you for sharing'?*

"I don't feel alone anymore," I say. "I'm very grateful to you for letting me in."

It's the best I can do, and it seems to be enough, because everyone smiles. Then Nicole suggests that we all stand and join hands. Vince groans, but when everyone else gets up, he does, too. He's on one side of me, his hand cold, Bunny's on the other side, her hand warm.

"Our stories," Nicole proclaims as we raise our locked hands high in the air, "are the moral compasses that point to the truth. That is why we're here. That is why we're doing this." *This,* I repeat silently. Whatever this is.

We lower our hands, and Vince drops mine like he can't bear to touch it a second longer. Bunny gives my other hand an affectionate squeeze. She's letting me know I'm now part of this circle, this family, this group of people abandoned by the world and left to cling to each other, to nestle in each other's pain for relief and comfort, to reinforce each other's self-righteousness and need for vengeance.

"It's late," Vince says.

"And I'm hungry," Bunny says. "Can we eat now?"

"Might as well. Too late to do anything else tonight anyway." His sideways scowl points the finger of blame directly at me, as if the late hour is my fault. "We'll finalize our plans in the morning."

TWENTY-SEVEN

"Smell the rain," I hear Corey say to Nicole.

"Umm. Nothing like the earthy smells of pine and birch after a thunderstorm," she says. "Always so glorious."

I pull the sleeping bag up to my chin and stare at the ceiling, listen to the sound of their voices out on the deck, the birds chirping and tweeting outside the window above my head, Bunny's breathing next to me, Freddie snoring over in the corner. Who would ever guess that such an idyllic morning scene—a cabin on a remote wooded island where friends gather to enjoy nature and each other—is really an assembly of the wounded seeking justice, a secret place for plotting retribution? And who would ever guess that I had the audacity to infiltrate such a group?

My eyes close and hold on to what happened last night. How close I came to flushing nineteen years down the toilet. How I almost broke my vow to never let anything or anybody in this world become more important than my recovery. How I almost forgot that no matter how impossible and complicated life was, everything was workable as long as I didn't pick up a drink.

How I confessed to doing something that is still unknown to me.

Smoke from the potbelly stove outside and a piece of wood jabbing me in the back bring me back to the present. There's no point in looking back, no point in second-guessing my decision to let Vince record my confession. Right now I have to find out what it is I took responsibility for and then keep whatever that is from happening. This is not the time to worry about anything beyond that.

The smell of fresh coffee elevates me to an upright position. Next to me Bunny groans, unsticks a strand of thick black hair from her cheek, and flops over. When I drag myself out of the sleeping bag, every part of my body complains, loudly, that I'm too old to sleep on an uneven floor like this, too old to sleep on any floor. I crawl on all fours to the window and use the ledge to pull myself up.

I step out on the deck and my eyes absorb, one blink at a time, the glitters of sun on wet tree branches. Then I see Vince, sitting alone, his legs dangling over the edge, his eyes frozen in a snarl that forecasts the coming of a very different and much more intense storm than last night's rain.

Nicole sits on a tree stump a few feet from the potbelly stove, balancing a jar of black coffee on her lap like a veteran camper. Corey carries an aluminum percolator coffee pot over to her. "More?" he asks.

"I'm good," she says. She sees me standing in the doorway and her face brightens. "Good morning, Sylvia. Hey, Corey, she looks like she could use some fresh brewed java."

"Bathroom," I say. "My bladder is about to burst."

She places her jar on the deck and leads me to a stack of firewood covered with a plastic tarp, behind it a hidden path into the thick forest. My brain records the landmarks on the way—intertwined branches of two birch trees, a pile of rocks, a sharp left turn, the number of steps we take. At twenty, Nicole stops and reaches for a plastic bag hanging from the branch of a tree.

"If this isn't here," she says as she pulls a roll of toilet paper from the bag, "that means the bathroom is occupied."

"Where *is* the outhouse?"

Nicole laughs. "Right behind that big tree," she says as she hands me the toilet paper. "Straight ahead. You'll see it."

The bathroom, it turns out, is nothing but an uneven hole cut in the middle of a wooden plank, about two feet wide and six feet long, held up by a tree stump at each end. I'm strangely moved by the primitive attempt at civility when, for all the privacy afforded, we could just as soon squat in the woods.

Nicole waits for me by the tree, then hangs the plastic bag back on the branch. "I knew you were okay before I met you," she says. She slips her hand through my arm and we start walking back to the cabin.

"You did?" I want to know what Corey told them about me, but I don't dare ask, don't want to arouse suspicion by being too curious.

"So did the others."

"Vince?"

"Oh, Vince." She waves her hand dismissively. "He doesn't trust anybody."

I'm so worried that Nicole, like everyone else, is going to excuse and apologize for Vince's rude behavior that I take a risk and ask, "Why do all of you put up with him anyway?"

She gives me a knowing look. "For the same reason people always put up with someone who irritates them."

"Because you need him?"

She nods.

"Bunny seems to need his approval," I say. "So does Corey."

She nods again.

"But what about you and Freddie? Why do *you* need him?"

"He's the link to money for our . . . our operation. I guess you can call it that. He pays Bunny's medical bills for Princess, too. If it weren't for him, she'd have gone bankrupt after her divorce."

"Where does the money come from?"

She shrugs. "We don't ask, and he wouldn't tell us if we did. Freddie suspects it's his own money. Vince is a strange bird, but he cares. It's because of him we all found each other." She squeezes my arm and her astute green eyes radiate the wisdom of age. "As I say, he who pays the piper calls the tune." She winks. "Or has to think he does. Just don't let him bother you." She chuckles then and mutters, "I should probably follow my own advice."

I worry that Vince could be more than what she thinks he is—a provocateur of some kind or an FBI informant—and file that suspicion away, along with the other information she's given me, in a safe place in my brain. Later, when I have time to put the puzzle pieces together, I'll

173

pull it out again.

Back at the cabin, Corey is trudging up from the lake with two buckets of water. He drops one next to the potbelly stove and carries the other to an old wooden washstand at the far end of the deck. He splashes dirty water from the washstand's chipped bowl onto the ground and then refills the bowl with fresh lake water from the bucket.

"It's all yours, ladies," he says with a bow.

I look in the cracked mirror above the bowl at the craggy-faced and bristly gray-haired woman staring back at me. I dip my hands into the cool, clean water and splash it on my face, then yank the binder from my hair and comb through the tangled, coarse strands with my fingers, pull them into a fresh ponytail. I look back at the woman in the mirror and, when I smile, it sucks up the creases in my chin and makes me look ten years younger.

Nicole stands behind me with a jar of coffee. "You look fine," she says as she hands the jar to me. "Sorry we don't have any cream or sugar."

"Thank you. It smells delicious."

"You need to eat something," Corey says. "I'll make you a peanut butter and jelly sandwich. Not exactly bacon and eggs. In the meantime, you need to sit down." I wave him away and he says, "Back in a jiff."

Vince is still staring into space at the other end of the deck. I decide to talk to him, see what he's like when he's alone, maybe ask him about the money.

"Good morning," I say. "Mind if I join you?"

"Hmm."

I sit down next to him, not so close that our shoulders touch but close enough to smell his morning breath and wonder if mine smells as bad as his.

"It's beautiful here," I say.

"Hmm."

I stare at the little sliver of lake peeking through the trees and give my brain time to unscramble dozens of possible conversation starters. I toss out the irrelevant and dangerous, save the maybes for later, and finally settle on one that I hope will perk his interest.

"I keep thinking about what you said last night," I say.

It's enough of a hook that he glances at me, but not enough for him to give me the satisfaction of asking what I mean.

"About you digging in the radioactive dirt with no protection," I say.

He tips his head and winces.

"Norton didn't have any protection either. He said his commander . . . is that what you call the person in the military that gives the orders?"

"Hmm."

"He said his commander was cold and unfeeling . . . what was that man's name again?"

"Hell if I know," he mumbles under his breath.

I snap my fingers. "Trayne. That was his name. Master Sergeant Trayne."

An impatient *pffft* shoots from his mouth. It says, *Yeah, who cares, we all have our stories,* and even though his lips don't actually form those words, the sound he makes gives me enough encouragement to forge ahead.

"So Trayne told his men they were safe and didn't need any protection," I say. "But Norton wasn't stupid. He saw the officers were wearing high-density goggles. I don't know how that man could lie like that and still live with himself."

Vince rolls his eyes up at the sky. "Well . . . yeah . . . he was like that." He sighs, not like he's agreeing with me, more like he hopes that saying something, anything, will shut me up. But the several words he's just strung together imply something more.

"You knew him?" I say. "You knew Trayne?"

"Yeah, yeah, he was the commander of my unit, too."

"He *was?*" I do a quick calculation. If Vince did cleanup in the Marshall Islands in the 1970s, that would have been fifteen or twenty years after Norton was there, so it's possible. "He really *was?*" I say again.

His cold stare makes me shiver. "I just said that, did I not?"

"Yes, yes, of course you did," I say. "I'm just surprised. I mean, what are the odds that you and I would be here like this now, and you and

Norton would have served under the same commander . . . I mean, it's just hard to believe, don't you think?"

"Hey, Sylvia and Vince," Nicole calls out, "time to meet. We don't have all day. I have a flight to catch."

Vince's fingers dig into my upper arm and the sneer on his face makes my skin crawl. "Listen up," he says, in a voice too low for anyone else to hear. "You breathe a word to anyone about any of this, and that recorded confession of yours will be in the hands of the authorities so fast your head will spin."

"Don't you bully me." I try to hiss it, but it comes out sounding like a wheeze.

He tightens his grip on my arm and whispers in my ear, "You tell a soul, and I will make sure you are hunted down and eliminated."

TWENTY-EIGHT

A tight circle of six wooden crates has been set up in the middle of the deck for our meeting. I strategically place myself directly across from Vince, a safe distance away so our knees can't touch, and give myself a pep talk. I will not let him intimidate me. I will not let emotions cloud my thinking. I cede all authority to my brain with the following instructions: *As a new member of the group, your position will be tenuous at best, especially with Vince but with the others as well, so don't give advice or make suggestions. Instead, be supportive and positive. Ask questions. Pay attention. Listen and learn. Record everything in your head. And don't forget: first things first. Once you know what the plan is, then you can think about what to do next. Don't get the order mixed up.*

Vince, with his palms turned down as if to quell any disagreement, brings the meeting to order. "We'll begin with a recap of why we're here, shall we?" His clipped voice and outstretched arms extend his authority deep into the circle. "Two erratic and reckless government leaders are threatening nuclear war. The American people either think we can survive it or, mostly, they don't think about it at all." His gaze turns on me, his eyebrows high on his forehead. "Do you not agree, Sylvia?"

Of course, I agree about that. I mean, who doesn't? "I do," I mutter.

"Well, Sylvia . . ." drawing out my name, "then do you not also agree that ignoring the danger of nuclear war will not make that danger disappear?"

He's playing another game with me. I check to see if the others notice, but their faces are impassive. My brain kicks in with more instruc-

177

tions: *Don't let him set up you up to cause dissension in the group or for any other reason. Best not to say anything at all. If he pushes for an answer, ask him what he means. Wait for him to make the next move.*

But I don't have to do any of that, because in a little more than a second, Nicole's motherly scold breaks the stalemate. "Okay, Vince, okay. You know we all agree, so let's move on. *Shall* we?"

Bunny yawns and rubs the sleep from her eyes. "How did the test run go?"

Freddie shakes his head. His face looks ashen in the daylight and there's a sallow tinge in the whites of his eyes that suggests he may have a liver problem. "The bomb didn't go off," he says.

Corey is quick to interrupt, his words pressured. "But it's okay. We know how to do it now."

Vince pats him on the back. "Good job. Tricky to build explosives that are big enough and can still fit into backpacks."

Corey beams, but Freddie is less enthusiastic. "Well, at least we figured out what was wrong. Thanks to my old hazardous device manual from military training." His left thumb rubs the palm of his right hand like he's reviewing the steps they took to fix the problem to make sure they really did get it right.

My legs start vibrating. I was right to come, but my God, now that I know they're making bombs, what am I going to do about it? I take in a deep breath and blow out my fear. My brain kicks back in. *Okay*, it tells me, *so now you know they really are planning something violent, you need to slow down and listen. There's more to learn before you'll know what to do. Remember, first things first.*

"We'll do it at Nectaral Plaza, a day or two before the hearing," Vince says.

I jump to attention. If they're talking about the hearing that's scheduled for the fifteenth of next month, in DC., then there isn't much time to stop them. *Breathe*, my brain says. *Slow down.* "What hearing?" The voice coming out of my mouth, all upbeat and innocent, doesn't sound like mine.

"A congressional hearing in DC," Nicole says. "About the government's plutonium storage contract with Nectaral."

Corey rubs the heel of his palm against his chest as if to contain the grief in his heart and allow himself to hope at the same time, maybe even feel a bit of excitement. "Let's do it! And just before the hearing is the perfect time. It'll show them what could happen if there was an explosion at the Nectaral storage site and it released radiation into the air."

I swallow the lump in my throat, force my voice to sound calm and curious. "So when is the hearing?"

Everyone looks at Vince. He lifts his shoulders and says, "I'll find out."

I can't believe he doesn't already know. I'm no longer in the information loop, and even I know the date, time, and place of the hearing and that the Peace and Justice Coalition is planning a huge rally at Nectaral Plaza two days before. Corey should know that, too, but maybe, with Pickles's death and his recent bout of heavy drinking, he missed the news, or his memory got clouded. Or maybe he's just deferring to Vince.

"Here's a map of Nectaral Plaza," Corey says.

"You drew this?" Vince looks pleased.

Corey's chest puffs up. "At the last rally." He passes copies of the map around the circle.

Now I know what he was doing when I saw him there with his Guy Fawkes mask. The map is crude and out of proportion, with squiggly lines marking the perimeter of the plaza and carving out the garden spaces, buildings, entrance gates. Corey has drawn a cluster of circles on the expansive lawn where the protesters gather, a megaphone where the speakers are, and several cars where the police descended on the crowd when things got out of hand that day. Red X's designate explosion sites—one at the main gate, one at the bottom of the steps to the executive building, one by the tower, a few scattered around the perimeter. But it's the large X right in the middle of the cluster of circles that sends shockwaves through me. I can't believe that Corey, who was so upset after what happened at the last rally, would consider setting off a bomb in the middle of thousands of people.

"Good job, son," Vince says. "And now, here are the numbers." He

179

passes copies of another piece of paper around the circle. "We all agreed that the damage should be substantial enough to get people's attention, did we not?" He leaves no space for an answer. "So here are the calculations for our best option. All it will take is two bombs strategically placed, one here and one here." He holds up Corey's map and places his finger first on the largest X in the middle of the crowd and then the X on top of the police cars.

The words and numbers on the page blur, but after a blink, a squint, and another blink, they emerge with horrifying sharpness. Injuries: two to three hundred. Deaths: five to ten protesters, two to four police officers. Property damage: at minimum, one million dollars. My hands fly up to my mouth but don't reach it in time to silence a gasp. Fortunately, my brain kicks in quick enough to disguise the gasp as a cough.

Nicole slams the map and the calculations down on her lap. "Not in the middle of the crowd. Not there."

"We all agreed, did we not—"

A swift slice of her hand cuts him off. "Vince. There will be children at the rally."

Like the two-year-old girl who died at the last one. My pressed lips hold the words back. Pink lines move up Corey's neck, and his mouth opens, but then he glances at Vince and closes it again. If he's having second thoughts, he's going to keep them to himself. Freddie scratches at the flag tattoo on his neck. *Why don't they stand up to Vince?* My heart—exploding with the flash of thousands of protesters flying, falling, dying—demands that I say something, do something, anything. But I defer to my brain and stay silent, instead prepare to record what happens next.

Vince slaps his knees and laughs. "Yup. Top news story. Nationally *and* internationally."

Bunny's head shakes like a frizzy-haired dog after a bath and she splashes him with a nervous chuckle. "Not funny, Vince. Stop playing games." She gives his knee a teasing tap.

But I know that this time it's not a game. This time he's dead serious.

"We want to shock people, do we not," he says. "So what we do is this. We hand out flyers right after the bombing that say: 'Are you horrified by what just happened? Then open your eyes and face the worse horror of nuclearism.' Or something like that. If we want to wake people up, let's not be stupid about it. A couple little firecrackers won't do anything but make people think it was the work of some nut job."

"*Not* in the middle of the crowd." Nicole stands up, plants her feet on the deck in a wide stance. "Off. Limits. Period." Then she sits back down.

Vince jabs his finger at her. "Off-limits? Really? Has the government set any limits on all its shadowy stuff? Has it set any limits on the numbers of people who have died? Don't we have a duty to make sure their suffering was not in vain?"

Bunny leans toward him, a weak smile on her face. "What the government's doing is horrible, Vince. But do we have to stoop to their level to get our point across?"

"As a matter of fact, yes, we do. It has always taken violent action to make change in this country. Come on, people. Think. It took a civil war to end slavery, for God's sake. And how did we end the Vietnam War? Remember Kent State? How many people died before we got any civil rights legislation? Assassinations. Murders. Riots. Looting. Conspiracies. CIA plots. FBI—"

Nicole says, "That's enough, Vince," but his hand waves her away. "Things have to get out of control! Nothing else works! It never has." He crosses his arms over his chest, his fingers fluttering under them as if to say, *I can't believe I have to explain any of this to you.*

Nicole mirrors his arm crossing and finger fluttering with her jaw set and her brow furrowed, just like his. "No deaths. End of discussion."

When his palms go up in a gesture of surrender, a balloon of relief rises from the circle and floats away. The others think he's given up, but not me. I don't believe that for a minute.

After a few seconds, Freddie's forefinger taps on the map. "How about by the gate. By the tower would be good, too. In front of the executive building, definitely. Maybe three or four around the perimeter."

"Too many," Nicole says.

Bunny ventures in. "It seems that one could do it." She hesitates, glances at Vince. "I mean, depending on where we put it."

He grunts. "Sure. If it's right in the middle of the crowd."

My hands hide under my thighs to keep me from lashing out and my tongue pushes itself to the back of my throat to keep me from saying anything. Bunny sips her coffee while peeking at Vince over the rim of her jar. Freddie's finger moves along the map like it's trying to find its way to another solution. Corey squirms in his seat, studiously avoiding everyone.

The silence is broken by Nicole. "We're all in agreement that we want to make the biggest impact, right?" Everyone nods. "*And*," she says, "with the fewest injuries and deaths." She stomps her foot. "Let's not forget that part. *No* deaths."

Nicole and Vince glance at each other sideways like competitors waiting for the starting gun to go off. Bunny tentatively asks couldn't they maybe explode a really big bomb just outside the plaza gate, and Freddie offers to calculate the blast area. That does it. The race is on. Ideas stumble over each other and clamor for attention—conciliatory ones, technical ones, adamant ones, hesitant ones. Whenever Vince makes one of his deadly suggestions, Corey nods and studies his hands. But Nicole, Bunny, and Freddie band together and shoot it down like clusters of torpedoes hurled at a morally rudderless ship. I stay alert. Record everything in my head.

Finally, Nicole throws up her hands. "I give up."

Bunny wrings hers. "Maybe, I mean, I think, we should decide about other things and then come back to this later?"

Everyone but Vince nods.

"Well," Freddie says, "we do need to decide what to do if there are security checks at the entrances to the plaza."

They come up with a plan to get the backpacks through if there's security and then move on to deciding what to wear so they'll look like normal protesters, how to coordinate with each other once inside the plaza, how to get away safely before or after the blast or blasts, and other details that will remain irrelevant as long as there is no plan. When I was still working, this common group behavior in meetings would either amuse or irritate me, depending on my mood. Now is no time for such musings. I deploy every neuron in my brain, a virtual army of interconnected scribes, to record in my memory every single detail, every intuitive thought I have, every observation I make. Like what Vince is doing right now, just leaning back on his crate with his face to the sun like he's singularly disinterested in, even bored by, the details. Like he's biding his time. Waiting for his chance.

"Oh my," Nicole says with a quick glance at her watch. "It's noon already." She jumps up. "We have to get going or I'll miss my flight."

"Give me your maps," Freddie says. "The calculations, too." With the help of his cane he pulls himself up and walks over to the potbelly stove. Using the sleeve of his jacket as a hot pad, he lifts the lid on top and tosses all the evidence into the flames.

Vince stops sunbathing and stretches. "I'll find out when the hearing is and then call all of you."

That's it. Everyone stands. Then they scurry around, carry the wooden crates back into the cabin, roll up the sleeping bags, rinse out the jars and the coffee pot, tidy up, collect their things. I watch, aghast. The meeting has ended with no decision made, which I'd like to hope is a good sign. Except for one thing. Vince is still doggedly in charge.

TWENTY-NINE

Corey whistles for attention. "Sylvia and I will be heading out now."

Vince stands off to the side. His crossed arms and threatening eyes trigger a battle inside me between panic and self-control.

"Are you all right," Nicole asks.

I force a smile. "I'm fine. Just shouldn't be sleeping on a hard floor at my age."

Freddie chuckles. "Tell me about it," he says as he shakes my hand.

Corey cups my elbow and says, "I better get you home."

I let him help me down the steep incline to the lake. *Think, think, think. Get away. Write everything down. Figure out what to do.* When we reach the lake, he brushes away wet leaves on a boulder and helps me sit down.

"I'm fine, Corey, really."

"Wait here," he says. "I'll scoop the water out of the boat."

Sounds of grunting and swearing, the whoosh of water and scraping of metal against wood, soon fade away and dissolve into words in my head, vague and without form but all pointing in the same direction. *Figure out what to do, what to do, what to do.*

After a while, I feel Corey's hand on my shoulder. "That was some downpour last night." He helps me up and into the boat. My sandals splash in an inch of water on the bottom. "I'm sorry. I couldn't get all of it out."

I collapse onto the seat, and a white pain shoots through my spine from what feels like a nail jammed into my back. Corey's at my side in a flash, his face contorted with worry.

"It's okay. Arthritis is all. No big deal."

After a while the pain subsides and I'm listening to the purr of the engine and watching the shoreline whiz by. As the boat sways, another mantra rocks back and forth in my head—*have to stop them, have to stop them*—until a splash of cold water over the bow of the boat slaps me in the face. I check and see that the used stopwatch I bought on a whim at a thrift store a few years ago didn't get wet.

Corey sees me studying my wrist and shouts to me from the back of the boat. "Everything okay?"

"Just checking the time."

I face the front, away from him so he can't see me press the start button on the stopwatch. Five minutes and thirty seconds: a two-story log house with a neatly trimmed front lawn sloping down to the shoreline. I engrave the data in my brain until the next landmark appears. Eleven minutes and two seconds: an island to the left, a pontoon boat peeking out of a boathouse at the end of a long steel dock, a concrete sidewalk winding its way up to the three-season porch of a palatial house. I make a mental note—sparsely populated lake, privately owned islands, prime real estate. Just then, as if confirming my assessment, a floatplane flies over our heads. It has white stripes along the sides of its slender red pontoons, and some words I can't make out.

Corey points and waves. "It's them! Hey, guys!"

The floatplane swoops down. I catch a glimpse of Bunny's face through the window. She's blowing kisses. Then the plane soars up and flies away.

"Where'd they get a plane? Did someone come to get them?"

"That's how they got here," Corey shouts back. "It was parked on the other side of the island from our boat."

"Who's flying it?"

"Vince."

"Is it his plane?"

"Don't know."

Fifteen minutes and three seconds: rugged shoreline with no distinguishable structures, only bold rock outcrops high above the lake covered with forests of pine and birch trees. Twenty minutes and nineteen seconds: an opening in the trees, a gravel beach.

Corey cuts the engine and I turn off the stopwatch. The boat floats toward shore and, with his jeans rolled up to his thighs, Corey jumps into the knee-deep water and pulls it the rest of the way onto land. His truck and trailer are just where he left them last night.

"Let me help you out of the boat." His voice, like a solicitous son attending to his mother, makes my teeth hurt like fingernails on a chalkboard.

"I'm not infirm," I say. He smiles and holds out his hand. As soon as I'm out of the boat I pull away. "I'm *fine*, Corey." He looks confused, maybe a bit hurt, so I add, "That warm sun and the breeze on my face invigorated me."

"So, you okay standing for a few minutes while I hook the boat to the trailer?"

"I'd rather help."

He ignores me and goes about hooking a cable to the U-bolt on the bow, cranking the boat up onto the trailer, and attaching a safety chain. I sigh, the impatient sound of elderly people who refuse to be rendered invisible, and run my hands along the underside of the boat.

"There it is!" I yank out the plug and hold it up in triumph. Water pours from the boat onto the sand.

"Huh," he says. The corners of his mouth turn up ever so slightly.

"I've pulled boats out of lakes hundreds of times," I say. Then I climb into the truck before he has a chance to assist me.

He smiles. "You hungry?"

"Famished."

"You like pie?"

"Who doesn't?"

He starts the truck, and I press the button on my stopwatch again. Twenty minutes: we pull up in front of an unpainted wood building with a sign over the door that says Luncheonette—Best Pies in the County. Inside, a counter with six stools. Several tables with plastic tablecloths, red and white checked, blue and white striped, a tangle of wild flowers. Menu on a whiteboard behind the counter. Today's specials on the left, pies on the right.

"Raspberry," I mutter. "No one has raspberry pie these days. It's my favorite."

"Didn't I tell you?"

His boyish smile seeks my approval, wants me to say, "Good job, son," like Vince did. But it has the opposite effect on me. It sets me off instead, releases what I can no longer ignore.

"Why did you tell Vince about my drinking?"

The smile falls off his face and he looks down at his lap.

"How dare you? What I told you was in confidence. You had no right to tell anyone."

His face crumbles like glass shattering into a million little pieces of shame. "I'm sorry. I didn't think Vince would do that." His voice trembles. He can't look at me.

"He's not who you think he is, Corey."

"You don't know who I think he is."

"Why did you tell him?"

"I don't know."

"I think you do."

He twists a paper napkin in his hand, then tosses it on the floor. "I'm not you, Sylvia."

"What's that supposed to mean?"

His head jerks up. "I'm not a teetotaler, that's what it means. I'm not a Big Book thumper. I drink, okay? I *choose* to drink. Do you understand?"

"Of course I understand." How could I not understand? On the day I put myself into treatment, more than nineteen years ago now, a good part of me didn't want to quit drinking either. And even though there was a bigger part of me that did want to, I still wasn't ready to admit that I had a problem or that I needed help.

"I'm sorry, Sylvia. I just don't want . . . I'm not like you. I can't be."

I nod. "Of course not," I say. "But why did you betray me?"

188

"I don't know." His chin trembles. "I didn't think. I'm sorry."

His shoulders hunch over and he looks like he feels like a pile of shit. I lean across the table and place my hands on top of his. "I know you're a good person, Corey."

He seems to freeze for a second. Then he smiles. His shy little-boy smile.

Our food comes, and while we eat, he gets talkative again, very much like I get after I've made a decision and no longer have to worry over it. He asks what I think about the people in the group, and I tell him I like them, that I think they're good people. He asks what decision I think they'll make, and I tell him it's not for me to say, since I'm new and they've been at this for a long time.

"Only a few months," he says.

Then he talks about the sincerity of everyone in the group, how he feels bad for them with all the troubles they've experienced, especially Bunny. He asks me if I think she's pretty and when I tell him I do, he gives me a nervous smile like maybe he's attracted to her but doesn't want to say so, maybe doesn't think it's appropriate. He doesn't ask me if I think she likes him. I hope she does.

"If it weren't for Weppler," he says, "Bunny would be homeless."

"Weppler?"

"Vince doesn't like us to use his last name. He's really a good egg, you know. He gets me. He really does get me." The raspberry pie tastes sour, even bitter, on my tongue. I push it away. "I know he can be a jerk," Corey says, "and sometimes he's way too bossy, but he's the one that brought us together, you know. And he takes care of the money."

"Where does the money come from?"

"Don't know. Never asked."

He's quiet for a few seconds and then, out of the blue, he says, "Pickles's favorite book was *Cloudy with a Chance of Meatballs*. He made me read it to him at least twice every night." He studies the French fries on his plate. "He was a picky eater. All he wanted was hot dogs and pancakes and never broccoli." His nostrils flare. "He was so brave. So little. The big hospital bed swallowed him up." He pounds his fists on the table. "It's so wrong, Sylvia. It's so unfair. It's so . . . so . . . ."

He stops, a surprised look on his face. "You know what? Nicole reminds me of you," he says. His grin, tentative at first, expands as if he's letting that awareness sink in for the first time.

"I like her." I say. Then I chuckle. "Maybe because she reminds me of me."

"Do you regret coming, Sylvia?" I hesitate, struck by the naiveté of his question in the face of my deception, my gaining membership in the group under false pretenses. "You aren't having second thoughts, are you?" he asks.

I shake my head. If only he knew. "No," I say, "but I gotta tell you, Corey, I'm like Nicole and Bunny. I don't want any children to get hurt."

His nod doesn't signal agreement or disagreement, just acknowledgment that he's heard me. He pours some ketchup onto his plate and dips a French fry in it just like his father used to. I hand him my napkin and say, "It's dribbled in your beard," and he swipes at it in the same absent-minded way his father used to. But it isn't just his resemblance to Norton that defines him for me anymore. There are many other fragments unique to him. Some are found in his words and the all-pervasive passion and pain in his eyes when he speaks, some in the smell of alcohol on his breath, some in his love for his son, some in the way his face lights up when he talks about Bunny. When I piece all the fragments together, like a puzzle, an image of love emerges. My breath catches in my throat when I realize that I've come to love him as if he were my own son.

He notices I'm staring at him. "What?"

"I'm thinking," I say. "We should probably get going."

THIRTY

Seventy-five minutes and twenty-two seconds. That's how long it takes for us to get from the luncheonette to my apartment. I give Corey a quick peck on the cheek, tell him we'll talk tomorrow, and rush inside, where I grab a yellow legal-size pad of paper from my desk drawer and start to write down everything I've stored in my head. Several times I think I'm finished, but when I flex my fingers and work out the cramps in my hand, I suddenly remember something else. Sometimes it seems inconsequential, but I write it down anyway. The smallest, most insignificant detail could make all the difference. Finally, I put my pencil down for the last time, place the legal pad on my lap, and let my arms and hands rest limp at my sides.

Staring up at me is a veritable blueprint of death and destruction. A design I'd actively searched for and now an execution I must actively prevent. I sag into the couch, start rocking back and forth. Whatever made me think I could do this alone? My hand automatically reaches for my iPhone, and my finger presses the numbers it knows by heart.

"*New York Times.* Harrell here."

My tongue feels thick in my mouth. "It's me, J. B. I need your help."

He gives a little chuckle. "So, what are you going to drag me into next, Sylvia?"

The last time he said that to me—twelve years ago, when we found out who had killed a student of mine in the Bronx—I reminded him that when we first met, after an American Indian boy died in a foster home, *he* was the one who'd dragged *me* into it, not the other way around.

"This is serious, J. B. I'm in trouble. *Real* trouble."

"You're not going to almost get me killed like you did last time, are you?"

"Other people could get killed. A lot of people."

"Wait a minute, Sylvia. I just saw you, not so long ago, and you never mentioned any trouble, certainly nothing as serious as this."

"I didn't tell you everything. I didn't know it would come to this."

"Come to what?"

"A group of people is planning to bomb the Nectaral Corporation just before the congressional hearing next month. I'm the only one who can stop them, and I don't know how." My iPhone flies up in the air and my fingers fly after it, manage to grab it in midflight and bring it back to my ear.

"How do you know this, Sylvia? And why do you think you're the only one who can do anything about it?" He's dead serious, no trace of humor in his voice now.

"I was worried about what Corey might be getting himself into, so I infiltrated a group he's gotten involved with. That's how I found out. I'm the only one who can stop them because I'm the only one who knows about their plot . . . well, except you, now . . ."

"Slow down, okay? How about we take this from the top?"

I draw a deep breath and pull myself together so I don't repeat myself. "I was alarmed by Corey's need for vengeance," I say, "especially when it sounded like he and some other people were planning to do something violent." I fill J. B. in about how I met Corey, how Corey's son Pickles died recently from a cancer that Corey traces back to Norton's exposure to radiation, how I tried to dissuade Corey from doing anything violent. I even tell him about opening Norton's briefcase. I finish with how, in desperation, I made the decision to infiltrate Corey's group and how I'd managed to do it.

J. B. listens like a friend, without judgment or comment, but when I start to tell him about the planning meeting at the cabin, he gets impatient and asks, "So what exactly *is* their plan?"

"I wrote everything down as soon as I got home. Just a minute." I flip through pages of notes on my legal pad, stopping to take photos on my iPhone. "Okay, I'm sending you two pictures. One is their map of Nectaral Plaza and the other is a list of their damage calculations."

"Got 'em."

"Look at the map first. The red X's are potential explosion sites. See the X in the middle of the protesters, that little cluster of circles? And the X where those police cars are drawn on the map? The other photo shows estimates of the numbers of people who would be injured and killed and the amount of property damage that would be caused by explosions at those two places."

J. B.'s silence is deafening. Doesn't he believe me? Finally, he clears his throat. "Who *are* these people, Sylvia?" I let out the breath I've been holding in. It doesn't sound like he thinks I'm crazy.

"All I have are first names . . . Nicole, Bunny, and Freddie . . . except for Corey, of course, and a guy named Vince whose last name might be Weppler." I flip several pages into the legal pad. "I wrote down every detail I could remember about each of them—their stories, personalities, physical characteristics, how they behaved. They're good-hearted, J. B., they're well-meaning people. But their suffering, desperation, and thirst for justice have made them dangerous . . . and vulnerable . . . and I—"

He snorts. "Good people don't explode bombs that kill people, Sylvia. Terrorists do that."

"It's Vince," I say. "It's his plan. Everyone wants to do something that will wake people up, but Nicole insists that no one should get hurt or killed, and I think the others are having trouble with it, too. They made a lot of other suggestions at the meeting."

"So what did they decide?"

"They didn't. The meeting ended without a final decision. The problem is, they left Vince in charge, and he's very determined. And influential."

I flip the pages on my legal pad. "I have lots of notes about the meeting here. I can make a copy for you. It's all written down, every specific item they discussed, what was decided, what wasn't decided, all the suggestions made and by whom, who agreed, who disagreed, the group dynamics. Everything I could remember."

The sound of pencil scratching tells me J. B.'s listening has shifted from that of friend to that of investigative journalist. "So you have all this information," he says at last, "and I'm the only one you've shared it with."

His reproach comes through loud and clear. "Come on, J. B. Think about what would happen if I turned all this over to the authorities. You think the police are going to believe a strange woman in her seventies who traipses into their station with a bunch of notes in shaky handwriting and says someone is going to bomb Monrow City's biggest corporation?" I pause, absorb the absurdity of how all that would sound to the police. "Let's say they don't laugh at me. Let's say they don't ignore me, but instead they say they'll bring the others in for questioning, and I don't even know their last names, much less where they live. Even if the police managed to find some of them, they'd deny everything. And then the police would think I was either delusional or suffering from dementia."

"Would that be so bad if it scared the others into calling off the bombing?"

Maybe J. B.'s right. Maybe I should go to the police. But then what would happen to the others? What would happen to Corey? I can't bear to think about how hurt and angry he'd feel if I betrayed him like that. Even worse, that he'd end up in prison.

"Vince is the ringleader," I say. "Maybe I could go to the police and only tell them about him. The others are decent. He's not."

I recognize J. B.'s sigh as a patient prelude to him pointing out the flaws in my thinking without being critical. "The trouble is," he says, "if you left the others out of it, you'd have to delete everything about them from your notes, and that would be seen as withholding evidence."

I should have thought of that. Of course he's right. "Going to the police would be my death sentence anyway," I say. "Vince said if I told a soul about any of this he would have me hunted down and eliminated."

"Hunted down? Eliminated?" His tone of voice is not only surprised, there's also a sense of foreboding in it.

"If Vince even found out I was talking to you now—oh, J. B. . . . I've put you in danger now, too."

But instead of sounding frightened or intimidated, J. B. seems energized. "Okay then," he says in his *Now we're getting somewhere* tone of voice. "Tell me everything you know about this Vince character." I hear him scratching a line down the middle of a piece of paper, dividing it into two lists like I've seen him do in the past. "First we write down everything we know. Then everything we don't know and need to find out."

"Corey says his last name is Weppler." I pause. "I don't know if that's his real name or not. He's the leader of the group. Well, I'm not sure that's true or if he just thinks he is. Maybe the others are just humoring him. I know he threatened me." I stop to think. "He's an airplane pilot. No, I don't know that. But I did see him fly a floatplane. He's about six feet tall and not a heavy man. He has droopy eyebrows and a cold stare that sends shudders through you. Let's see . . . I don't know much . . ."

"Let's not worry about distinguishing fact from fiction from conjecture right now. Just tell me what you think you know. The truth will sort itself out later."

"Okay, then he either finances the group himself or gets the money from someone else. He's helping Bunny pay her daughter's medical bills. Corey says he brought the group together but I don't know how. He claims he cleaned up radioactive waste in the Marshall Islands in the seventies and that he and Norton served under the same commander. Time-wise, that would be possible, I suppose."

J. B. blows out a little whistle sound. "There's a whole lot we don't know about this guy, and what we do know about him doesn't quite ring true."

My heart skips a beat when I hear him say *we*, not you. "So you'll help me?"

"I thought that's what I was doing." I hear the smile in his voice.

"We don't have much time," I say. "The congressional hearing is next month."

J. B.'s pencil goes *tap-tap-tap* like it does when he's thinking hard.

"So, about how to stop them," he says. "Do you think Corey's need for vengeance could be satisfied some other way? Maybe if he testified at the hearing he wouldn't need to explode bombs."

"I think he trusts me now," I say. "So maybe he'd be open to the idea. If I could convince him to testify, maybe he could convince the others, too. Do you think that's even a possibility?"

"I'm covering some . . . um . . . I'm working on a related story in Washington right now and have some sources who could get them on the agenda." He goes silent for a second and then adds, "And, uh, Sylvia, you did the right thing by calling me. Thank you."

I wonder why he's thanking me when I'm the one who should be thanking him, should have already thanked him. But before I have a chance to say that, he says, "Try the idea out on Corey. I have to run now. I'll get back to you."

Feeling grateful and relieved, I sit back on the couch. Time to do some serious thinking about the idea of offering Corey the alternative of testifying at the hearing. It's possible he'd get some temporary relief from directing his rage at members of Congress. But the problem with that, based on what I've learned from my experience as a social worker, is that when people bleed on people who didn't cut them rather than on those who caused the pain, it can make them feel worse instead of better. Healing is more likely to occur when people can confront the source of their pain, the person or persons who hurt them, directly. And with that thought, everything suddenly becomes clear, and I know what I have to do. I have to find the person directly responsible for the radiation exposure that took the lives of Corey's father and his son. I have to find Master Sergeant Trayne, the man who gave the order way back in 1956.

THIRTY-ONE

"*New York Times.* Harrell here."

"Glad I caught you," I say. "I have another idea. If Corey could confront the man who gave the order, in 1956, that sentenced his father and his son to death, there's a better chance of him healing so he won't need to get revenge. I'm going to try to find Master Sergeant Trayne."

"Uh, Sylvia, I hate to burst your bubble," J. B. says, "I doubt if he's still alive."

I scribble some calculations on my legal pad. "Well, let's just say he is alive and he's one hundred years old. That would have made him thirty-seven years old when he was in charge of Norton's unit. Hmm, could be possible. Or, let's say he's alive and he's ninety-five years old. He would have been thirty-two then. Even more possible. It's worth a shot, don't you think?"

"I guess you could try doing an Internet search," he says with a little more enthusiasm. "All you need are his first and last names and the state where he might be living . . . or where he was born."

"All I have is his last name," I say. "How about I use Master Sergeant as his first name."

He chuckles. "There probably is someone out there named Master Trayne."

"I'll get back to you," I say.

He says good luck in that tone of voice people use when they don't think there's a chance in hell of you having any. But if I'm on the right track, it could change Corey's mind. I have to at least try.

I find eight million free search engine sites that promise to do the work of hunting, crawling, and accessing all online databases, archives, and public records. I choose one. It turns out J. B. is right, of course. The search yields not only one, but eleven people named Master Trayne, and all of them are way too young to be the sergeant. I narrow the search to someone with only a last name, Trayne, but who was born between 1919 and 1931, and up pop the names of nine men between the ages of eighty-eight and one hundred: Elbert, Henry, Michael, William, Thomas, Robert, James, Paul, and Anthony. It's possible that one of them is *the* Master Sergeant Trayne; it's equally possible that none of them is. To find out, I'd have to first locate and then contact each of them, and I don't have enough time to do that. I pick up the phone. Maybe Corey knows something that will help me narrow the search.

He answers on the fourth ring, his voice thick and slurry. "Are you all right, Sylvia?" He yawns. "I knew it was too much for you."

"I'm *fine*, Corey."

"Do you know what time it is?"

I glance at my watch. Two o'clock in the morning. "Oh, I'm sorry. I haven't looked at the time since you brought me home."

"Why you calling?"

"I wanted to talk to you about something but . . . it can . . . wait . . ."

"I'm awake now."

"Did your dad mention his commander in his journal? I was trying to remember what his first name was."

"Michael," he says without hesitation.

"Did he say where he was from by any chance?"

"No, but he did mention that he had a New Jersey accent. Why?"

"I was just wondering. Come for dinner tonight. We can talk then." I hear him sigh. "Bring the journal with you."

He yawns again. "I wonder how Dad would feel about the two of us reading it together."

"I think he'd like it," I say. "Dinner at five, okay? Sorry I woke you. Go back to sleep."

I look at the list of nine men, and there he is. Michael Trayne, nine-

198

ty-six years old, born in Paterson, New Jersey. That's him. It has to be.

Now all I have to do is find out where he's living and how to contact him. But before I can figure out how to do that, exhaustion takes over, and the next thing I know I'm waking up on the living room rug. My left eye tries to open and makes it halfway, wide enough to complain about the noonday sun streaming through my patio doors and cooking my face. My stomach is next to complain. I haven't eaten anything since yesterday afternoon when Corey and I stopped at the luncheonette on our way home.

I drag myself into the kitchen and, while the coffee's brewing, devour a piece of toast with a slab of high-protein peanut butter on it. Then I bring my mug and the coffee pot to my desk and sit down at the computer. Time to find out where Michael Trayne is living and how to contact him.

I remember hearing that the military archives is chock-full of information about veterans, but when I search for Michael Trayne, born in New Jersey and stationed in the Marshall Islands in 1956, I get no response, no other names, not even a message. It's like a total information blackout. I scroll down a list of websites using the keywords *veterans* and *Marshall Islands* and find a 2013 article called "The Year of the Disappearing Websites." In it, a technology institute professor writes about how an extensive collection of military and civilian reports and correspondence related to U.S. nuclear testing in the Pacific disappeared. He speculates that much of the absent content, which had previously been readily available to him on a Department of Energy website, was related to the work done in the mid-1990s to compensate victims of atmospheric testing. But why did the websites go missing? The professor doesn't know. And why is there no information at all about the servicemen who served in the Marshall Islands? He doesn't say. I download the article and save it on my computer so I can check it out later.

On a whim, I go on Facebook. It's unlikely that someone Michael Trayne's age would be wired into social media, but I've found people I went to high school with that way, so why not try it. I type his name into the search line, and bingo, there he is: the right age, even a picture of him in uniform as a young man. There are only a few posts on his page, birthday wishes and a few social events at Lakeside Terrace Independent and Assisted Living, where he lives. I go to the Lakeside Terrace Facebook page, and there's the address. I've done it. I've found him. I grab my iPhone and punch in J. B.'s number.

"*New York Times.* Harrell's desk. Leave a message."

"I found him, J. B. His name is Michael Trayne and he lives in rural West Virginia, about fifty or sixty miles from Washington, DC. I'm going to try to convince Corey to go with me to see him. I'll let you know what happens. Bye."

I glance at my watch. Four o'clock. My stomach's rumbling and I feel weak from hunger. I bring my mug and the now-empty coffee pot to the kitchen and stuff a few pieces of bread in my mouth to hold me over. To add to the package of spaghetti noodles and jar of organic tomato and basil pasta sauce I already have, I run to the store around the corner for ground Italian sausage, a frozen loaf of garlic bread, and a bag of salad fixings. While the meat sauce is simmering, I shed, finally, the soiled and wrinkled dress I've been wearing since Corey took me to the cabin and stuff it in the garbage can. After a nice hot shower, I throw on an old pair of bell-bottom jeans and my ancient black No Star Wars T-shirt from the 1980s.

I'm still waiting for the spaghetti to boil when Corey arrives. He stands in the hallway, shifting from one foot to the other, his left hand pressed against his thigh, his right hand clutching Norton's journal. I smile and touch his arm ever so lightly. "Come in," I say. "Dinner's almost ready." He tucks in his chin with that shy little-boy smile that looks awkward on his man-size face.

He lays the journal on the kitchen table, then stands with his back pressed against the doorframe. I drain the spaghetti and take the garlic bread out of the oven, put the pot of sauce and the drainer of noodles on the table. He doesn't sit down until I tell him to.

"Smells good," he says.

I laugh. "Straight out of the jar."

As if we've lost the ability to speak, we serve ourselves with hand motions and furtive glances. A half smile when he pushes the drainer toward me after helping himself to a huge pile of noodles. A nod when he loads up on meat sauce. Raised eyebrows when I hand him the Parmesan cheese. The air is heavy with the significance of who we are to each other now, the meaning of which neither of us fully understands nor would be able to put into words even if we did. I look down, as if somehow a picture of the shift in our relationship will emerge from the arrangement of food on my plate and tell me what to do next.

"Mmm." He wolfs down his spaghetti like a ravenous teenager, then wipes the remaining sauce from his plate with two pieces of garlic bread. When he reaches for more, I pass him the bowl of salad instead.

He grins. "Thanks, Mom." His voice is trying to be sarcastic, but he doesn't quite pull it off.

"Greens," I say, smiling back. He grunts. Places an obligatory clump of lettuce on his plate. Glances at me before putting the servers back in the bowl. I raise my eyebrows. He looks up at the ceiling, then places another helping of lettuce onto his plate.

My hands cover my mouth to hide my amusement. "You didn't like vegetables when you were little either," I say. "Your dad would laugh about it."

A thoughtful look takes over his face. He rests his fork on his plate. "If Dad hadn't died, maybe he and Mom would have divorced. Then you'd be my stepmom."

My head jerks from side to side. "No. No. I never would have broken up your family. Neither would he."

He raises his fork up and down like it's nodding or questioning or maybe just acknowledging what I've said. "Why'd you want me to bring his journal?"

I get up and walk over to the freezer. "I'll tell you why," I say, "but first, how about some spumoni ice cream. With coffee?"

He clears the table while I prepare the coffee and dessert. I would like to tell him that I don't want him to explode bombs, that instead I want him to confront the man who killed his dad and son. But I don't think I should be that direct. I need to be strategic, take it one step at a time.

"I asked about Trayne," I say between a slow spoonful of ice cream and little sips of coffee, "because I was trying to find out if he was still alive."

"Why?"

"Because he's the one who killed your dad, that's why." Anger unexpectedly rushes in and takes over without any resistance from me. "He's the one who gave the orders. He knew what was going to happen. What kind of a bastard protects himself and leaves his men unprotected? I mean, how does a man like that get to live a long life after what he did? Should he get to die without being held accountable?"

Corey's fists clench and unclench. "No. He doesn't get a pass. No one does. He doesn't get to say he was just following orders. Everyone is responsible for what they do."

My hands strike the table. My spoon falls to the floor. "Damn right!"

He opens Norton's journal then and starts reading.

May 5, 1956. Yesterday Trayne told us we had nothing to worry about, but we weren't stupid. Today we all talked about how we saw the officers wearing eye protection during the test. How come we weren't? Why were we given radiation badges to measure our exposure but nothing to protect us from it? We wanted to ask him now that the test was over but none of us dared.

Corey looks at me, his eyes filled with rage. "So, did you find him? Is Trayne still alive?"

I nod. "He's ninety-six years old, and I know where he lives."

"Let's go get the bastard," he says.

I nod and smile. I hadn't expected it to be this easy.

THIRTY-TWO

Two days later, we're on our way to the airport. Each time the taxi driver switches lanes in the heavy rush hour traffic, Corey cracks his knuckles and expels a whiff of alcohol through his lips. He's impatient, eager to get his hands, literally, on his dad's former commander. I'm worried about what will happen when Corey does confront him—*if* he confronts him. *If* Michael Trayne is even home when we get there. *If* we should have contacted him ahead of time, *if* it's such a good idea to surprise him, *if* he'll talk to us . . . and *if* he'll remember anything at age ninety-six anyway.

At the airport, Corey yanks our carry-on bags from the cab, slams them down on the sidewalk, and taps his foot on the pavement while I pay the fare with my credit card. Inside the terminal, he takes one look at the long check-in lines and drops our bags on the floor, throws his arms up in the air. I'm worried he might go over the edge before we even get there, have a nervous breakdown or a stroke or something.

I reach into my purse, slowly, and pull out our boarding passes. "Good thing we're not checking baggage," I say in a cheery voice that doesn't match what I'm feeling inside. "Let's see, our gate number is 13B. That's the security checkpoint over there." He grunts and rubs the back of his neck, picks up our bags again.

The TSA screener takes one look at me and says, "You may keep your shoes on, ma'am." Spots of pink pop up on her round cheeks as if to apologize for assuming that I'm over seventy.

"You'll need to remove *your* shoes, sir," she says to Corey. He glares at her, nostrils flared. "I don't make the rules, sir." With an aggrieved groan, he bends over, takes his sandals off, and tosses them in a plastic bin. He doesn't empty his pockets or take off his watch, so she makes him walk through the metal detector again. "Thank you, sir."

"Sure, any time," he mumbles under his breath.

"She's just doing her job, Corey. Probably a single mom with two little kids. Give her a break." I return his scowl with a smile. "We're plenty early. How about some breakfast."

The restaurant is crowded, folks in a rush, suitcases blocking spaces between tables. Someone bumps into the waitress, and a few drops of coffee spill onto Corey's napkin. He snaps at her.

"I'm sorry, miss," I say. "It's a bit of an anxious morning for us."

I order two eggs over easy with toast and bacon on the side. I'm too nervous to eat much, if anything, but it's my way of encouraging Corey to eat something. He orders French toast with an indifferent shrug like he's doing me a favor by ordering anything at all.

"It's only a three-hour flight," I say. He grunts. "We'll have time to pick up our rental car and get out of DC before rush hour." He grunts again. All through breakfast I make similar half-hearted attempts at small talk, only to have them go nowhere. I feel like a parent trying to engage a sulking teenager to keep him from acting out. Corey doesn't say anything, but he does eat all his breakfast.

On the plane, his anxiety escalates. "It's too cold in here," he complains to the flight attendant. She brings him a blanket, and a few minutes later he says, "It's too hot," and balls it up and shoves it under the seat in front of his. He orders a glass of orange juice and two shots of vodka from the beverage cart. The flight attendant glances at her watch and he flashes her a tight smile that doesn't reach his eyes. I stare at the clouds out the window, listen to him make a big production of pouring the vodkas into his orange juice and taking several gulps of his screwdriver. There's never a good time to confront us alcoholics about our drinking, but there are some really bad times, and this is without a doubt one of them.

He pokes me with his elbow. "I dreamt about Pickles last night," he says. "He was in the hospital bed and calling out to me, 'Papa, Papa, make it go away.'"

I reach out to touch his arm, and he gapes at my hand like it's a strange object he's never seen before and doesn't know what to do with. "Then Pickles disappeared and there was this old man in the bed. I ask him what happened to my son and he smiled. He *smiled*, Sylvia." He reaches for his drink and sees the glass is empty, slams it back down on the tray.

"I ripped the pillow from under that old man's head and covered his face with it. He started blubbering, and the more he blubbered, the harder I pressed down on the pillow until finally he went still."

My tongue feels like sandpaper. There's nothing I can say that won't grate on him, nothing that will make a difference. Not in the state he's in.

"I want to hurt him, Sylvia. I want to make him pay. I want to beat him senseless. I want to make him bloody." His teeth are bared, the vein in his neck pulsing. Little hairs stand up on my arms.

I reach for the glass of water on my tray and brace myself for more. But he's finished. Exhausted. He falls back in his seat and almost immediately starts snoring. His slack face and open mouth turn him back into a vulnerable and innocent child, incapable of killing anyone. My hands grip the armrests, tight, holding onto my trust in that child.

"Ladies and gentlemen, we are beginning our descent into Ronald Reagan Washington National Airport. The temperature on the ground is a sizzling ninety-five degrees with ninety percent humidity. Please fasten your seat belts and make sure your tray tables and seats are in an upright position. Thank you for flying with us today."

Corey yawns and sits up. The rage and violence I saw reflected in his eyes before are gone now, replaced by a combination of anticipation, excitement, and resolve.

"J. B. is going to meet us there," I say. "I'm looking forward to seeing him."

"Who is he, again?"

"J. B. Harrell. He's the prize-winning reporter I told you about, who came to the diner that night, but you'd already left. The two of you need to meet. He's working on a story about the consequences of nuclear testing in the Marshall Islands. He'll be coming to West Virginia from Pennsylvania. He's interviewing someone there."

"An atomic veteran?" he asks.

"Probably," I say. "He'll want to interview you, too. And . . . depending on what happens . . . maybe Trayne."

"So how long have you known this J. B. guy?"

"A long time. Our relationship started out rocky, but we're good friends now. We solved two murders together more than a decade ago. I'll tell you all about it sometime."

What I won't tell him is that J. B. knows everything. I won't tell him that the two of us are working together again, right now, to stop him and his group from bombing Nectaral Plaza. I won't tell him that I asked J. B. to come today to help me in case things get out of hand—like Corey lunging at Trayne and him falling and hitting his head, or Trayne having a gun that goes off by accident, or who knows what else.

THIRTY-THREE

The one-and-a-half-hour drive from the DC airport to Morgan County, West Virginia, takes us through lush, rolling hills that are widely touted as some of the most scenic in the country. But Corey doesn't even glance out the window.

"I'll stop if you want to take pictures. Just let me know."

He stares at his hands.

"Hungry?"

He doesn't answer. I can't think about eating anything myself right now either. Seems like the door to my stomach locked after letting in a few bites of eggs and toast at the airport this morning. One of my favorite things to do when I'm on road trips is to stop at a quaint roadside café to try its hot roast beef sandwich special. But this is no normal road trip. There isn't anything normal about anything we're doing today.

Corey tenses up more and more with each passing mile, and by the time we get to the Lakeside Terrace Independent and Assisted Living complex, he's like a spring in a toy that's been wound up so tight it's at the point of either exploding or breaking down. His tension is contagious. By the time I pull the car into a visitor spot in front, my knuckles have turned white from gripping the steering wheel and my neck is frozen.

"You know, Sylvia, you could have let me help you drive."

I look at him over the top of my sunglasses, consider asking him if he's gotten his driver's license back yet, but he's already getting out of the car.

Before us, a vision of perfectly crafted grounds, complemented by the aromas of orange, red, and white flowers.

"Disgusting," he mutters with a flip of his ponytail.

We stand next to an artificial pond in front of the main entrance. It's lovely and depressing at the same time, the sparkles of sunlight in the dancing spray beautiful; the aerator pushing those water droplets into the air fraudulent. Sweat from Corey's brow trickles down his cheeks and disappears into his beard.

"This is sick. It's not right. My dad and son are dead and that *bastard* gets to live out his life in the lap of luxury."

"We can wait a few minutes before we go in," I say.

He throws his arms up. "Hell no! No way I'm waiting."

I catch the door before it closes behind him, and when I walk through it, I'm hit by a blast of frigid AC air. While it's a welcome relief from the thick, suffocating heat outside, it won't be long before I'll wish I'd brought a sweater.

The lobby is both welcoming and unpleasant, in equal measure. On the one hand, there's a homelike atmosphere, with comfortable chairs and sofas, the soft glow of reading lamps, and a burning fireplace. On the other hand, there are the revolting smells of rotten eggs and farts and low-calorie poached chicken being cooked in large quantity.

One lone person is in the lobby, sitting in a chair in front of the fireplace with his back to us. I recognize the perfectly straight salon cut of the black hair at his neck, the perfectly stiff shirt collar, the squared shoulders. "J. B.," I call out.

He turns around. His smile, the one that broke my heart when he was seven years old, warms me down to my toes now. He walks toward me with his arms outstretched. The only other time he's hugged me was at his wedding reception, when he thanked me for bringing Mentayer into his life.

"Thank God you're here," I whisper. "He's a basket case."

Corey coughs into his hand.

"Nice to meet you, Corey," J. B. says. "I look forward to—"

"Yeah, you too. You can interview me later. Gonna take care of some important business now."

I tell him I have to go to the restroom first, and I walk away before he has a chance to object. On my way down the hall, I pass a chandeliered and carpeted dining room and a luxurious billiard room, and when I think about how Norton was denied such amenities of senior living, a fusillade of anger is unleashed in me. Yet I know my anger doesn't compare with the injustice-fueled rage burning inside Corey right now—to the point of exploding. I splash cold water on my face, then lean against the wall of the women's restroom and scribble a note to J. B. *Stay close but don't let Corey know. If I text you come right away.* On my iPhone I type *help* in a text message, then set it up so I can send it later with the touch of my finger if I need him. He'll know what to do. I fold the scrap of paper several times, tuck it in the palm of my hand, and go back to the lobby.

Corey's already at the elevator, holding the door open with his foot. "Let's go, Sylvia."

"Wait, we have to get the apartment number."

"I already told him," J. B. says as I slip the note into his hand. "It's 801."

Every time the elevator stops, Corey swears and punches the button for the eighth floor with his fist. But the elevator is immune to his angry outbursts; it's been programmed to stop at every floor, even if no one is waiting, and then to open and close the door at a snail's pace to allow plenty of time for walkers and wheelchairs. When we reach the eighth floor, Corey jumps out like a wild horse bolting through a gate.

"You're going the wrong direction," I say.

He stops, his body rigid, and turns around with a stomp of his feet. I slip my hand through his arm and we walk together awkwardly, with him trying to get me to go faster and me trying to get him to go slower. All the apartment doors we pass are decorated with summer floral wreaths and colorful pictures, until we get to the end of the hall. The door to number 801 is bare except for a small gold plaque on which is engraved, in black letters, M. Trayne.

Corey's face turns ashen and his feet plant themselves hard on the floor. He glares at the door, pulls his arm back, his fists curled into tight cannonballs.

I grab his hand just in time and pull his arm down. "No, not that way," I say. He raises his fist again; he either doesn't hear me or is ignoring me. I get a firm grip on his arm and squeeze. "Listen to me, Corey." His eyes widen. "Let *me* start."

He jerks away from me, raises his arm again. I jump in front of him. "Look at me." I raise my voice and look him straight in the eyes. "*Corey,* look at me."

He drops his arms and tucks his chin into his chest. Then he presses his back against the wall with his knees bent like he's about to slide down onto the floor.

"It's going to be all right, Corey." His body collapses like a deflated balloon and leaves behind a frightened four-year-old. I touch his cheek. "But you have to let me talk first." I place my hands under his chin and lift his face up. "That will give you time to know what to say." He nods. "Okay?" He nods again.

He draws himself up, straightens his T-shirt, and faces the door. I pull my iPhone from my purse and slip it into my pocket. The weight of it makes the front of my lightweight cotton dress sag. I take Corey's hand in mine and press the doorbell. When the door starts to open, I squeeze his hand and then let it go.

"How can I help you folks?"

I don't know what I thought a ninety-six-year-old man would look like, but this man's chiseled face, while certainly well lived-in and sporting a few age spots, looks like it's being held in place by the less-wrinkled skin of someone much younger.

"Are you . . . Uh, we're looking for Michael Trayne."

"Well, then, ma'am, this is your lucky day."

Corey seems to be as taken aback as I am by Trayne's deep blue eyes—clear, not rheumy like I expected, and surprisingly warm, not cold and unfeeling as Norton had described them in his journal. Could this be Trayne's son? Or a younger brother, perhaps?

"My name is Sylvia Jensen," I finally manage to say.

He takes my hand and holds it between both of his. "My pleasure to meet you, Sylvia Jensen."

I pull away, unsettled by how soft and warm his hands feel. "And this is Corey Cramer." I suck in a quick breath, and then let everything I planned to say tumble out all at once. "His father was Norton Cramer. He served under you in the Marshall Islands in 1956. Norton was a dear friend of mine."

Michael Trayne squeezes his chest with both hands. He stumbles forward, then finds his balance and stands like a wiry statue with his mouth open. "Sorry, son, you're just the spitting image of—"

"Son?" Corey makes a sudden forward movement. I grab his arm and pull him back. He's trembling.

"So you remember Norton," I say.

"I remember all my men."

"May we come in?"

"Of course, of course, where are my manners?" He steps back and urges us inside with a circular motion of his hand. "Please, it's Michael. Well, Mike actually, to my friends." His voice trails off and he stares down at his hands like he's just realized his mistake.

I feel the heat of Corey's anger at my side. "This isn't a social visit, Mr. Trayne."

"Yes, I . . . I suspected as much. Please do come in."

I feel Corey's breath on the back of my neck as we pass Trayne's bedroom. The room is spare and immaculate. Sheets stretched tight on a single bed. A blanket at the foot folded as neatly as if, like the creases in Trayne's khaki shorts and crisp cotton shirt, it had been ironed. One wall of the living room is a window. Across from it, a wall-sized mirror reflecting the panoramic view of the West Virginia hills and creating the illusion of a room much larger than it actually is. Not much furniture. An overstuffed brown leather sectional. Across from it, a matching recliner. In the middle, a heavy mahogany coffee table, and next to the recliner, an end table with a gooseneck lamp, a book, and a pair of reading glasses. The room is warm and stuffy, unadorned and pristine, and somehow fitting.

I sit on one end of the sectional and pat the spot next to me. But Corey remains standing, his arms bent at his sides and hands opening and closing, making fists like a wrestler ready to pounce on his opponent. "You and I need to talk," he says. His voice is tight, like it's taken everything out of him to control himself.

"Very good. I'll put the kettle on. We'll have a chat."

Corey surges forward. I slip my hand in my pocket, place my finger on my iPhone. "A chat? Oh my, yes, Mr. Sergeant Major, let's do have a chat. Let's see, how should we start? How about how you killed my dad? Or don't you remember?"

Michael Trayne's body crumbles into the recliner. He holds his head in his hands and groans, a long, resigned groan like he knew his day of reckoning would come someday, and now it was here.

"I'll never forget, son," he says at last.

Corey flings himself across the room, screaming, "I'm not your fucking son." He pins Trayne's head to the back of the recliner and, with his face only inches away, spits out slurred, incoherent, rage-filled words. "Murderer . . . brain tumor . . . four years old . . . my son . . . my dad . . . no protection . . . But *you* . . . you were protected, weren't you . . . selfish son of a bitch . . . you don't deserve to be alive."

"Stop! Corey! Stop!" I grab the back of his shirt and try to pull him off Trayne. He shoves me away with his elbow. I stumble backward. My iPhone flies out of my pocket.

"Let the boy be," Trayne says, his hands raised in surrender. "I deserve it."

A blue vein bulges in Corey's neck and I see his arm go up, his fist raised above Trayne. He's going to kill the man.

I grab Corey from behind and squeeze his neck. He coughs and pries my fingers loose, grabs my hand, and throws me off. My wrist hits the edge of the coffee table and I double over, face down on the sectional, nauseated. Before I can straighten myself up, I hear pounding. Shuffling feet. A door opening. Voices.

"Hey, Mike. Everything okay in there?"

"Sorry about that, Sam. Got a little carried away in here. Thanks for checking on me. Everything's okay. And you are . . . ?"

I hear the door close, hear garbled words. "Come in. That was just my neighbor."

Then I hear a voice in my ear. "Sylvia?" J. B.'s hand is on my back.

I open my eyes. "I'm okay," I say. When I roll over, there's a searing pain in my left wrist. I grab it with my right hand, blink back my vision, and sit up.

J. B. looks down at me. "Wiggle your fingers."

"I'm okay," I say. Then I see Corey, on his knees next to the recliner, his eyes red, his face puffy. "*He's* not okay, though," I say. "Look at him."

"Wiggle your fingers, Sylvia." I try, and I can't. "There must be a medical clinic here," he says.

"I'll call them," Trayne says.

"No! Just put some ice on it. We need to finish what we came here for."

J. B. throws up his hands and sits next to me on the sectional. He knows better than to argue. A few minutes later, Trayne hands me a bag of crushed ice. Then he lowers himself down on the recliner next to Corey, who's still on his knees, with sweat streaming down his face. Trayne leans forward and places his hands on Corey's shoulders.

"I'm sorry, son. I'm so, so sorry. I know saying that doesn't make it right. I knew I was putting my men in danger, and I did it anyway. I live with the shame of that every day."

Corey tucks his chin into his chest and his upper body into his knees like he's trying to make himself disappear. Trayne's hands move to his back like he's going to make sure he doesn't succeed.

Seconds pass. Finally, I cut into the silence. "You *knew*?"

Trayne nods. He takes a breath and makes a sound like a wounded animal.

"You *knew*?" I say again. "Exactly what did you know?"

"I knew it was dangerous to expose anyone to radiation without protection. I knew some of my men could die. I knew there could be health consequences in the future."

"But . . . but how could you know that? Norton wrote in his journal that the government claimed the dangers of radiation weren't known at the time of the tests."

Trayne lets out a long breath. "That was a lie," he says. "They did know. Even before Hiroshima and Nagasaki, physicists at Los Alamos understood the bombs would cause radiation sickness and other fallout effects. And, after the bombings, reports from Japanese doctors confirmed it. In 1953, forty-five hundred sheep died after exposure to fallout from our continued testing. The government knew. It was all top secret."

I lean forward. Corey sniffles, still curled into himself next to Trayne.

J. B. stands in front of them. "Mr. Trayne, you should know that I'm an investigative reporter. May I ask you some questions? Off the record if you wish."

"*On* the record, Mr. Harrell. Please."

"All right then. If it was the government that lied about the dangers of radiation, then why do you feel guilty? I mean, if it was top secret, like you say, then *you* couldn't have known."

Corey's head shoots up, and the rest of his body follows. He turns toward J. B. "Why are you letting him off the hook?"

Trayne holds his face in his hands and moans, then looks up as if toward the heavens. "Oh God. Oh God. Oh God. I did know. God help me, I did know."

"How?" I ask.

He blows out his breath. "I got a memo with instructions to check my men for signs of radiation poisoning, after the tests. It told me to look for things like vomiting and diarrhea, red or purple spots on the skin called petechiae, wounds that didn't heal but just broke and bled, sudden hair loss." He lets out a sharp sound like a dog's yelp. "I knew enough to be afraid to have children of my own."

Corey grabs his stomach like the wind has just been knocked out of him. Then he pulls out his wallet and opens it, takes out a picture of Pickles. "This is . . . was . . . my son. *You* may have escaped losing a child because of what you knew, but *I* didn't. I didn't."

Trayne crumbles into his pain. "I told my wife we couldn't have children, but . . . my daughter . . . she was an accident . . . she died of cancer. My wife died of a broken heart." His chin trembles. "I didn't escape God's punishment, son."

Corey sits back on his heels. He's crying. Trayne is crying.

"I'm sorry about Pickles, son. I'm sorry about your dad. I wish there was something I could do."

I move to the edge of the sectional. "Maybe there is. Did you keep that memo? Do you still have it?"

"I kept everything," Trayne says. He stands up and walks over to the mirror, which, it turns out, is a sliding door to a closet the length of the wall. Inside are at least a dozen gray file cabinets. He opens the top drawer of the first one on the left and pulls out a file. "The memo is in this one. No one knows I took it." He reaches inside. "Here it is."

He goes to the third file cabinet and opens the top drawer, pulls out a thick folder. "Corey," he says, "all the newspaper articles about your dad when he was on trial and after he died are in here. Plus all the copies of his FBI file that I got through the Freedom of Information Act." He shuts the drawer and brings both folders to Corey. "It took courage to do what your dad did. He was a hero, son. A real hero."

Corey sits on the floor, his legs straight out in front of him, and stares at the folders on his lap. His fingers move across the top of Norton's file, slowly, lovingly. I wonder what he's thinking but then realize, from the look on his face, that he's unable to think about anything at all right now.

Trayne starts to close the sliding door, but J. B. jumps up and places his hand on the old man's shoulder to stop him. "What else do you have in there, Mr. Trayne?"

"Everything I could get my hands on," he says. "These seven cabinets are packed with U.S. government and non-government documents about nuclear testing. Stuff no one knows about. Environmentalists will be particularly interested in this stuff about the Runit Dome in the Marshall Islands. Did you know that more than one hundred thousand cubic yards of radioactive debris was left behind after the nuclear tests and it's now leaching out of the crater and about to spill into the ocean? I've got the evidence here. And this file"—he points to another cabinet—"documents all the government standards for storing nuclear waste, including recent evidence of how the safe level," he snorts, "yeah, *safe*, a tricky word that. Anyway, there's recent stuff in here about how the government's planning to change the *safe* level at Hanford nuclear waste storage site so cleanup will be easier and cheaper and they can walk away from it."

"Do you have any information there," I ask, "about the Nectaral storage contract?"

"Oh my, yes. In this cabinet here. Some shady business going on there. Some information you have to grab up fast. It's on a website one day and then disappears the next. Like some of the studies in that file at the end about the health effects of atmospheric testing." He opens a different drawer and pulls out another thick folder. "Here. Proof that there's a link between radiation exposure and cancer." He pulls out some articles. "This study connects thyroid disease in schoolchildren with their exposure to fallout at the Nevada test site in the 1950s. This one estimates that hundreds of thousands of deaths can be attributed to atmospheric nuclear testing. Here's another one that predicts 2.4 million people could eventually die as a result."

Trayne jerks open another drawer. "Top secret medical experiments to study the effects of radiation exposure on downwind Marshallese people from the infamous Castle Bravo bomb test." He pulls out a file folder and slaps it down on the top of the cabinet. "Instead of providing medical care, they gave people placebos so they could study them."

My mouth drops open. My blood is boiling. "I can't believe—"

"Mr. Trayne," J. B. says. "What were you planning to do with all this evidence?"

"Well, Mr. Harrell." He pauses and glances over at Corey, who's now hugging his dad's folders to his chest. "I'm beginning to think God sent you folks here to help me with that."

THIRTY-FOUR

I've never seen J. B. like this before. He's staring at Trayne's cabinets, practically salivating over the gold mine of evidence inside. An investigative reporter's dream. His excitement is so contagious it catches me and lifts me to my feet. But then the bag of ice falls to the floor and a sharp pain shoots through my wrist and knocks me back onto the sectional.

Corey hovers over me, a look of horror on his face. "Oh dear God, I'm sorry, Sylvia. I didn't mean, shit, I didn't want to hurt you."

"I know, Corey, I know."

"We need to get her to a doctor," J. B. says to Trayne.

"Oh, for heavens' sake, J. B., I'm fine." He looks amused. Just like that time years ago when I ended up in a Bronx hospital with a concussion and kept insisting I was okay. I was wrong then; maybe I'm wrong now, too.

"I'll call for a wheelchair," Trayne says. "The clinic's a bit of a walk."

"I don't usually walk on my hands," I say, "and I have two perfectly good legs."

Corey's skin stretches tight with worry over his face. "I'm going with you."

They all look at me. It's three to one. I can't win this one. "Okay," I say, "but I walk. No wheelchair."

"I'll call the clinic and tell them you're on your way," Trayne says.

J. B. looks at me with that lopsided grin of his and says, "Probably a good idea to warn them about her." I slap his arm with my good hand, and his grin blossoms into a full smile.

To get to the medical clinic, Corey and I have to walk through a maze of inside corridors, cavities in a beehive that connect people living in different nests in the complex based on their capabilities. The clinic is a square white building a city block away from the main buildings, so for the last leg of our journey, we have to wade through the 99-degree soup outside. Stepping into the clinic waiting room is like walking into a freezer. The same design as the main lobby. A fire burning in a gas fireplace. Flanked by overstuffed chairs. I collapse in one of them, about ready to pass out.

"You must be the folks Mike sent over." The twenty-something-year-old, white-uniformed blond has the smile of someone who loves old people but doesn't ever want to be one. "The doctor is finishing her notes from her appointment with . . ." Her eyes light up, keen to share some juicy gossip, but she thinks better of it and says instead, "It shouldn't be long."

Corey's eyes are stuck on my wrist. "Does it hurt real bad? Do you think it's broken?" He tucks his shoulders and elbows into his sides like a child expecting to be chastised.

"I'm *fine*," I say.

I pat his arm with my good hand and try to retreat into my thoughts about everything that's happened, but his foot tapping on the floor distracts me.

"You thinking about Trayne like I am, Corey?"

He pulls on his ear, then strokes his beard. "Uh . . . sort of . . ." His eyes go back to my wrist.

"He's certainly not what I expected," I say. "I don't know whether to be more moved by his remorse or by his need to atone for what he did by collecting all that evidence."

Corey scrunches his eyes together. "What he did can't be undone." He spits out the words, staccato sharp.

"That's true."

He frowns and moves to the edge of the chair. "His feeling guilty doesn't make him a victim."

"No, it doesn't." I pause and take in a bit of air. "But maybe losing

218

his daughter and wife does." I wait a second and then say, "Do you think maybe we're all victims?"

His hands fly out, palms up, like he's maybe wanting to push that idea right back to me. "I don't know what to think," he says at last.

I nod. "It's going to take time to digest all this."

"The doctor is ready to see you now." The blond stands in the doorway, ready to take me to the examination room.

"I won't be long," I say to Corey.

The doctor comes in almost immediately. "I'm Stephanie Mills," she says, with a smile and outstretched hand. "We generally only provide clinic services to our residents, but I understand this is an emergency. And who can say no to Mike? Certainly not me."

"I wouldn't call it an emergency," I say.

"Well, let's take a look and see. I understand it's your left hand. Or is it your wrist?" She lifts my arm and I wince, force myself to focus on her white, Chiclet-perfect teeth instead of the pain. "Hmm, we better X-ray this," she says.

"I'm sure that's not necessary," I say.

"May need a cast," she says.

"I'm sure not. A splint or a wrap should be enough to hold it in place. Probably just a sprain."

She smiles and says, "Doctor's orders." I take in her just-shy-of-six-feet height. She has the body build of a jogger in her thirties who snacks on fruit and nuts and undoubtedly has a nutritious yogurt drink for breakfast every morning. What does she know?

"You don't want to make me answer to Mike, do you, if it's broken and I don't take an X-ray?" she says. I give her a look intended to remind her she's talking to an adult, not a seven-year-old.

She smiles and goes about being efficient. I watch her do it: squareish jaw and golden brown skin, cuffs of blue jeans and Nike running shoes peeking out from the bottom of her long white lab coat. I wonder what a young and vibrant doctor like her is doing in a clinic like this.

She pulls up the X-rays on the computer screen. "Your wrist is broken. See that bone right there?"

"No. They all look broken to me."

"We're going to have to cast it." Her voice makes it clear that this is not up for debate.

I sigh. "How long will that take?"

"Not long. We'll have you out of here before you know it. I'll give you something for pain and have you lie down while we do it so you can relax."

I close my eyes and succumb. Before I know what happened, Dr. Mills is saying, "Okay, that should do it," and helping me sit up. "Don't rest anything on the plaster for the first forty-eight hours until it's fully dry. Keep your hand raised above your elbow as much as possible for the first week. Here's a list of exercises. Do them four times a day. Check with your own doctor as soon as you get home. I'll give you some pain medication to hold you over."

"Tylenol is fine," I say. "That's all I ever take."

She smiles and fills out a prescription form, hands it to me. "We have a wheelchair for you."

"I'm fine," I say.

"Mike can bring it back to us later. No problem."

The blond nurse comes in with Corey and a wheelchair. I get in it, albeit not without embarrassment, and they send us on our way, at which point I almost immediately fall back asleep.

"Okay, Sylvia, here we are."

When I open my eyes, I'm pleasantly surprised to find my head feels as clear as it did in my younger days after a ten-minute power nap. The door to Trayne's apartment is open and I hear him talking.

"If only they'd allow themselves to imagine the devastation, the pain, the loss they've caused. If only they'd see it isn't just what they call collateral damage. It would break their hearts. At least it should."

We leave the wheelchair out in the hall and go inside. J. B. and Trayne are in the kitchen, each holding a glass of wine, a very expensive-looking bottle of Château Lafite sitting in the middle of the table. J. B. sees us and presses the button on his iPhone. He's been recording Trayne.

He points to my cast. "That's what I thought."

"Just a little break," I say. "A tiny little bone."

Trayne gets two glasses from the cupboard and raises the bottle. "My niece gave me this truly extraordinary wine for Christmas. I've been saving it for a special occasion, but nothing's been worthy of it until now. May I?"

I shake my head no. "It's wonderful of you to share it with us," I say when I see how crestfallen he looks. "I don't mean to be rude, but I'm one of those people who can't drink one glass without drinking the whole bottle." He looks confused, so I smile and add, "I'm in recovery. Nineteen years."

"Ah, yes," he says. "Good for you. Good for you." He looks at Corey with his eyebrows raised. "And you, son?"

"Thanks, but I don't drink either. I want . . . I'm . . . I'm trying to stop." Corey's sheepish grin makes my heart skip a beat.

"Iced tea then?" Trayne says.

"Great," Corey and I say in unison.

We bring our drinks into the living room. The three of us sit on the sectional, and Trayne sits in his recliner. The closet door is still open, some cabinet drawers ajar, a few folders scattered on the floor.

"Mike and I have been talking about the congressional hearing that's coming up," J. B. says with a wink.

"About the plutonium storage contract with Nectaral?" How easy it is to fall back into the rhythm of one of our teamwork strategies, this the one where, for the benefit of a third party, I ask questions, and J. B. answers as if he thinks I don't already know.

"It's been rescheduled for two weeks from now. I was talking to Mike here about being an expert witness. All this evidence about the dangers of plutonium." He motions with a sweep of his hand toward the wall of file cabinets.

"And I was just saying," Trayne says, "that if he used my research for his *New York Times* story instead, the information would get out to a whole lot more people. You can come here to study the files any time, J. B. Stay as long as you want. There's a guest room on the first floor. I can't let you take anything with you, though. Can't risk anything getting lost or stolen or anything bad happening to you."

J. B. narrows his eyes at the file cabinets like they're ominous and threatening creatures; like he knows delving into them is entering dangerous territory.

"Glad you understand," Trayne says.

The two of them maintain eye contact for a few seconds. I can tell J. B. has more to say but knows this isn't the time to say it. He refocuses, flicks his eyes toward me. My turn.

"Why not both?" I say. "Your testimony could be part of the newspaper story." J. B. nods in a way that tells me he knows what I'm thinking—that the congressional hearing might not be enough for Corey, but if he knew Trayne's testimony would also appear in the *New York Times*, maybe that *would* be enough.

Trayne stares out the window and rubs his chin. J. B. and I look at each other sideways, a signal that it's time for tag team.

He starts. "Think about how powerful it would be if you read the memo to them."

"You could wear your uniform. Do you still have it?"

"You could tell them why you did all this research."

"How you were trying to appease your conscience."

"You could tell them how painful it was for you to learn about the suffering that's been inflicted on generations of families."

"And about your own wife and daughter."

Trayne lets out a slow, sad breath, turns away from us, and looks at Corey. "I would like to tell them about the suffering I inflicted on *your* family, son."

A moment of silence follows. I nod to J.B, a signal for him to do the heavy lifting now. "Corey is part of your personal story, Mike," he says in a drawn-out, deliberate way, like he's thinking out loud. "Maybe he could testify *with* you." He pauses and turns to Corey. "Wouldn't that be powerful? The two of you together?"

Brilliant, I tell him with my eyes. I imagine the two of them sitting side by side in the hearing room, perpetrator and victim, Trayne's guilt and shame next to Corey's bitter anger.

Trayne walks over to Corey and gets down on his knees before him. "Would you consider doing it, son?"

"It won't make things right." Corey says. He massages his forehead and shakes his head.

Trayne's voice is shaky, and for the first time he sounds his age. "I'm not asking you to do it for me."

"Do it for yourself, Corey," I say, "and for Pickles. And your dad."

"I can get you on the witness list," J. B. says. He pulls out his iPhone and starts texting.

"He has sources," I explain to the others. "But he'll never tell you who they are."

Trayne stands up, places his hand on Corey's shoulder. "You need to do what's right for you, son. I understand."

A few minutes later J. B. gets a response to his text. "Good news," he says. "Should be no problem getting the two of you on the witness list plus four or five others." He pauses. "That is, if you know any other atomic veterans or family members who might want to testify?"

Corey crosses his arms and sits back on the sectional. J. B. and I glance at each other. We've done our best. Now it's time to back off. With everything that's happened today and no time to process any of it, we can't expect Corey to make a decision right away. But, from the look on his face, it could go either way.

THIRTY-FIVE

Saying good-bye to Trayne is awkward and complicated. I reach out to shake his hand and he hugs me instead. We step back, both of us embarrassed.

"Thank you for saving me," he says.

I want to thank him for helping me save Corey, but of course I can't do that, so instead I raise my casted arm up in the air and mumble, "Doctor's orders," as if my broken wrist has anything to do with what he said or with me showing my appreciation.

Corey gives Trayne a curt nod and stuffs his hands in his pockets, making it clear that he will not be granting forgiveness with a handshake.

Then J. B. steps in and pumps Trayne's hand. "I'll be back to dig in those files, Mike."

Trayne pats him on the back. "And you can expect good food when you get here."

We leave Trayne at the Lakeside Terrace Independent and Assisted Living complex with his burden of guilt lightened a bit, with J. B. radiant with the magnetic sense of a man on a hunt, with Corey plunged into confusion and ambivalence, and with me carrying a strange and uneasy sense of foreboding.

I reluctantly agree to let Corey drive from West Virginia to the DC airport. Even though he might not have his driver's license back yet, it wouldn't be safe for me to drive with my right hand on the steering wheel and my left hand up in the air. I don't talk to him, let him focus on his driving. I try not to worry about what might happen next or what he's thinking or feeling. I wait until we're finally on the plane to ask him, but as soon as I lean back in the seat and close my eyes, I'm gone, like the-sleep-of-the-dead gone, like anesthesia-induced gone, like passing-out-drunk gone.

I wake to Corey shaking me. I pry my eyes open but they slam shut again. "Sylvia, we're almost there." He shakes me some more. "Did the doctor give you pain pills?"

"I'll take a couple Tylenol," I say, bending down to get my purse from the floor under the seat in front of me.

"I've been awake the whole way thinking," he says. "I know what to do." I sit up, forget about my purse.

"Oh?"

"Our group needs to meet," he says. "We need to tell them everything. They should know what happened."

I cross my fingers. "Good idea. Maybe everyone should testify."

"What? No, Sylvia. I just think we should meet and talk."

My brain kicks in, tells me to slow down, not appear too eager. "Okay, but could we meet at my place maybe? I'm really not up for going back to that cabin, Corey."

"Sure. I'll call Vince. He'll set it up."

My mouth shapes itself into an O and I shake my head. "You and I can do that."

The flight attendant announces that we'll be arriving shortly. Corey checks that his seat belt is fastened and then says, matter-of-factly, "Vince always sets up the meetings."

Alarm bells clang in my head. "I'm happy to do it this time," I say. "If we meet at my place, I can save him the trouble." For a second, I entertain the idea of inviting everyone but Vince to the meeting.

"Naw," he says. "Vince is the only one who has all our phone numbers. It's easier to let him do it."

I lean back and watch as the ground moves closer to the plane. Okay, so Vince sets up the meetings. Nothing I can do about that. But there's a lot I can do when we meet; I can convince the others to testify at the congressional hearing as an alternative to the bombing plan. Or, at the very least, I can convince them to testify first, and after that decide if they still want to go ahead with the bombing. If the idea comes from Corey, I think the others, except for Vince, will listen. So the first thing I have to do is convince him. I think I can do that.

"Let's talk more tomorrow," I say as the plane is landing. "I have something to show you."

##

The next afternoon, he comes to my apartment as agreed. We sit for a while on the bench out on my balcony with our shoulders touching, soaking up the sun. We don't speak, as if in silent agreement that words will diminish the magnitude of what happened yesterday, that talking about how we've changed won't make the full extent of it any more fathomable. And yet, the difference, in both of us, is undeniable. Another shift, another step in the right direction. I reach for Norton's briefcase on the floor next to me and open it.

Corey looks confused. "That's what you wanted to show me? Is there something in there I didn't see the first time?"

The mimeographed booklet, *Radical's Guide to Homemade Bombs and Improvised Explosives*, is on the top. I tell Corey to take it out. "Open it to a page marked with a sticky note," I say, "then read the note in the margin."

"'What if it's trip-wired,'" he reads. "Wait a minute. That looks like the handwriting in my dad's journal."

"It is. I discovered your dad's scribbles when I went back and looked at the booklet again. Go ahead. Read the others. I put a sticky note on each page he wrote on."

His fingers caress his father's handwriting as he reads each entry to himself. When he gets to the last one, I ask him to read it out loud. "'I hope I never have to defuse or deal with any of these.'" Corey's voice is so soft it's barely above a whisper. A tear drops onto the page, and he blots it with his shirtsleeve.

"Your dad was learning how to dismantle bombs, Corey, not set them off."

He nods and stares at the booklet for a long time. Finally he closes it and places his right hand on the cover as if taking an oath on a Bible. "Dad wants me to testify."

I place my hand on his. "That's what he did. In court. It was something he had to do."

He exhales, releases a long, drawn-out breath as if it's his last, the battle over. "It's what I have to do, too." Then, almost immediately, a worried look jumps in and takes over his face. "Do you think the others will understand?"

"Yes. I think they will. Everyone wants to make an impact, and your testimony will have a huge impact. Imagine the exposure. All the national TV networks will show you and Trayne together. And your testimony will be in J. B.'s story in *the* most respected newspaper in the country. Talk about getting people's attention! Maybe the others will want to testify, too."

"They might be okay with me doing it, but I don't think I could ever convince them to testify. Not Vince, for sure. He's dug in on his plan."

I squeeze his hand. "I'll help you convince them. And so will your dad. The three of us will talk to them together."

"I'll get Vince to call the meeting," he says, still looking worried.

"We have to meet soon," I say. "We don't have much time."

THIRTY-SIX

Two days later, a call from Vince wakes me up. "Corey told me everything. We're meeting this morning. Ten o'clock at your place. See you then."

"Nothing like telling me at the last minute," I say, but he's already hung up.

Yesterday Corey told me he'd had a long conversation with Vince and that it had gone well. I was skeptical, but he insisted that Vince was fine with the idea of him testifying. Corey was still worried about how the others would feel about it, though, and I told him I was more concerned about how Vince might try to *get* the others to feel about it. I call Corey now, but he doesn't pick up.

"It's me. Where are you? Vince just told me we're meeting this morning. We don't have much time to prepare. How early can you get here? Call me. Or just come."

I look at the clock. He's probably at the seven o'clock AA meeting he said he was going to start going to every morning. The meeting ends at eight o'clock, so if he takes the bus, he could get here half an hour later. That should give us enough time to talk before the others come.

I take a shower, pull my wet hair back into a neat ponytail, and put on a plain white T-shirt and a pair of lightweight jeans, a neutral run-of-the-mill outfit. I grab a piece of toast and gulp down some stale leftover coffee and then run to the bakery. After arranging fresh pastries on a platter, starting the coffee, and making a pitcher of orange juice, I sit down and stare at my phone. No word from Corey. He should be here by now. I send him a text in caps. *WHERE ARE YOU?* I watch the minutes pass at a snail's pace on my phone. *Come on, Corey,* I think. *We need to talk. Get here. Come on.*

At nine o'clock, he finally knocks on the door. I trip over my feet going down the hall to let him in. "How do you always manage to bypass the security system anyway," I tease while unlocking the door. I pull it open with a flourish. "Where have you—"

My foot shoots out to block the door and my good arm tries to push it closed, but Vince is quicker and stronger. He barges in, pushing me back against the wall. "What's wrong?" His lips curl up in a sinister grin.

"The meeting is at ten, Vince. It's only nine."

"Well, what do you know. I thought it was ten. Oh my, must have forgotten to change my watch to Central Daylight Time." His foot kicks the door shut behind him. "Is that fresh coffee I smell?"

I nod. What else can I do? I can't tell the group's self-appointed leader to go away and come back later.

He points to the cast on my wrist. "You fall down or something?"

"Something like that," I say.

He waits for me to lead the way inside, but I motion for him to walk in front of me instead. He spots the tray of pastries on the kitchen table and raises his eyebrows. With his eyes unblinking and his lips pressed tight like he knows exactly what he's doing, he snatches the almond croissant, my favorite. I pour him a cup of coffee, careful not to turn my back on him.

"Corey will be here any minute," I say.

"You and I need to talk." He sits down at the table. "Alone."

"Oh?" I keep my voice light. My phone is on the table. I reach for it. "That's probably him now."

He covers my phone with his hand. "He told me about your trip to West Virginia."

A chill runs through me as I watch my phone slowly slide away and drop onto Vince's lap. I take a step back, bump into the counter behind me. I pour coffee into my mug, a source of energy to help me deal with him if he's just being his jerky self, or a weapon to defend myself if he's up to more than that. I blow on my coffee and take a sip, then hold the mug with my right hand like a weapon.

"It was *your* idea, wasn't it?"

I blow on my coffee again and take another sip, try to keep my hand steady. "If you mean was it my idea for Corey to confront Trayne, the answer is yes, as a matter of fact, it was."

His chin goes up then drops down like I've just confirmed what he already knows. "And I imagine you thought that was a good idea, did you not."

"I thought it might help him heal."

"And the idea of testifying? That was yours, too, wasn't it."

"It came up," I say.

He grips the edge of the table and pushes his chair back a few inches, then a few more. I press my back against the counter, take in a deep breath, and then bolt. "I have to go to the bathroom," I shout from the hallway. "Pour yourself more coffee if you'd like."

Just then there's a loud rap on the door. *Thank God!* "There's Corey now," I call out in a flash of triumph. Over my shoulder I see Vince leaning against the kitchen doorframe, watching.

I fling the door open and my heart stops. "J. B.! What are you doing here?" I've never been so happy to see anyone in my life.

He glances over my shoulder, then reaches out to me like I'm his long-lost friend. He laughs and kisses me on each cheek. Totally out of character. "Thought I'd surprise you. Mentayer sends her love. She's sorry she couldn't come with me. Couldn't get away from work. You know how she is about that school." All of a sudden he takes a step back, and his eyes widen with mock surprise. "Oh! I didn't know you had company. I'm sorry, have I come at a bad time?"

His performance is as good as and even better than any I've seen in a theater. "Not a bad time at all," I say. "In fact, your timing is perfect. Our meeting doesn't start for another hour, so until then, I'm free. Please come in. Come in."

I return his *No need to overdo it* smile with a *You should talk* chuckle. "J. B. Harrell, meet Vince Weppler," I say. "Vince is here for the meeting.

Early."

Vince shrugs. "On a different time zone."

"Sylvia's a good friend of mine," J. B. says. "We go way back." Then he turns to me and winks. "So, are you going to make my day and tell me your meeting is about the next protest at Nectaral?" I give him a *Sort of* shrug and a half smile. He claps his hands and then winks at Vince. "Much as Sylvia might want to believe I came all this way just to see her . . ."

"Now you know I would never believe that, J. B." We both laugh.

Vince's eyes turn dark, and one of them crosses inward as if it doesn't trust the other and has to watch out for it.

"J. B.'s a journalist with the *New York Times*," I say.

"And the truth is," J. B. says, "I'm here on a story about the plutonium issue. I've come to Monrow City to interview a few top Nectaral executives. It would be good to get your take on the CEO. I suspect you think he's more of a villain than the saint portrayed in their corporate materials. Mind if I sit in on your meeting?"

Vince scowls and folds his arms over his chest. "It's closed."

J. B.'s eyes brighten and his eyebrows shoot up. "Maybe we could ask the others when they get here? If they say no, I'll be happy to, well, not exactly happy, but I *will* leave."

He saunters into the living room and heads for my antique pulpit chair. After all these years, I still don't know if it's his favorite because it's the only classy piece of furniture I own or because it comes from the Bronx and reminds him of how he met Mentayer. Vince tips his head toward the door, his eyes commanding: *Get rid of this guy.*

"Would you like some coffee," I say. "Maybe a donut?"

J. B. shakes his head and pats his stomach. "Mentayer tells me I eat too many desserts, and I've had my limit of coffee for the day."

He sits down, all cheerful. "So, Vince, what's your story? How'd you get involved with this issue?"

Vince mumbles, "Personal experience . . . like everybody."

"And what is your personal experience?"

Vince leans against the wall and picks at his fingernails. J. B. flashes me a look that says, *Your turn, Sylvia.*

"Vince was part of the cleanup crew in the Marshall Islands after the nuclear tests," I say. "In the seventies, right, Vince?"

"Really?" J. B. almost falls off the edge of the red velvet cushion. "Would you mind if I ask you some questions about what that was like? Off the record if you prefer."

Vince glowers. J. B. glances at me. My turn again.

"Vince actually served under the same guy Norton served under," I say.

J. B.'s eyebrows go up so high they almost fly off his forehead. "Michael Trayne? You served under Michael Trayne?" *Oh, you are good,* I tell him with my eyes.

Vince walks over to the sliding glass door and stares out at the patio. J. B. gets up and stands next to him. "I interviewed Trayne for my story. Interesting fellow. What was it like to serve under him?"

When Vince doesn't answer, J. B. gives me another sideways signal with his eyes. "I've always assumed, Vince," I say, "that you felt pretty much the same way about Trayne that Norton did."

Vince shoves his hands in his pockets. His eyes dart up and to the right. "I don't remember much about him," he mumbles.

"That's *interesting,*" J. B. says, in a tone of voice I know only too well. His eyes narrow. I know that look, too. I shake my head, but he ignores my warning and forges on. "Trayne doesn't remember you either. Which is strange, actually, because he told me he remembers every man who ever served under him."

I hold my breath and give J. B. my *What the hell do you think you are doing?* look. Vince bares his teeth and cracks his knuckles.

I look at my watch and gasp. "Oh my, look at the time. Everyone will be here soon. Where's my phone? I need to call Corey."

Vince blinks, and with a jerk of his head, he pulls out his own phone. "I'll call him," he says in a voice that won't take no for an answer. "Hey, Corey," he says into his phone. "Yeah? Right now? Great! Okay then. Come on in." He slips the phone back in his pocket. "He's here."

Air shoots out of my lungs and propels me down the hall like I've been fired from a cannon. I open the door. "Corey, where the hell—"

Two men push their way inside and almost knock the breath out of me. They shove me up against the wall and shut the door. Then they grab me under my arms and drag me back to the living room.

THIRTY-SEVEN

The two men throw me onto the couch, then yank me up to a sitting position and stand in front of me with their hands clasped behind their backs like soldiers taking their ease until the next command. But unlike soldiers, they look more like recently released prisoners trying to fit in on a college campus by hiding their cropped haircuts and bulging arm and leg muscles inside preppy polo shirts and khaki shorts.

"You, over there."

From the corner of my eye I see the flash of a gun, J. B.'s hands up in the air. "I'm going, Vince. I'm cool."

"Yeah, you're cool all right, Mr. Harrell. Cool collateral damage. I have no interest in you. I came for her." He points the gun at me. "So I gotta tell you, I don't take too kindly to having to deal with you, too. But lemonade out of lemons, as they say. The public's going to care a lot more about what happens to a *New York Times* reporter than they will about what happens to an old lady. Sit!"

The two men make space for J. B. to lower himself onto the couch next to me. Then they close ranks again. J. B. gives me a nudge that says, *Don't worry, I know what I'm doing,* and then looks at Vince. "Corey's not coming, is he?"

Vince's lips flicker into a smile. "Finally figured that one out, did you?"

"You told him the meeting was postponed, didn't you?" J. B.'s fingers run through his black hair and then linger there. "No, that's not it, you told him the meeting was tomorrow, not today, right?"

"Nice try, Mr. Reporter."

J. B. rubs his chin and smiles. "Ah, I know. You told Corey there wasn't going to *be* a meeting."

Vince laughs out loud. "Nailed it!" The barrel of his gun tips up and down as if nodding.

I swallow hard. If Corey thought Vince wasn't going to call a meeting, he would have told me . . . unless he couldn't. I swallow again. And he would have returned my call by now . . . unless he can't. Oh God, what did Vince do with him? What have I done? And why is J. B. talking about Corey like he's okay? Doesn't he know Vince is lying?

"So tell me," J. B. continues in his most pleasant voice, "was Corey okay with that?"

"He was quite happy, in fact, to hear that when I called everyone in the group, no one felt any need to meet until after the hearing."

"Come on," J. B. says with a roll of his eyes.

Vince waves the point of his gun inches from J. B.'s forehead. "You're not saying I'm lying now, are you, Mr. Reporter? And just when I thought we were getting along so well."

"That would be very unwise of me." J. B. flashes a conciliatory smile. "Given the circumstances."

"But . . . but," I stammer. "The rally is before the hearing. Don't we have to meet to decide what we're going to do at the rally?"

"Already decided. Corey knows. Everyone else, too. Except you."

"You mean . . . they're going along with your plan? The two bombs?"

"Boom," he whispers with glee. "And I'm sure you'll be happy to know that the two of you are going to have front-row seats."

I shake my head. No. No. The others would not have agreed to explode bombs in the middle of the crowd. Corey wouldn't either. Not after . . . No, he wouldn't.

"What have you done with Corey?" The question comes out like a dirge and then changes its mind and shouts instead. "Where is he?" The two men take a step toward me.

Vince waves the gun back and forth. "Enough with Corey, Corey, Corey."

J. B. leans forward. "Enough with everything, whoever you are. Your name is not Vince Weppler. Michael Trayne wasn't in the Marshall Islands in the 1970s, and neither were you. You never served in the military at all. So who are you and what do you want?"

Vince presses the barrel of his gun into the side of J. B.'s neck. "What do I want?" he hisses. "I want to kill both of you right now."

"No! Don't! I'm the only one you want. Isn't that what you said? Go ahead and shoot me. I deserve it. Just let J. B. go." Short breaths shoot in and out of my mouth and I can't get them to stop. *What have I done? What have I done? Corey's dead. I know he is. Now J. B.'s next. Then me. Then more people, at Nectaral Plaza. Why didn't I go to the police? What was I thinking?*

Vince lets out a snort, followed by a loud laugh that almost knocks him off his feet. One of the men reaches out to make sure he doesn't drop his gun. The other man steps in front us, arms outstretched and hands up and at the ready to make sure we don't jump from the couch. Then Vince stops laughing and leans close to me. The two men go back to standing with their hands clasped behind their backs. I feel cold metal pressing into my cheek, the barrel of the gun, warm breath on my face, and then all of a sudden it's gone.

Vince steps back and grins down at me. "Much as I'd like to," he says with a sigh, "I have other plans for you." Then he signals to the two men with a tip of his head. "Take her out first."

One of them reaches in his pocket and pulls out a syringe. The other one grabs my casted wrist and covers my mouth with his other hand so I can't scream. The man with the syringe holds my hair back. I feel the needle go into my neck and come out, then two sets of hands rough under my armpits lifting me up from the couch.

"Make it look like she's walking."

Vince's voice, a foghorn far, far away. Room spinning. Feet flip-flopping over each other. Brushing the floor without landing. Elevator plunging. Stomach lurching. Door opening. Air. White-hot pain burning my wrist. Door slamming. Then nothing.

237

THIRTY-EIGHT

I scream, rattle the bars of my crib. *Help! Is anyone there?* There never is. I'm alone in the dark. Again. Just like all the other times, only this time there's a stench like moldy, damp clay trapped in a swamp at the bottom of an outhouse. My nostrils close, open, release tiny whiffs of the putrid smell of desperation, then close again. A valve in the back of my throat blocks the stink from my churning stomach. My head turns, my mouth opens, but there's no sound. This is not my usual dream. This is not a dream at all. The smell is unbearable and all too real.

"Sylvia?" J. B. is an arm's length away from me, his voice tight, a tense echo in the middle of a chamber. Slivers of dim, almost nonexistent light peek through tiny cracks in a curved stone wall and land on his face.

I roll onto my side. Try to pull myself up. Fall back down. "I can't get up," I say.

J. B. stands over me. Splatters of dirt on his face instead of his usual grin. His clothes grimy, wrinkled, no crease in his pants now. His hands under my arms gently pull me up to a sitting position. My cast is smeared in muddy brown, gray, and black.

I press my back against the hard, cold wall. "Where are we?"

He sits down, folds his legs up against his chest, rests his chin on his knees. His forehead is unusually smooth, as if he's been kneading it. "Inside the tower. At Nectaral Plaza."

My hand touches the floor. My eyes take in the circle of packed dirt. In the middle, propped up against a giant riding lawn mower, garden hoes, rakes, tools, landscape equipment. Nectaral Tower, for all its exterior medieval grandeur, is just a storage shed.

"Vince's henchmen drugged us. They brought us here two days ago," J. B. says.

My fingers dig into my temples, try to dredge up scraps of information. But all I find are sensations. A fog in my head, lifting, then engulfing me again. Grogginess, everything going black. Losing time, seconds, minutes, hours. Waking up nauseated. A woman's voice: "Drink this juice." A straw pushed between my lips. Sucking. Shivering. Then deep, peaceful, wonderful sleep. The woman's voice again: "Swallow this." Who was she? Where did she come from? Something mushy sliding down my throat. Sleeping again.

J. B. sighs, and it's like the sound of someone releasing his last breath. "Today's the rally," he says.

I slap the ground with my good hand. "And these are the front-row seats Vince promised us."

"He stopped by yesterday and sat here laughing and making up newspaper headlines. His favorite was 'Terrorist Sylvia Jensen Dies from Own Bomb at Nectaral Plaza, *New York Times* Reporter Collateral Damage.'" J. B. coughs into his hand. "I suggested 'Bombing Threat Thwarted, Alias Vince Weppler in Custody,' and he laughed and said, 'You wish, Mr. Hotshot Reporter.'"

It starts to come back to me. I must not have been drugged the whole time, must have gone in and out of consciousness. "I heard one of his headlines," I say. "'Terrorist Sylvia Jensen Takes Sole Responsibility for Planning and Carrying Out Bombing.'"

"That was a good one, wasn't it?" J. B. says.

"Oh God, J. B.! I did."

"Did what?"

"I confessed. Vince recorded it on a burner phone. At the cabin. It was a test I had to pass in order to get into the group. If I hadn't, I never would have found out what they were plotting."

J. B.'s mouth opens, shuts. He shakes his head. "So *that's* Vince's plan. After the bombing, he gives the phone to the police and then leads them to you in the tower and they arrest you. But then you'd tell them how you got here. No, he needs you, both of us, dead, so he'll have to let us out of here just when the bombs explode. That'll be our one chance to escape. Either way, you'll be held responsible."

Either way, dead or alive. J. B.'s knees are pressed against his chest, his arms wrapped around them. He's strategizing, his brow furrowed, trying to figure a way out. But there isn't one. Not this time. My shoulders curl into my chest and I rock back and forth. This is it. It's over. Nothing to do but wait to be released to our fate. The noonday sun's sharp rays drip down on us from an opening at the top of the tower like a form of slow water torture. Sweat oozes from my pores like blood from open wounds.

I hear a low rumble outside. It's the protesters, starting to gather. Their voices roar inside me, tell me it's not over, not yet. I stand up and press my mouth against a small crack between the stones in the wall. "Help! Somebody, please help! We're trapped. In here! Please!" My screams hit the opposite wall and bounce back at me. I stumble over to the door and kick it, then fall to the ground.

J. B. exhales, long and slow.

With a grief locked inside me as tight as the door to this tower, I press the back of my head against the stones, my fingernails into my upper arms. No point in calling out. No one can hear. Nothing left to do but pray. I tip my head skyward. And then I see it. A small black backpack dangling from the top of the tower by a rope. A cell phone duct-taped to its side, one wire sticking out.

"Oh my God! Up there! A bomb!"

J. B.'s eyes follow my point. The skin on his face sags. A man defeated. His last hope gone. "Looks like Vince thought of everything," he says. "He knew these stone walls would be thick enough to protect us from the explosions outside. Well, now we know." He turns away from me.

I crumple forward, face in the dirt. *Now we know.* We're going to die. I scrape the palm of my good hand on a rock. I sit back up, bring it to my mouth, lick the open wound, taste the iron on my tongue. I stare up at the backpack, at least twenty feet over our heads. Too high. Impossible to reach. *What have I done?* The perspiration on my skin freezes into a million icicles. *It's over. Corey's dead. Soon we'll be dead. How many others?*

J. B. interrupts my lament. "Michael Trayne is dead," he says, even now reading my mind. "He died suddenly at home. That's what I came to your apartment to tell you. His heart was strong, and he was in good health for his age, so I'm suspicious. There was no autopsy, and someone who said they were from the VA had him cremated right away, so we'll never know what happened."

No, no! Not him, too.

"Sylvia." J. B.'s voice, gentle but firm, cuts through my despair. "It's not your fault. This thing is bigger than you could have known, bigger than anyone could have known."

I don't ask him what he means. Whatever he's been investigating doesn't matter anymore. It will never be published anyway. Someone was making sure of that. We sit in silence, nothing more to be said.

A few minutes later, the door squeaks. It opens a crack. Slowly. An inch. A creak. A sliver of light. My heart races. Another creak. J. B. jumps to his feet, a thick-handled hoe in his hand. Ready to attack.

Another inch. A ray of light. Light? Moving toward the light? The door opens. The brightness blinds me. Is this it? Is this how it ends?

THIRTY-NINE

"Sylvia? J. B.? Are you in here? It's me, Corey."

A black silhouette against the blinding light. Not real. The open door must be the gateway to wherever Corey is now. He's come to lead us to the other side. But then he comes closer, and the sweaty hair sticking to his cheeks and forehead looks real. So does his flushed face. And when he reaches out to pull me up from the ground, the trembling in his fingers feels too real not to be. Then he laughs. His breath warms my face.

"Hey," he says, all casual-like and grinning like he knows something we don't know.

"We have to get out of here!" J. B. is on his feet. He waves his hands, points frantically to the backpack over our heads. He pushes me out the door with one hand, pulls Corey out with the other. "Run!"

J. B. grabs one of Corey's hands and I grab the other and we pull him with us to a square concrete building fifty yards away from the tower. When we reach it we run around the corner and press our backs against the wall.

Corey leans forward with his hands on his knees, laughing, catching his breath. "It's okay, guys. Really. Everything is okay. We took care of them."

"What?" J. B. and I both say.

"The bombs. We defused them. Well, Freddie did. There he is, over there."

Freddie's standing on the edge of the main plaza, now packed with thousands of peaceful protesters, old, young, middle-aged, with their children and grandchildren, people in wheelchairs, babies in strollers.

Corey whistles to him, and he waves back, runs toward us. Just then a microphone squeals and a deep voice thunders through the loudspeakers. "Everyone clear the area! You are in danger! Clear the area now."

All hell breaks loose. Screaming sirens. Screeching brakes. Shrieks from terrified protesters. Feet trampling grass, stomping through flower beds, tripping and falling. Babies wailing. Children screaming. Mothers yelling.

Freddie reaches us, smiling, his hands raised. "Stay where you are. It's okay."

Corey pumps his fists in the air. "Way to go, Nicole!"

"Yup, she did it!" Freddie's grin stretches from ear to ear and takes over his face. Then he sees our baffled looks. "Nicole called the police and reported seeing a suspected terrorist in the plaza who looks like Vince," he says with a little chortle.

Corey explains. "It was her job to tell them he had a couple of backpacks and that she was scared he'd planted bombs or something. Bunny's job was to call us if she saw Vince. My job was to save you. And Freddie's job was to defuse the bombs."

I'm so relieved I almost fall to my knees before them. "What? So you all changed your minds about the bombs? When?"

"For me it was when I found out Vince lied," Corey says.

"But how did you know about the bomb in the tower?" I say.

"Thank God you did," J. B. adds. "We didn't know you'd defused it. We were sure we were going to die!"

I reach out to hug Freddie, but instead of falling into my arms, terror takes over his face, and before any of us realizes what's happening, he disappears.

"You can't get it down," J. B. calls after him. "It's too high."

Suddenly realizing that there was another bomb, Corey's face turns ashen. Then he grasps what that means and his eyes turn black with horror. He takes off running toward the tower, yelling, "Don't, Freddie! Come back! Come back!"

J. B. runs after him, pulls him back around the corner of the concrete building and tackles him to the ground. I'm spinning in circles, screaming out for help, but all the police are outside the plaza gates, busy corralling the fleeing protesters to safety. "What are we going to do? What are we going to do?"

"You're going to kiss your ass good-bye, *that's* what you're going to do." I freeze. Vince smirks. His hand moves toward the bulge underneath his No Nukes T-shirt. "Yeah, that's exactly what you think it is, and I am *really* going to enjoy using it this time."

My eyes dart every which way for help, but the area's been cleared. There's no one around to see Vince pull the gun from under his shirt. No one to hear him say, "Okay, up against the wall, all of you." We do as he says.

He points the gun at me first and sneers. "I don't take kindly to anyone who tries to set me up. Until now I was just doing a job. Only you had to go and make it personal, did you not." Then he points the gun at Corey. "Or to someone who lies to me." He lets out a snort. One side of his upper lip twists. "I love the way you all hate the government so much." He laughs and the shiny silver fillings in his crooked teeth look like little bullets. "Such silly people you are. Who do you think's been keeping Bunny's little princess alive? Where do you think your money's been coming from? All they needed was for you to set off a few bombs. After that, they could have done whatever they wanted to anyone who dared to protest and no one would have complained." He points the gun at J. B. "And you, Mr. Big Shot Reporter. You just couldn't resist such a juicy story, now could you." He purses his lips. "Well, enough of that. You first, Sylvia."

He points the gun at my heart, then has a change of mind and aims it higher, at my head. I take in a deep breath, wonder if I'll feel the shot before I hear it or hear it before I feel it. Determined to face the devil head on before I die, I stare into Vince's eyes just as a bright red dot appears on his forehead. I hear J. B. gulp. He sees what I see. I stay very still and wait, keep my eyes on the laser-type light. I hear a *ping* and close my eyes. It's over.

Then I hear a boom. The earth quakes. The tower explodes. I'm thrown off my feet and onto the ground. I taste grass on my tongue. Hear screaming in my ears. See J. B. leaning over Vince's body—checking to see if he's dead? Reaching into his pocket—maybe for his gun? There's the sound of sirens, people yelling, the warmth of Corey breathing on the back of my neck as he moans, "No, Freddie! No!"

FORTY

I'm in the back of a police van, sitting on a hard bench between Corey and J. B. Nicole and Bunny are on the bench across from us. No Freddie.

"What happened?" I ask. "I must have passed out."

Just then the van comes to a stop and J. B. puts his hand on my arm. "We're at the precinct, Sylvia. They're going to take our statements."

A heavyset woman with sympathetic eyes leads me to a tiny room inside. Only two places to sit, a bare cot and a metal folding chair. I sit on the cot. I'm filthy and I stink—my hands and feet muddy, my jeans and T-shirt soiled and grass-stained, my hair greasy and matted, the cast on my arm covered with grime. But, thanks to the throbbing in my wrist and the empty hole in my stomach, I know I'm still alive, and for that I am grateful.

The kind woman leaves and comes back with a bologna and cheese sandwich, a bag of potato chips, and a bottle of water. "Thank you," I say. "I haven't had anything to eat or drink since . . . since I can't remember."

"Is there anything else I can get you?"

I grin. "A shower? Some clean clothes?"

"You *are* a sight, ma'am." She smiles her apology. "But I'm afraid we only have those for prisoners, not for witnesses."

"Can I see the others?"

"Your friends are fine. Waiting to be interviewed. You'll be called when it's your turn." She starts to leave, then turns around. "I was sorry to hear about that older man who died in the blast."

"Freddie. He was one of us."

She says she's sorry again and closes the door. I lie down on the cot and fall asleep thinking about him. A knock on the door wakes me. Another knock. Then a wrinkly-faced police officer peeks through the partially opened door.

"Come in," I say.

"Evening, ma'am." He extends his hand, then sees how filthy I am and pulls it back. "I'm Officer Renton, but you can call me Officer Burt." I'm warmed by his midwestern-nice smile and the way he covers up his disgust at the sight of me. "Sorry you had to wait so long. Took a while for us to roust the FBI and get their agents here." He chuckles. "And then we couldn't roust you, so we interviewed all the others first. But we're ready for you now, ma'am."

He takes me to a windowless, gray-walled room with a rectangular table in the middle and pulls a chair out for me. Two men, dressed in identical navy blue T-shirts with FBI emblazoned in yellow on the front, sit across from me. Their eyes scrutinize me and, I'm quite sure, determine that a woman in her seventies who looks like she lives on the streets is going to be an unreliable witness.

"I'm *Senior* Agent Henry Fantell," the man on the left says. I scrutinize his seasoned look—gray hair, cool eyes, creased face, wire-rimmed glasses—and determine, based on both his appearance and his remote demeanor, that he wishes for me to be intimidated by him. "This is Leonard," he adds. His sidekick's smooth, shiny head reminds me of pink frosting on a round white cake, and that image, plus his muscular and painfully handsome physique, leads me to think he isn't all that sharp.

Officer Burt places a cup of coffee and two little plastic containers of fake creamer in front of me. Then he sits down at the end of the table. "If you're feeling up for it now, ma'am?"

"We'll be recording your statement," Senior Agent Fantell says. "So please speak up."

Handsome Leonard pushes a black audio device closer to me. He picks up his pen and I'm thinking he's going to ask me to sign a permission form or something. But when he positions his pen on a yellow legal pad instead, I realize he's going to take notes in addition to recording my interview, which seems redundant to me.

"Tell us everything," the senior agent says in a no-nonsense tone. "From beginning to end."

I expected them to ask specific questions, not to leave it wide open like that. "How far back do you want me to go," I ask, not knowing if the beginning for me is the same as the beginning for them.

"Everything," the senior agent says.

I start with how I met Corey and the concerns that led me to infiltrate his group. Whenever Senior Agent Fantell interrupts to ask a question, which he does often, to my increasing annoyance, I hear my voice getting stronger, steadier, and louder. All Leonard does is take notes and check every once in a while to make sure the recorder is still on.

Officer Burt nods encouragingly but doesn't ask any questions. Until I talk about the group and its plan to explode bombs at Nectaral Plaza. Then he pushes his chair back with a screeching scrape on the concrete floor.

"You say you wrote everything down as soon as you got back from the cabin," he says, "but I don't believe the police heard anything about any of that before just now."

"I didn't think you would believe me."

He crosses his arms over his chest.

"And I was afraid for my life."

Officer Burt nods and sits back.

"Keep going," the senior agent says, his eyes and voice even colder than before.

I talk for a very long time about Vince. I want to make sure they know how evil he was and how the others in the group stopped him. Finally, I run out of things to say and push a greasy strand of hair off my face, tuck it into my ponytail. "I think I've told you everything I know."

"Okay, then," Senior Agent Fantell says. "Now, you told us that Corey saved you and Mr. Harrell, but you didn't tell us how he knew you were locked in the tower."

"That's because I don't know," I say. "You should ask him. I haven't had a chance to talk to him yet."

"Okay, then. You also told us that Freddie deactivated the bombs, but you didn't tell us how or when the group members decided to do that."

"All I know is what Corey told me before the tower exploded. He decided to stop the bombings after he realized Vince had lied. I don't know about the others. And Freddie . . ." I choke on his name, and Officer Burt reaches over and pats my arm. "Like I told you, Freddie ran into the tower. I never had a chance to talk to him."

"Okay, now then, about this Vince, or whatever his real name is. You think he wanted to kill you."

"I don't just think it. I know it. He threatened to kill me two times. At the cabin. At my house. He tried to kill us by locking us in the tower with a bomb. And when that didn't work, he tried to shoot me, all of us, with a gun."

"Okay, now, so, he obviously didn't succeed, and you think it's because he may have been killed by a sniper."

"I don't just think it. I *know* it."

Senior Agent Fantell and Officer Burt glance at each other. Leonard presses his pen even harder on the yellow legal pad.

"He was shot right in front of me." I tap my forefinger on my forehead. "J. B. saw it, too."

Leonard underlines something on the legal pad. Twice. Senior Agent Fantell purses his lips. Officer Burt studies his hands and then leans toward me. "Is there anything else you can remember about that, ma'am?"

"Of course I can. As I already told you, before the bomb exploded in the tower, Corey, J. B., and I ran for safety behind this concrete building. Then, while the police were busy clearing the plaza, Vince showed up with a gun and threatened to kill us. Me first. I looked him straight in the eye, and that was when I saw this laser-type light on his forehead. Then the bomb in the tower exploded and I saw Vince on the ground. After that, I passed out."

"And you're sure he was dead," Officer Burt says.

I ball my hands into fists. "I am not only sure he's dead, I'm *glad* he's dead."

"And, so," Senior Agent Fantell, says, leaning in on me, "who do you think shot this Vince guy?"

"What? How should I know? You don't think I had something to do with it, do you?"

"Just answer the question. Who shot this Vince guy? What's your best guess?"

"I don't know. I guess . . . uh . . . well, Corey said Nicole called the police and described Vince to them so . . ." I look at Officer Burt. "I guess I must have thought you guys shot him. To stop him from killing us."

Once again Senior Agent Fantell glances, this time with a slight rolling of his eyes, at Officer Burt. Then he slaps his hands on the table and motions to Leonard to turn off the recorder.

"Okay then." He pushes his chair back. "Don't leave town. We may have more questions later. In the meantime, I suggest that you think very seriously about what you saw and what you didn't see."

FORTY-ONE

At midnight, Officer Burt ushers me out to the precinct lobby and into the hands of the others, who have been waiting for me there. Bunny is sleeping with her head on Corey's shoulder. Nicole is lying on her side on an adjacent bench. J. B. slips his iPhone into his pocket and rushes to steady me before I even realize that I'm a bit wobbly. Nicole sits up, makes room for me on the bench.

"You look a fright, Sylvia." J. B.'s grin says more than his words.

"What do you mean? You looked just as bad as me the last time I saw you."

"Oh no, I have never looked that bad."

I laugh. "Very funny." I point at his shiny, tapered hair, his crispy clean light blue shirt, and the casual tan slacks with his signature crease down the front. "So what's with this?"

"Well, *some*body's interview took so long I had time to go to the hotel, take a shower, and change clothes. Would've had time for a four-course dinner, too."

I slap his arm. Everyone chuckles. Except Nicole.

She rubs the back of her neck. "We need to talk," she says. "Seriously."

Bunny moves her head in circles and it makes a sound like the bones in her neck crunching loose. "Please, can we eat," she says. "I'm famished."

"We can go to my place," I say. "I've got a bunch of all-night delivery menus."

"Perfect," Corey says. "I'm dying . . ." His voice trails off.

Bunny reaches for his hand and brings it up to her lips. "We know, Corey."

It's only a short ten-minute ride from the precinct to my place. The five of us squeeze into a taxi, J.B. in the front seat and Bunny on Corey's lap next to me and Nicole in the back. When we get to my apartment, I usher them into the living room and show them where the bathroom is. Then I open a desk drawer and pull out a stack of menus.

"We can order food from several places through one delivery service." Everyone stares at me like they haven't heard, so I add, "So each of us can get whatever we want."

"What I want," Corey says, "is to know who the hell Vince was." His eyes flash, his arms flail, and his words burst out like water suddenly released from a dam. "What was he up to? Where did he get the money? How did this all happen?"

"We all want to know that," Bunny says.

"But why did I fall for it?" Corey drops onto the couch and curls into himself. "Why? Why? Why?" He grips clumps of his hair with his fists and whimpers.

Bunny puts her arm around him. "We were all taken in by him, Corey."

Nicole sits on the other side and puts her hand on his back. "He used all of us."

"But why?" Corey unfolds himself and sits up. "The FBI agents kept asking me that, and I didn't know what to say. I don't think they believed anything I told them about Vince."

"They didn't believe me either," I say.

"Or me," Nicole says.

"So they think we made him up?" Corey is incredulous. "So that's it. No one knows who Vince was."

J. B. clears his throat. "Someone does," he mumbles. All eyes turn to him. Up until now he's been sitting in the pulpit chair, saying nothing, just looking down at his iPad.

Nicole shakes her head like she doesn't believe he knows any more than the rest of us do. "Well, I would certainly think *some*one does," she says. Then she looks at me and points at J. B. "Who is this guy anyway, Sylvia?"

"Someone who only says things," I say with a smile, "that he can back up."

J. B. doesn't respond, just keeps looking at his screen. "It's on the radio right now," he says. "One of those late-night talk shows." He touches the speaker icon and turns up the volume. We all lean forward and listen to the booming voice of the radio talk show host, a well-known conspiracy theorist.

"Yesterday a man was killed in a terrorist bombing at the Nectaral Corporation headquarters in Monrow City. The attack took place at a rally of supposedly peaceful protesters. But do not be fooled, these people are really terrorists, and their only goal is to distract us from what we must do. Countries like North Korea and Iran are out to destroy this great nation of ours, and even though we have a defense system that can knock their nuclear missiles right out of the air, it needs further development. And that takes money, folks. Money these terrorists don't want us to invest in a strong defense system. So if we are to learn anything from today's attack, it's this. If we are to survive, we have no choice. Today's bombing, folks, is a wake-up call."

Nicole's lips purse. "That is so . . . so . . . twisted! It's the exact opposite of the message we wanted to communicate."

"But maybe the exact message Vince wanted to get out there," J. B. says.

"The guy on the radio didn't even get the facts straight," Bunny says.

"Yeah," Corey says. "Two men were killed, not one."

"Obviously he didn't care about the details," I say.

J. B. closes his iPad with a click. "Or maybe Vince *isn't* dead."

Corey jumps up so fast his knee hits the coffee table and he winces. "Are you saying Vince is alive?"

"The FBI agents didn't believe me when I said he was shot by a sniper," J. B. says with a shrug. "And if he was dead, wouldn't they have his body?"

Corey's nostrils flare, then he spins around as if checking for an intruder in the hallway. "Do we need to call the police? If he's alive, he knows where Sylvia lives. He knows what we've done. What if he comes to finish us off?"

"No, no, no." I shake my head. "Vince is dead. I saw it with my own two eyes. I heard the shot. The FBI may think we're covering something up, but they're wrong."

"Maybe it's the FBI that's covering something up," J. B. says.

Nicole leans forward and slams her hands on the coffee table. "What we don't need right now is more conspiracy theories. Holy shit. Anyone else want some coffee?" She stands up and stomps off to the kitchen.

The platter of pastries and pitcher of orange juice I prepared the morning Vince and his men abducted J. B. and me—how long ago was that? Two days? Three? A lifetime?—are still on the kitchen table. Nicole picks up a hardened donut, sniffs it and makes a face, throws it back. She looks inside the pot of stale coffee and curls her lips.

"For the meeting that never was," I say. She gives me a blank look. "I'll tell you all about it when we talk."

"We need to go over everything Vince did to trick us," she says. "I'm really worried that each of us may have told the FBI a different story. Maybe that's why they're suspicious. But first, I need coffee. And food."

"Before I touch anything," I say as I head for the bathroom. "I need a shower and clean clothes."

Nicole gets everyone moving. Bunny finds out what they want to eat. Corey calls in the orders. J. B. goes out to the patio to make some calls. In record time, we're all sitting around the coffee table drinking freshly brewed decaf coffee and passing around cartons of Thai food, slices of pizza, and foot-long Subway sandwiches.

Nicole claps her hands. "Let's compare stories now," she says. "We already know that Corey told Vince he'd changed his mind about the bombing and that he wanted to testify at the congressional hearing instead. So, let's take turns talking about any interaction each of us had with Vince after that. What he did, what he said, everything. Okay?"

An eye-popping exchange of information follows—myriad disclosures, questions asked, feelings expressed—as we piece together all the steps Vince took to lure us into his trap. J. B. records everything on his iPad, and when we're finished, he reads a summary of his notes.

"Okay, this was Vince's strategy," he says. "Let me know if I got something wrong or missed anything. Once Vince knew a change of plan was in the works, he told Corey he would set up a meeting and then sent him off to Chicago, supposedly to apprise the donor about the possible change of plan as a 'matter of courtesy.' He drove Corey to the airport and on the way, stole his phone."

"I didn't know he took it, though," Corey says. "I thought I'd lost it."

"Right," J. B. says. "So that's how Vince got Corey out of the way and made sure he couldn't communicate with the rest of you."

"And, just to add," Corey says, "Vince told me the donor was going to meet me while on a layover at the Chicago airport, but no one showed up."

"What'd I say?" Nicole mumbles. "What'd I tell you?"

"Okay," J. B. goes on. "Then Vince called Bunny, Nicole, and Freddie and said the donor had ordered them to proceed with the bombing and told them where to place the bombs for the greatest impact. He didn't say anything about a meeting or Corey's change of heart, just told them he'd see them at the rally."

Nicole raises her hand. "I was sure it was *Vince's* plan, not the donor's, and, just for the record, I had no intention of carrying it out."

J. B. nods and goes back to his notes. "Then Vince called Sylvia. He said Corey had told him everything and you were all going to meet at her apartment. But, of course, there was no meeting. It was Vince's way of making sure Sylvia would be home alone. His plan was to kidnap her."

I let out a long sigh. "I suspected Vince all along," I say. "But when Corey told me Vince was fine with him testifying, and he was going to set up a meeting, well, I have to admit I fell for it. I'm afraid I really did think you were all going to come to my apartment. I called Corey and left a message for him to come early so we could talk about how to convince the rest of you to testify at the hearing with Corey and Trayne. But then of course none of you showed up, because Vince never called a meeting."

"I did show up, fortuitously, and that spoiled his plan," J. B. says.

"Then I almost got us killed on the spot when I let him know I was on to him. The only reason he didn't kill us then was because his plan was for Sylvia to die in the explosion, and then he would turn her taped confession over to the police." He looks up from his notes and smiles. "I was just collateral damage. So that's how I ended up in the tower with Sylvia and a bomb hanging over our heads." J. B. looks up and closes his iPad. "Did I miss anything?"

"Pretty ingenious strategy," Bunny says. "You gotta be impressed." She reaches for a slice of pepperoni pizza and devours it in three ferocious bites.

Nicole jumps to her feet and pumps her fist in the air. "That bastard may have been clever, but we outwitted him. He blamed some fictitious donor for everything, but I knew Vince was calling the shots all along."

"I wouldn't rule out a donor," J. B. says with raised eyebrows.

"Vince *did* say he was just doing a job for someone," I add. "He even implied that the government was paying the bills. Of course, that could have just been another lie."

"Well!" Nicole's hands pinch her waist. "Like I said. I wasn't about to follow his instructions regardless. I made that clear at the cabin. I already knew he was up to no good, and then, yesterday morning at the plaza, before Vince got there, Corey told us all about his trip to West Virginia and how Vince sent him on that wild goose chase to Chicago. My suspicions were confirmed when Corey said he was sure Vince had killed Sylvia and J. B. while he was in Chicago. Then he played the recording on J. B.'s iPhone, and we heard him threatening you two. Well, that did it for all of us. That's when we came up with our plan to defuse the bombs and report Vince to the police."

I cover my forehead with my good hand. "What? Wait a minute. J. B.'s iPhone? What am I missing?"

"When I returned from Chicago," Corey says, "Vince gave me my phone back, said I'd left it on his car seat. Yeah, right. I listened to all those messages from you, Sylvia, and realized Vince had been lying to me the whole time. I called you back. I kept calling and calling, and finally I came to your apartment. You weren't here, so I talked your neighbor into unlocking the door. J. B.'s iPhone was on your bed . . ." His eyes fill with tears and he stops to wipe them away. "I was sure you were dead."

My jaw drops and I feel my eyes straining to pop out of my head. "J. B.! You recorded everything Vince said in my apartment?"

He gives me a little grin and then breaks out in a full smile. "After Vince's henchmen took you away, I told Vince I had to go to the bathroom, and on the way I tossed my phone on your bed. I hoped someone would find it and listen to the recording in time to save us."

"But I was sure I was too late," Corey said.

He tugs on his beard like he's trying to rip it off, and Bunny puts her hand on his cheek. "But you weren't, Corey. You *saved* them. Tell them how you knew to look for them in the tower. Go on, tell them."

"Vince tipped me off without realizing it." He shakes his head like he still can't believe what happened. "I asked him where Sylvia was, and he said he didn't know, but he did that evil smile thing and his eyes flickered off to the side, toward the tower. So as soon as he left, I ran over to it."

"But the door was locked," I say. "How did you get it open?"

"That was the easy part. There's only a sliding latch on the outside. No padlock or anything. The hard part was getting up the courage to look inside. If you were dead—and I was sure you were—it was my fault. I couldn't bear . . ." His body sags from the weight of his shame. "I never should have gone to Chicago. Because of me, Sylvia and J. B. almost died. And Trayne is dead, too."

J. B. leans forward. "How do you know about Trayne?"

Corey sighs. "I called him when I couldn't reach you or Sylvia, and his niece answered. She said he died suddenly of unknown causes. She had just talked to him the day before and he told her he was coming to see her before he testified. She said he was excited about it. I can't help but—"

"Trayne's death is not your fault, Corey," J. B. says. "But it's not a coincidence either."

What does he mean by that? What isn't he telling us? He obviously knows a lot more than he's letting on. I know from what he told me when we were in the tower that he thinks someone killed Trayne, but does he know who? I can tell he thinks Trayne's death is connected with Vince, but how? And now that Trayne is dead, what will happen to all his files?

Corey shakes his head. "But what if Vince isn't even dead . . . or, okay, maybe he is dead but . . . what if he already sent that recording of Sylvia's confession to the police . . ." He wraps his arms around his middle and starts rocking. "Maybe it's not over. Maybe it's not anywhere near over." Bunny makes soothing sounds in his ear, runs her fingers through his hair.

"Oh my God," I say. "Maybe that's why the FBI didn't believe me. Do you think they already have Vince's burner phone with my confession on it?"

J. B. reaches in his pocket. "This phone?" He holds it up with a smile. "The one I took out of Vince's pocket when the tower exploded?"

At first I'm in shock. Then I start laughing. Then I can't stop. "You tampered with evidence in a federal investigation," I finally manage to say.

"Yup." He takes the burner phone apart and stomps on it, crushes it to pieces.

Nicole's eyes shine with the radiance of someone who has just seen the light. She runs over to J. B. and kisses him on each cheek. He blushes. Then she goes back and sits down. "Look at what we did. Once we were faced with the truth, we instinctively knew what was the right thing to do, and we did it. *All* of us."

"Because *that's* the kind of people you are," I say. "The kind of people who want to *save* lives, not take them. Isn't that what you wanted to do all along?"

"Freddie gave his life to save lives," Corey says.

Nicole pats his hand. "And if he were here, Corey, he'd want us to think about what we're going to do next."

"National news is coming in now about what happened. Lots of stuff about domestic terrorism." J. B. turns the screen towards us so we can follow the live news coverage. Then he reaches into his briefcase for his laptop, opens it, and starts typing on it instead of his iPad.

All of a sudden Corey jumps up with the relieved and determined look of someone who has been set free. "That is *not* going to be the story. We'll tell our *own* story. We'll get the truth out there. We'll all testify at that congressional hearing. And after today, the media will really be interested in covering it, don't you agree, J. B.?"

J. B. nods. "Absolutely."

"Even without Trayne . . ." Corey's voice trails off.

"Oh, Trayne will be there, too," J. B. says with a smile. "I recorded his testimony. I have the memo he saved. All his files, too." Then he smiles and winks at me, clearly enjoying my surprise.

I lie down on the floor. I'm beyond tired. Beyond hungry. There's nothing more I can do. Nothing more I need to do. I close my eyes to the sound of snippets of ideas about my friends' testimony playing in my ears like a musical symphony: The risks of radiation exposure were known beforehand . . . plutonium from the Enewetak tests has been found as far away as China . . . scientific findings . . . close to one million persons consigned to plutonium-induced lung cancer . . . long-term studies about the carcinogenic effects of nuclear testing on atomic veterans' families . . .

"Sylvia."

I open my eyes and see J. B. looking down at me. He looks troubled.

"The story I'm working on could lead to an investigation into the corruption and criminal behavior of powerful people, even at the highest level of government," he says in a low voice intended only for me. "You need to watch your back."

I open my eyes. "Pffft. Why would anyone bother with an old lady like me?"

"Because," he says, "your infiltration of Corey's group led me to uncover critical information that I never would have found otherwise. You *all* need to be careful."

My eyes won't stay open; I'm too tired to respond, too tired to worry. The click-clack of J. B.'s fingers on the keys to his laptop tell me that he's protecting the others from things they can't know or don't need to know or that would place them in danger if they did know. I hear the

261

voices of good, well-meaning people doing their part, assuming their place in the course of history, playing a role they never anticipated playing and don't even know they're playing. And I see Bertha Pickering, in her floppy-brimmed hat with its kick-ass buttons, looking down on me. "You—all of you—are the torchlights you were meant to be in this increasingly dark world," she says. I drift off to sleep then, knowing that that is enough.

Notes

1. I'll never forget the day I met Bertha, thirty-nine years ago. She held something in her hand that looked like a hollowed-out metal ball. "You know what this is?" I shook my head. "It's a cluster bomb. The Nectaral Corporation designs them." She shoved it in my hand. I almost dropped it. "About six hundred and sixty of these bomblets . . . cute name, huh?. . . are shot out of large bomb containers. Imagine, almost seven hundred of these bomblets spinning out at warp speed all around us, little steel balls exploding from each one, indiscriminately killing, injuring." She paused. I handed, almost threw, the cluster bomb back to her and she caught it with one hand. With her other hand, she held up a photo of a dead Vietnamese baby. "*This* is who they kill." She looked down at the metal shell in her hand. "You see, not all the bomblets explode right away. No, they lie in wait. In the ground. And when little children pick them up . . . Boom!" She whispered the word. "One more dead kid." (page 6-7). This speech is inspired by a quote by Marv Davidov published in Carol Masters and Marv Davidov, *You Can't Do That! Marv Davidov, Non-Violent Revolutionary* (Minneapolis, MN: Nodin Press, 2009), 130–131.

2. UN treaty to ban nuclear weapons (page 13). Landmark United Nations agreement to ban nuclear weapons, known officially as the Treaty on the Prohibition of Nuclear Weapons, was adopted by 122 nations on July 7, 2017. (https://www.un.org/disarmament/wmd/nuclear/tpnw/).

3. Meridel Le Sueur (page 21). Midwestern writer and activist Meridel Le Sueur (1900–1996) was a voice for oppressed peoples worldwide for more than seventy years.

4. *Child, child, child, child* (page 39). The song "Child, Child" (origin

unknown) is included in the Women's Encampment for a Future of Peace & Justice, the oral herstory digital archive of the Seneca Women's Peace Camp in Romulus, New York (1983–2006), collected & curated by the PeaCe eNCaMPMeNT HeRSToRy PRoJeCT, 2005–2015. https://peacecampherstory.blogspot.com/2018/07/song-index.html

5. There are *hundreds of thousands* of us. (page 72). From 1946 to 1962, the United States conducted about 200 atmospheric nuclear tests. The approximately 400,000 servicemen in the U.S. Army, Navy, and Marines that were present during these atmospheric tests, whether as witnesses to the tests themselves or as post-test cleanup crews, are called atomic veterans. At the time of the tests, many of these servicemen did not know about the effects of radiation exposure and did not question if their health was at risk. After leaving the armed services, many developed serious health complications, including cancer. More information about can be found at the Atomic Heritage Foundation website (www.atomicheritage.org).

6. But now the veterans are organizing, (page 72). The National Association of Atomic Veterans (www.naav.com/) was founded in 1979. In their words, the association's purpose is to allow "the U.S. Atomic Veteran Community to speak, with a single voice, to their inability to get a fair hearing related to their developing (radiogenic) health issues that may have been precipitated by their exposure to 'ionizing' radiation while participating in a nuclear weapon test detonation, or a 'post-test' event." It continues to organize veterans and their spouses and children today.

7. Nuclear Radiation and Secrecy Agreements Act (page 99). Repealed by U.S. Congress in 1996, which released atomic veterans from their oaths of secrecy. See www.publichealth.va.gov/docs/radiation/atomic-veteran-brochure.pdf and www.aarp.org/health/conditions-treatments/info-11-2011/atomic-veterans-special-benefits-radiation-exposure.html.

8. The Year of the Disappearing Websites (page 197). The disappearance from the Internet of previously available reports related to U.S. nuclear testing in the Pacific is documented at http://blog.nuclearsecrecy.com/2013/12/27/year-disappearing-websites/.

DISCUSSION GUIDE
Questions Raised by Nuclear Option

1. Unlike the first two Sylvia Jensen mysteries in which the story of a murder is told within the context of a social issue, in *Nuclear Option* the social issue (nuclearism) *is* the story. What are your thoughts and concerns about the nuclear threat today? When and how did you first become aware of the threat? How concerned are you about it?

1. *Nuclear Option* tells the story of how Norton Cramer, and the members of the group his son Corey joined, were impacted by atomic testing. How and when did you first learn that atomic veterans in this country were used as nuclear guinea pigs? Do you think the program was justified? Why or why not?

2. In the Prologue and in chapter nine, reference is made to the Marshallese people who were evacuated from Enewetak island prior to the nuclear testing. When and how did you first learn about the impact of the testing program on them, both then and now?

3. Norton Cramer's son Corey is the epitome of the maxim that "hurt people hurt people." How does Sylvia try to help him heal and what do you think about her approach?

4. Corey joins a group of people who are atomic veterans or family members of atomic veterans. How is his motivation (need for revenge) different from the other group members? How would you characterize the others? As good-hearted people whose pain makes them vulnerable, as Sylvia does? Or as terrorists, as the media does?

5. Vince, the self-appointed leader of the group, stood out from the beginning as different from the others. Who do you think he real-

ly was? What do you think J.B. Harrell knows about him that the others don't know?

6. During a meeting of the group Vince argues that social change has never been and can never be accomplished without violence and gives examples like the Civil War and the civil rights movement and Corey struggles with whether his father was truly nonviolent or not. Do you believe violence is necessary to bring about change? What historical changes inform your opinion?

7. In *Nuclear Option* people protest the Nectaral Corporation's role in the arms race, both in the present and thirty-five years ago. What corporations can you name that are profiting from the current escalation of the nuclear arms race?

FURTHER RESOURCES

Books

Atomic soldiers. Rosenberg, H. (1980). Boston, MA: Beacon Press.

GI Guinea pigs: How the pentagon exposed our troops to dangers more deadly than war. Uhl, M. & Ensign, T. (1980). New York, NY: Wideview Books.

No place to hide: 1946/1984. Bradley, D. (1948). Hanover, NH: University Press of New England. Includes quotes from Alan Cranston (former CA Senator), Helen Caldicott MD (former President of Physicians for Social Responsibility), John Kemeny (former Dartmouth College President), Eric Chivian (former president International Physicians for Prevention of Nuclear War) and Father Theordore Hesburgh, (former president of Univ. of Notre Dame) that speak to addressing the consequences of nuclear capability, medical consequences of nuclear war.

Films

Atomic Veterans Were Silenced for 50 Years. Now, They're Talking. (May 27, 2019). https://www.youtube.com/watch?v=qbBu6cWczTY

Original Child Bomb, a 2004 documentary about the aftermath of the atomic bombings of Hiroshima and Nagasaki. The title of the film was inspired by Thomas Merton's poem of the same name, which is quoted throughout the film. The documentary employs color footage that had previously been labeled top secret by the US government. Directed by

Carey McKenzie and produced by Holly Becker. https://www.imdb.com/
title/tt0415193/

Organizations And Actions

Ground Zero Center for NonViolent Action www.gzcenter.org

National Association of Atomic Veterans, Inc. https://www.naav.com/
Founded in August, 1979, to give voice to the U. S. Atomic Veteran Community's inability to get a fair hearing about their developing
radiogenic health issues related to their exposure to "ionizing" radiation
during a nuclear weapon test detonation or a "post-test" event.

UN Treaty on the Prohibition of Nuclear Weapons
https://www.un.org/disarmament/wmd/nuclear/tpnw/
As of July 7, 2017, 122 nations adopted this landmark agreement to ban
nuclear weapons. While the nuclear nations are not among the nations
supporting the treaty, it strengthens the global norm against the posses-
sion and use of nuclear weapons and establishes a legal standard aimed
at stigmatizing nuclear weapons and compelling nations to take steps
toward disarmament.

WPSR Statement of Support for Health Justice for the Republic of the
Marshall Islands -- September 11, 2019
https://www.wpsr.org/wpsr-blog/2019/9/11/wpsr-statement-of-support-
for-health-justice-for-the-republic-of-the-marshall-islands
This Washington Physicians for Social Responsibility statement acknowl-
edges the profound health impacts experienced by the people of the
Marshall Islands as a direct result of U.S. nuclear weapons testing during
the Cold War, and calls for support of the Marshallese people in their
efforts to establish adequate healthcare for their communities, particularly cancer care.

Union of Concerned Scientists

On January 23, 2020, the Bulletin of the Atomic Scientists moved its Doomsday Clock to 100 seconds to midnight—which is closer to an apocalyptic end of civilization than ever before.

https://thebulletin.org/doomsday-clock/

ACKNOWLEDGMENTS

My deepest gratitude and respect goes first of all to the many atomic veterans and their families whose stories inspired, infuriated, and informed me while writing *Nuclear Option*. I am deeply indebted to Professor Betty Garcia, California State University at Fresno, whose extensive research interviews with atomic veterans (*Ideological Change in Nuclear Witnesses*, 1985) helped ground the novel in real people and historical events. While *Nuclear Option* is a work of fiction and all persons, geographic locations, agencies, and community organizations are entirely the creation of my imagination, the too often ignored and invisible injustices inflicted on atomic veterans are imbued in every character developed and every storyline plotted.

Nuclear Option would not exist if it were not for the Women Against Military Madness (WAMM) women whose unstoppable demands for a peaceful and just society have inspired and called me to action for forty years. I am deeply grateful to Marianne Hamilton and Polly Mann for founding WAMM at Loretta's Tea Room in Minneapolis in the Fall of 1981 when they brought together eight other women – Cathy Anderson, Pam Costain, Moira Moga, Eleanor Otterness, Pat Powers, Mary Shepard, Lucille Speeter, and Mary White – who, like them, were committed to challenging the shift in national priorities taking place at that time from human services to military spending. In January 1982, WAMM's founding conference ended with more than one hundred of us braving the freezing cold weather to walk along University Avenue near the University of Minnesota in a march that was covered by *The New York Times* and published in newspapers across the country, along with photos of us with our "Moms Against Bombs" and "Women Against Military Madness" signs. The spirit of that day is imbued within me and reflected in the character of the unstoppable protagonist of *Nuclear Option,* as well as in several other characters.

The revolutionary spirit of Marv Davidov, founder of the Minneapolis Honeywell Project who spurred me to commit civil disobedience several times, permeates the story and some of the characters in *Nuclear Option.* Special appreciation to Carol Masters whose book *You Can't Do That!* (Nodin Press, 2009), sparked both memory and creativity in me with its rich documentation of Marv's extraordinary life and the nuclear disarmament movement. Deep gratitude to the Court Reporter who, moved by the testimony of my co-defendants and myself during one of our trials, provided us with copies of the full court transcript, which proved to be, decades later, an invaluable resource for the 1984 trial scene in *Nuclear Option.* Thank you to all the women who were at Women's Peace Camp near Seneca Falls, New York, in the summer of 1983 when I was there, and to Louise Krasniewicz whose insights in *Nuclear Summer: The Clash of Communities at the Seneca Women's Peace Encampment* (Cornell University Press, 1992) provided perspective to my personal experience.

I am grateful to all the many social workers, educators and professional organizations that, over the decades and today, understand and support the role of social workers as peacemakers. A special shout out to Dr. Frederick L. Ahearn, former Dean of the National Catholic School of Social Service, The Catholic University of America, who mentored me when I was Chair of the National Association of Social Workers' Peace and Social Justice Committee in the 1980s. His support shaped my thinking about the nuclear threat, enabled the publication of *Incorporating Peace and Social Justice into the Social Work Curriculum* (Van Soest, 1992), and influenced the development of Sylvia Jensen, the social work sleuth in *Nuclear Option.*

Writing books is always a team effort. For providing a welcoming and serene Mexican island retreat from which to write every year, I am forever grateful to the late Miriam Nates Greenstein. I continue to be indebted to two outstanding writers, editors, and teachers who have been critical to my development as a novelist. Hal Zina Bennett coached me through those first fledgling steps many years ago, and the wizardry of Max Regan helped transform *Nuclear Option* into the mystery you now hold in your hands. Thank you to my writing group members, Mary Kabrich and Roger Roffman, who as always provided wise feedback at every stage of development. A special thank you to readers of drafts of the manuscript: Lucia Wilkes-Smith (former director of WAMM), Dr. Betty Garcia, Mary Hansen, and Mary Swigonski. For the final stages of production I am grateful to Kyra Freestar for her outstanding copy-editing. A special shout out to the Apprentice House acquisitions team for suggesting changes to the manuscript and deep gratitude, as always, to Kevin Atticks and the entire Apprentice House publishing team. As always, I am indebted to my wife, Susan Seney, whose eagle eye doesn't miss a thing and whose unwavering love and support makes everything in life possible.

ABOUT THE AUTHOR

Novelist Dorothy Van Soest, professor emerita and former dean at the University of Washington, holds a B.A. in English Literature and a Masters and Ph.D. in Social Work. *Nuclear Option,* her third Sylvia Jensen mystery, is grounded in her activism in the nuclear disarmament movement in the 1980s and her concerns about the increased risks of nuclear war in the present. Van Soest has twelve books published and over fifty journal articles, essays and book chapters. Her three previous novels, *Just Mercy* (2014), *At the Center* (2015) and *Death, Unchartered* (2018) were published by Apprentice House. www.dorothyvansoest.com

Apprentice
House Press
Loyola University Maryland

Apprentice House is the country's only campus-based, student-staffed book publishing company. Directed by professors and industry professionals, it is a nonprofit activity of the Communication Department at Loyola University Maryland.

Using state-of-the-art technology and an experiential learning model of education, Apprentice House publishes books in untraditional ways. This dual responsibility as publishers and educators creates an unprecedented collaborative environment among faculty and students, while teaching tomorrow's editors, designers, and marketers.

Outside of class, progress on book projects is carried forth by the AH Book Publishing Club, a co-curricular campus organization supported by Loyola University Maryland's Office of Student Activities.

Eclectic and provocative, Apprentice House titles intend to entertain as well as spark dialogue on a variety of topics. Financial contributions to sustain the press's work are welcomed. Contributions are tax deductible to the fullest extent allowed by the IRS.

To learn more about Apprentice House books or to obtain submission guidelines, please visit www.apprenticehouse.com.

Apprentice House
Communication Department
Loyola University Maryland
4501 N. Charles Street
Baltimore, MD 21210
Ph: 410-617-5265
info@apprenticehouse.com • www.apprenticehouse.com